For the embers that will become flames...

First published in Great Britain by Hey Presto Publishing 2021
This paperback edition first published in Great Britain by
Hey Presto Publishing in 2021
Hey Presto is a registered trademark
www.heypresto.com/publishing

10 9 8 7 6 5 4 3 2 1

Temper the Flame
Text copyright © Jade Church

The author asserts the moral right to be identified as the author of this work.

Paperback Edition - ISBN 978-1-909678-16-3

JADE CHURCH

TEMPER THE FLAME

HEY PRESTO®
www.heypresto.com

I
IVY

IT was yet another painfully boring Wednesday and Ivy had just started her shift at the local One Stop shop. The day was passing infuriatingly slowly, as she was sure anyone who'd worked in retail would know. The usuals came and went with near Groundhog Day banality. Ms. Gray came in at 4pm as usual, picked up her semi-skimmed milk and left – as usual. Then a guy covered in blood slammed through the door, smearing bloody handprints along the glass and promptly collapsed – not so usual. Well, it finally seemed as if her day were about to get more entertaining.

Now, she wasn't some crazy sadist who took pleasure in the misfortune of near-death clientele.... but at least she now had something to *do*. Even if it was just to call out 'clean up in aisle two' sardonically down the tannoy system and watch morbidly from the side-lines – after all, they didn't have a code word for entrails by the chocolate bars. Luckily, gore didn't really phase her. When you had as much blood and death in your past as Ivy did, there was very little that could.

Technically speaking, she was the highest-ranking member of staff in today, so she should probably do something more than stand by and watch. But it was not every day she saw a bloodied man come into the shop and collapse with half his stomach hanging outside of his body and third-degree burns. Therefore, she thought she could get a pass for her delayed reaction.

Sighing and pinching her nose against the smell of piss and well, whatever that slimy stuff was, she warily made her way over to the mass of guts and blood that vaguely resembled a man. The sight of overwhelming redness and the tang of metal in the air was hauntingly familiar, but she was rooted firmly in the present. A different day, a different body, she told herself. Strangely, after taking a glimpse at him, she had the curious urge to gouge out her eyes with a blunt spoon. Mostly so she didn't have this moment etched into the back of her eyelids forever. The thought of adding to the therapy bills she already had were enough to make her retch, but after seeing the messed-up state of his face she nearly did vomit all over him. She'd had more than enough therapy for one lifetime but something about the intensity of the poor man's wounds reminded her of another day, another floor soaked with blood. *Breathe, Ivy, just breathe.* Affecting a blank look and a nonchalant step with practiced ease, she pushed those feelings down deep. Clearly the therapy had done her a world of good. It was then that she noticed the horrified look on poor Ms. Perkins' over-powdered face (back in again for her late-night shop, every Wednesday like clockwork) as she blanched and swayed on her feet.

Ivy got the feeling Ms. Perkins wouldn't be in as often after this ordeal. It wasn't the sort of thing that occurred in soft (or boring, as she frequently thought), rural England.

Frowning, she tried to decide what to do with this mess of a man – *for god's sake take his pulse, Ivy.* She eyed his bruised and shredded skin and felt reluctant to touch him at all. Everything looked doubly exposed under the harsh fluorescent lighting –

though admittedly the softest lighting in the world wouldn't have helped. She settled for prodding him with one – now bloody – black combat boot. She received a choked, gargling groan in response. Good. He wasn't dead. The paperwork would have been a bitch.

"HANK!" she shouted, "call an ambulance! Some guy's stumbled in who looks like he fell into a mincer!"

Hank, her colleague, ambled over and took a peek at Mince-Meat Man and actually did vomit all over him. Boy, he had probably thought his day couldn't get any worse – isn't it great when life proves you wrong?

Hank was a weedy man that vaguely resembled a mouse. His lank brown hair flopped onto his forehead and his overly large glasses permanently balanced on a long, skinny nose that made his beady eyes look huge. For all his mouse-like tendencies however, he was an okay guy. Hank turned to her with a dumbfounded look on his face, orange vomit and saliva hanging by a thread from his thin, quivering lips and once again her lunch threatened to make an appearance. However, she'd never live that down. She choked back her bacon sandwich and pretended all was well. *It's cool, Ivy.* She thought to herself as she slid a little in the gunk staining the floor – what would the ambulance crew do with that stuff? It looked important. She hoped they didn't leave it there.

She slipped over to the counter where the phone was located (as poor old Hank was clearly in too much shock to do anything right now) and gestured a still pale-faced Ms. Perkins over to be served. Hell, if paramedics could do CPR and talk at the same time, she thought she could handle serving whilst talking to the ambulance service.

"This is 999, what's your emergency?" An overly perky, female voice asked.

"Hi..." Ivy said slowly, thrown for a beat by this chirpy Barbie-esque operator, "I need an ambulance, some guy just stumbled into my shop, he's half-dead and vaguely resembles mincemeat." A little callous, but she wanted to knock operator Barbie down a couple pegs.

There was a noticeable pause on the other end before Operator Barbie responded, presumably where she tried to find the correct scripted response to Ivy's uncouth declaration. She smirked slightly at the distaste colouring the perky operator's voice, gave their address and hung up.

Ms. Perkins seemed to have recovered slightly as she paid, this was all undone the moment she turned around and saw Mince-Meat Man again, now also covered in Hank's vomit. Hank, having finally ceased puking, had thoughtfully put up a little yellow wet floor sign on the now red-stained, blue floor tiles. Bless him, he tries.

Ms. Perkins carefully made her way to the door, slipping in intestinal juice and blood only a little as she finally left. Her hands had shaken so badly it had taken three attempts to open the door. Poor thing... Ivy turned the open sign at the store entrance over to read closed until the paramedics arrived, they didn't need any more nosy customers coming in and slipping in people.

She sighed. Her earlier adrenaline had faded and the stink of blood was starting to seep into her while she waited for the ambulance. Fresh air would be nice, ideally before the metallic rot became too fused to her nose hairs. She knew she couldn't just abandon the shop though and so instead wandered over to check on Mince-Meat Man. It felt like the horror that was his face and body didn't dull with exposure, instead the more she stared, the worse he looked. Steeling herself, she prodded him with her boot once more. One honey-coloured eye opened suddenly and gave her a jolt of shock, the eye regarded her warily. It was easier to focus on the man in small parts, rather than one messed-up whole. The eye rolled back up into his head again as he passed out, most likely from the pain. She was pretty sure she could see the pale white gleam of an exposed rib in the mush at his side. She was now a little worse for wear, but it was possible that her visceral beauty and not the pain had made him see stars. Yeah, right. Nobody looked good in *this* much polyester. One Stop were cheapskates.

"So," she began, only slightly freaked out that she was basically talking to a corpse, "You got a name? I feel a bit rude thinking of you as 'Mince-Meat Man' or 'that-super-messed-up-dude-who-rudely-stumbled-into-my-shop'." This garnered no response except a slight twitch of his lips. She shook her head and started to stand up, "I can't believe I've resorted to talking to corpses for company."

"I'm not... a corpse," a gurgling voice responded wryly. She prodded him again and he managed to open one, long-lashed, eye to look at her irritably.

"I don't know man, you look pretty done-in to me." She received no response as the whites of his eyes showed and he passed out again. Not that she could blame him really. If some short woman with exceptionally large boots kept prodding *her* whilst she was laying on the floor in a puddle of her own blood, she thought she'd pass out too. That, or slug her.

The paramedics arrived shortly after he passed out and she rushed through her statement, already day-dreaming about that heavenly bed of hers at home. Admittedly, it was worth sticking around just to see the comical look of disgust on one paramedic's face as he saw what awaited them.

"Is that puke?" he called out and she shrugged and nodded in response. He shook his head, looking slightly green and she hoped for Mince-Meat Man's sake that he didn't puke on him too.

Doubling back before she left, she checked the floor for any stray, vital body parts, left a note for the cleaners and finally, she headed home, to her average flat after a not-so average day. One thing was for certain; her life would never be this exciting again.

II

IVY

HER alarm gave a shrill screech and she swore ferociously while repeatedly jamming her hand down over the grey snooze button. At last, the beeping stopped and she relaxed back into her pale pink covers until it started up again. It had been three days since Mince-Meat Man fell through the doors of the One Stop and life had returned to its normal, delightfully asinine self. Aside from the joy of adding a new horror-filled dream to her repertoire – well, change was good right? Her therapist had told her so. Plus, it could have been worse, she reasoned, at least she hadn't dreamed of her mother. She sighed in defeat and heaved all five feet, four inches of herself out of bed and into the shower, luxuriating in the soft feel of the carpet between her toes as she walked. Twenty-minutes and the strongest cup of coffee in the world later, she was ready to go. She yanked her flat door closed behind her and gave a one-fingered salute to her sometimes friend, always nosey, neighbour: Freddy. Against her better judgement, she liked Freddy. It was annoying, because she preferred not to like anyone. The little bastard had inexplicably begun to worm his way into her heart and that alone told her it was probably time to move on from her comfy little flat. He stuck up two fingers in return, she grinned as she blew him a kiss and made her way to work.

"£3.37 then please." Mr. Carlson blinked at her slowly, his mouth quivering as he chewed on his words, nearly showering her with spittle as he snapped his mouth open indignantly. Ugh. The joys of retail. It had already been the longest of days and she was only an hour and a half into her eight-hour shift. So far, Hank had dropped an entire case of pasta sauce (creating a gory looking spatter not unlike the bodily fluids that had coated the floor a few days ago, she had noticed Ms. Perkins eyeing it warily when she had stopped in earlier), a trolley of yoghurts (which also promptly exploded) and had short changed no fewer than seven, angry, customers.

"37?" he quivered. Fuck, here it came, "but the beans were on promotion!" Ivy wrinkled her nose, mostly due to the aroma of eau de flatulence that constantly surrounded him but also because he did this every. Single. Time. Honestly, did he *really* need beans? Maybe he'd eat too many and fart himself to death.

With that cheery thought in mind, she gave him her toothiest smile and said, "Sorry sir, I'll get Hank to check for you."

Hank, already expecting this due to it being a weekly occurrence, busied himself with the beans while she turned to her next customer and apologised for the wait.

Was she really apologetic? No.

Was it *her* fault Mr. Fartson was concerned about 37 fucking pence? No.

Alas, c'est la vie.

She paused and blinked at the next customer in line. He looked oddly familiar for some reason she couldn't quite place. It wasn't until he looked at her slightly warily and asked, "You're not going to come around the other side of this counter and prod me with your boot again are you?" that she placed him as the puddle of goo from the other night.

Her eyes bugged out as they slipped over his immaculate form from head to toe. She fondled her lip ring with her tongue, covering her shock with an indifferent smirk. "You clean up well."

He smirked right back at her, "Yes, well, it's hard to look your best when your intestines are on the outside of your body."

Smart ass.

"You were virtually dead, how can you be out of the hospital already? And looking like – well, *this?*" she said gesturing to him with her hands.

His smirk grew and she rolled her eyes, hoping he hadn't mistaken her question for interest, it was only natural to be curious.

"Apparently it looked a lot worse than it was. I think it was the vomit that *really* made things look bad," he widened his honey eyes innocently at her and she frowned at him, nauseated at the reminder. Maybe there was no coming back from seeing someone covered in blood and vomit – regardless of how glowy their honeyed skin was or how pretty the freckle above their mouth looked when they grinned.

There was no way he could have healed that quickly, but she let it go. She didn't even know the guy, didn't *want* to know him, it wasn't her problem where he decided to keep his intestines.

"So, what *is* your name? I'm still inwardly referring to you as Mince-Meat Man." she asked, darting a glance over at Hank to see if he was done checking the beans yet.

"You refer to me inwardly a lot then?" the man asked with a Cheshire cat grin and quirk of his thick black brows that made her bite her lip. She mentally cursed at herself, she'd walked right into that one.

Not wanting to show she was at all bothered, she gave him a deadpan stare and his entire face lit up with a genuine smile in return, making his skin almost seem to radiate light.

"Gabe," he said, and she blinked, caught in his golden stare – Gabe? Who the fuck was Gabe? And then she remembered. His name. She'd asked for his name.

After a slightly uncomfortable pause wherein she attempted to gather her thoughts, she smiled back at him.

"Nice to meet you, Gabe. I'm Ivy."

He gave a gentle laugh, "I know." he said and pointed at her boob. She was considering slapping the grin right off his face when it occurred to her that he was pointing at her store-issued name badge.

"Oh!" she laughed, flushing slightly with embarrassment, "Right."

Hank caught her eye, having finally finished fucking around with the beans and told her what both she and the till system already knew.

"Sorry Mr. Carlson, but that's £3.37 please, the original price was correct." She waited for it, and she didn't have to wait long.

"I don't want any of it then," he huffed. Fucking time waster. She took a deep, calming breath. *I am not going to lose my shit*, she chanted. 37p. Seriously?

Instead of clubbing him round the head with his own basket as she sorely wished to, she smiled.

"I'm sorry to hear that, sir. Have a good day!"

Retail was a game of deception. Unfortunately for her, she didn't have the patience to play the game. Ivy turned to resume her conversation with Gabe, but he'd left while she had been serving. Probably scared off by Fartson's arse. Although, she may forgive him seeing as the guy standing where Gabe had been was *hot*. Like, genuinely could melt-the-pantyhose-off-a-nun hot. He definitely didn't resemble the shop's usual clientele which mainly consisted of the elderly, the annoying and 'the youths' as Barry (the store manager) frequently whined.

No, a youth this guy was not. Everything about him screamed *bad* – the kind you know you shouldn't smile at but ended up fucking in the bathroom on a night out anyway. A wild shock of dark hair curled slightly towards his temples, it was thick, hair she was dying to fist and tug in her hands. It looked effortlessly rumpled but she'd bet money he'd styled it that way deliberately. A cocky smirk played on his mouth, the bottom lip a little fuller than the top, and something told her he wore that smirk often – especially when being eye-fucked by petite shop assistants. Nonetheless, she started her usual meet and greet, taking firm control of herself and doing her best to calm the flush she could feel moving through her. The heavy leather jacket he wore over a muscled physique and firm stance clearly screamed *troublemaker* and she wasn't surprised when he cut her off before she got even half-way through her rehearsed retail speech and she bit back her instant irritation.

"Hi... Ivy, is it?" he asked, reading her name badge with a flash of even, white teeth, his voice was rough and deep but could melt butter, and something deep inside liked hearing her name in his mouth.

"I'm looking for a guy. You might've seen him, came in about three days ago, My height, brown hair and eyes – answers to Gabe?"

His deep green eyes watched her with a cat-like intensity, framed by thick dark lashes and brows, she felt a stab of envy thinking of her own white-blonde lashes. He had gold skin, not unlike Gabe's, high cheekbones and she was surprised by the desire to kiss the hollow of that impressive jaw and feel the scrape of his stubble on her skin. Gabe was the furthest thing from her mind when she sent up a little *well done* to whoever had created possibly the most stunning man she'd ever seen.

She moved her mouth into a lazy smile and did her best to look bored, he sounded like he was looking for a missing dog rather than a person. He *definitely* hadn't been in the shop before, she would have remembered him. If he asked her to bail with him right then and there, well, she mused, who would win? Hank or one hot boi? Surely she could just *admire* him right? One look couldn't hurt? Though, that was probably what Orpheus had thought too.

She quirked her eyebrows at him and kept her tone as unaffected as possible, "He was quite memorable, that's for sure. What do you need him for?"

"Oh, he's family. Haven't seen him since he kicked me out of heaven." He said it with a grin, and she laughed but rolled her eyes, *what a fucking weirdo.*

"Sorry, I can't help" she said, "He came in not that long ago, but he was gone when I turned around." *Just when you showed up,* she thought but didn't say. "Besides, you definitely don't look like an angel to me."

The guy laughed in apparent delight. "Really?"

She shrugged back, the phrase *hotter than hell* certainly came to mind. He offered her a grin as if he heard her inner monologue and approved. He easily beat out every nameless one night stand she'd ever had. His eyes on her had her pulse racing, it made her wonder what exactly would happen if he touched her. She couldn't

fuck him in the staff-room here could she? No, no, that would be...
irresponsible. He was hot, sure, but she didn't get involved with the
ones that triggered this sort of response. Too dangerous, too easy to
get attached. Hurt.

"No worries," he drawled, "Just let him know Devlin is looking
for him if you see him?" The guy dropped her a quick wink that
made her blush all the way to the roots of her white blonde hair. An
attractive look for sure. Not that she should care.

"Yeah alright," she said, unsure whether or not she would actually
keep her promise. She didn't like to get involved with crazy, even
when it came in such a pretty package. She had enough of her own
to deal with.

He picked up her hand with a quirk of his lips and brushed a
searing kiss across her knuckles, looking up at her underneath his
lashes. Before she could say anything more, she was falling.

*"You don't know anything, Dev!" A voice screamed and as the
blinding white light faded slightly, she saw them.*

*Two boys - one with wings a dark auburn that matched his hair
and the second with wings so dark they were almost blue. The boy with
the magnificent auburn wings kept shouting at the other, presumably
'Dev'. She looked closer and gasped – it was the guy from the shop. He
seemed exactly the same aside from the enormous wings now gracing his
person, and maybe slightly younger. His face was fuller, lighter, than the
man she had just met.*

*"It's not right Michael! You cannot do this! I forbid it!" Devlin was
pleading with the other boy, Michael, his face rife with distress. There
was something alarmingly cold about Michael. The flint of his pale
blue eyes was unwavering and without remorse as they fixed on Dev*

like a predator sighting prey. A strange protective urge for Dev surged unexpectedly, she wanted to shield him from Michael's chilling gaze, certain that something bad was about to happen. She knew nothing about Michael, but something in the taut lines of tension framing his body told her he was someone who would stop at nothing to get what he wanted.

Michael laughed coldly, "You?" he asked, "You forbid it? You do not have the power, the authority to forbid me of anything!" Michael screamed out the words, his divine face was contorted with rage, spittle flying. He was completely wild, body trembling with the power he contained, and she saw despair cross Dev's face for a moment as he looked at the creature in front of him. Michael grabbed him by the throat and lifted him into the air. Dev hung limply in Michael's grasp, as if he couldn't bear to fight back.

"You will rue this day, Devlin. I curse you. May those humans you so revere whisper your name with fear. I strip you of your wings and cast you from this place, to never return while you know not of the love you so seek." He spat out the words and a gasp circled the two angels. For the first time, she realised there were others here in this white space, bearing witness.

"ENOUGH." Michael demanded, "See the price of those who challenge me; and should you choose him over me, the price that awaits you. Decide." So young, she thought, to be spewing such poison. To be so tainted and warped by what looked like jealousy and rage, lurking in those cold blue eyes.

With his final word, Michael wrestled Devlin to the ground and ripped those glorious wings from his back with the help of another angel with dusky brown wings. A large, jagged wound and shredded cartilage *was all that was left behind. She gagged at the sight of the flapping flesh as Devlin screamed and screamed, the sound burning like fire through her, she was sure it would haunt her dreams.*

"Leave!" Michael boomed, releasing and shoving Devlin forward into a swirling, shining doorway, like a crack in space and time itself. The brown winged angel kicked him until the doorway stopped pulsing, swallowing Devlin and a handful of others as they leapt after him.

Ivy came-to gasping for air and found Devlin crouched above her, his green eyes wide and breathing shallow, as if he too had seen whatever she just had. A fine sheen of sweat coated her face, and her legs shook when she tried to heave herself up from the floor. Surely it was a hallucination. Perhaps the stress and shock from Wednesday was finally affecting her. Angels didn't exist.

Devlin reached down to help her up from where she'd fallen, but she quickly brushed him off and hauled herself up the rest of the way with the remainder of her strength. He held his hands up placatingly and examined her from head to toe, seemingly unimpressed by the look on his face. He sighed at last and said simply, "I thought you'd be taller."

Then he left.

What the fuck?

III

DEVLIN

THEY were screwed. Some random girl from the convenience shop? *She* was the one supposed to help them get back home? Shit. She had been brimming with untapped energy, but clearly had no idea how to use it — why else would she have fainted when their energies collided? Who knew how long it would take to train her up, not that they had much of a choice. If it took ten years they would still have to try. Dev had been failing his people for too long. That changed now.

The image of her was already burned into his mind. Large, icy-blue eyes had appraised him from head to toe, he hadn't minded that stare. Not one bit. That in itself was a surprise, it probably should have told him straight off the bat that something was different about her. *Ivy*. His mouth ached to form her name over and over while he tasted her on his tongue. She was bold, cocky, infuriatingly distant. She had stood a good several heads shorter than him, but you'd never notice it from the sheer confidence she had exuded - after all, she hadn't been exactly subtle when she'd checked him out. Dev let out a soft curse as he walked, trying to drag his thoughts away from her tongue flicking over that damned lip ring. He had spent years imagining this moment, finally finding the psychic that some hokey prophet had foretold. Until now, he hadn't fully believed it was a real chance. Yet, here they were. He just had to keep his head in the game, and his dick in his pants.

He huffed and sped off, finally catching the trail he'd been looking for. Angelic energy left a certain taste in the air and this one's familiarity sent a twinge of pain through his chest. Following it all the way down a darkened alley that reeked of piss and despair; Dev spied him at last. Huddled behind some boxes like a lost lamb – a far cry from the being of almost ignorant innocence, blindly following his brother's orders that he remembered from before the fall.

"My, how the mighty have fallen," Dev drawled slowly, relishing the look of fear in Gabe's eyes that slowly faded to something else... relief?

He refused to spare a moment of mercy on this creature. After all, Gabe did help pluck out his wings, Gabe's foot had made the first blow – under Michael's watchful gaze, of course. Gabriel was no longer his brother. He had relinquished that title the moment he'd turned his back on Devlin. All that was left were the memories of who they used to be and the broken hope of who they could have become.

"Dev?" Gabriel's eyes were wide as he called out and Dev winced; just hearing his brother's voice after all these years was like smoke in his eyes and glass in his throat. He gave a sarcastic bow, "At your service, my liege."

Gabe's face lost any hope that had been building, he dropped his eyes to the ground and whispered, "I've missed you."

Dev let out a bark of a laugh that cut through the still night air, startling the huddled figure on the ground. He'd hoped that he'd learned to control his emotions a little more during his time on the Earthly plane, but one look at Gabe and Devlin was undone. Every old hurt, every terrible, cutting thought, unleashed all at once in his mind. "Really Gabriel? Missed me? *Missed?*" he shoved his hand through his hair and flung his arms out, wild. "If you had *missed* me as much as you say, you would have brought me *home,* Gabriel! Nobody else would have fallen if you had a decent bone left in your body."

Dev didn't let himself look away from Gabriel as he spoke, "So don't give me that bullshit, Gabriel. What do you want? Why are you *here?*"

Gabe couldn't even look at him and for some reason that was what pushed Dev over the edge, at last spurring him into motion. The loud sound of his shoes scraping against the concrete floor made Gabriel tense as Dev approached.

"For *fuck sake,* Gabriel! *Look at me!*" Dev roared the last with his hands under Gabriel's chin; tugging his head up none so gently so he would, at last, look him in the eyes.

What he saw stopped him cold. Dev dropped his hands from under Gabriel's chin like they burned. It was not the malevolent look of someone here on Michael's orders that was in his brother's eyes. It was the lost, disparaging look he'd seen countless times before. Of one who had fallen, of one who had lost their connection to the Heavens. It was his brother he saw — Gabe not Gabriel. His resolve crumbled as he rasped out his name.

"Gabe? Is it – have you-?" he could not bear to ask. To be trapped here, discarded, as Devlin had been. Like the others had been, as though they were not even worth the air they breathed. But the fall was not something he would have wished even on Michael. Gabe's honeyed eyes were glazed with tears as they stared into his.

"Are you here on his orders? Gabe, did Michael send you?" Dev wasn't sure he wanted to know the answer. Didn't know what it might mean for them all if Dev's instincts were right — that Michael had stripped his favourite angel, favourite *brother*, of his wings.

Slowly, Gabe shook his head. His tousled brown hair caught the dim light of a passing car giving it a red tinge, reminiscent of Michael's. His brother's face was pale, awash with the tears streaking down his face. He stood, and slowly turned facing the mouth of the alley, lifting the grubby grey t-shirt he'd somehow managed to acquire. Then Dev saw them. The long, bloody marks, still healing, carved deep into his back. He choked on his roar of anguish as Gabe turned to face him.

"He ripped them out." Gabe's broken whisper echoed around the dank alley and sank into Devlin's soul.

The dead, hopeless look in his eyes was all too familiar. Dev clenched his fists tightly, fighting the nausea that had settled deep inside him.

"He will pay." Gabe had fallen and Michael would know his pain. Dev would make sure of it.

He led Gabe home, to the compound. Since the original fall, many others had managed to attain Michael's wrath. They, like him, found themselves stripped of their wings and banished to the place his brother hated the most – Earth. A fitting punishment, to send them to the place Michael thought of as hell. A place where free will reigned, not the will of Michael. Michael was strong, stronger than Dev, at least in resolution if not in raw power. Michael would not hesitate to hurt anyone who got in his way, even his own brothers. It's why he had cursed Devlin. Well, that and maybe... just maybe, Michael had been scared. Devlin had been the only one who had ever dared to challenge him, it was a defiance that had cost Dev dearly.

Devlin's curse was a little more special than the rest of the fallen.

The others could be accepted back into the Heavens at any time — it was finding a portal there that was the hard part, without their wings it was near impossible to get home. It was why they needed the psychic, Dev didn't know exactly how she would help them get home, just that she could. He assumed she could sense the portal's energy somehow and lead them in the right direction. Only time would tell.

Dev flicked his gaze towards his brother, it was still hard to believe he was there.

"Gabe," Dev said softly, "I need you to tell me what happened." He couldn't risk everyone that had made this place a sanctuary by bringing the reason they had ended up there inside, not until he knew if he could trust Gabe. Gambling with his own life was one thing, but not theirs. Never theirs.

Michael had saved the worst punishment for Dev, for choosing humanity over his brother. The betrayal, as Michael saw it, was worse coming from Devlin than the others. Maybe it was why the rest could eventually return home while Devlin remained alone. Or maybe Michael hated Dev for openly defying him. Devlin would never know or understand why Michael did half the things he did and it was a waste of Dev's energy to try. They were brothers only in name now. Gabe, Dev understood. He was weak. He loved Michael too much to see his faults and didn't have the backbone to say *no*. That's why it was hard to understand Gabe's sudden appearance. Yet, however unlikely it seemed, there was no denying that Gabe had fallen.

Gabe looked at him with despair etched into the lines of his face and Dev knew that, at least, was real. The first days away from Heaven's energies, without the protection of your wings, was more than draining, it felt like your life force was leaking from you slowly. Like no matter what you did, any warmth inside would never reappear. Dev still had days when he felt like that.

"I couldn't do it any longer, Dev. Be his puppet. First you, then Freddy...I couldn't sit back anymore. Not when his plans meant I would never get to see either of you again." Gabe's eyes were wide as he pleaded, Devlin wasn't sure how genuine Gabe was but he wanted *so much* to believe him. To think that perhaps his youngest brother hadn't completely forsaken him, but up until now, he would have thought it a fool's hope.

For Dev, Michael had reserved the cruelest of punishments, ensuring he would never be accepted anywhere. Not only was Dev stripped of his wings and cast from his home, the people on Earth he had sought to protect from Michael could only see him as evil, practically the devil. Until a human saw through the glamour Michael had placed and fell in love with him, Devlin wouldn't be able to stay in the Heavens. Alone and unaccepted, forever. It was a powerful glamour and Dev had tried everything to break it. Nothing had worked. He'd yet to find a human who could see him as he was. So, he would remain on Earth, waiting, hoping. He would never begrudge the others for leaving him, the Heavens was where they belonged and he hoped that finally, with Ivy came the hope of their return.

Soon, Michael would get everything he had coming to him – doubly so now he had hurt Gabe.

Gabe stopped and looked at him evenly. "He needs to be stopped, I know that now. I can't change the things I did in the past but I can try to be more than them. You're the only one who can stop him, the only thing he has ever been scared of. Well," he said with a trace of his usual wry grin, "you and that psychic."

Dev froze. "How do you know about her?"

Gabe shrugged. "We found out about the prophecy the same time you did, I heard there's actually some truth in it. Mortals eh? Surprisingly resourceful bunch." Gabe quirked his brows, "Wait, did you say she? It's *true?*"

Shit.

"I'm not sure it's her," Dev started carefully, "and even if it is, I don't think she knows about her talents yet, so I may have inadvertently triggered a vision and freaked her out. Plus, she seemed a little more interested in someone else." he cast Gabe a pointed look.

Gabe looked puzzled for a second before he gave a delighted laugh, "Ivy? What are the chances," he had a shit-eating grin on his face as he thought about her and Dev itched to slap it off for reasons he didn't quite understand. Gabe must not have been on Earth for very long, just as Freddy had claimed, else he wouldn't have narrowed the suspects down so quickly. "I've spoken to her all of once, I stumbled into that shop she works at after I fell." Gabe said.

That explained why Gabe's appearance was so 'memorable', falling through portal energy without any protection from your wings was akin to jumping into a volcano. Losing them was a shock to the system that prevented any sort of mental fortification that might have worked in the absence of wings, allowing their bodies to be susceptible to the intense energy of the portal. Dev shook himself free of the burning memory of the fall and refocused his thoughts away from Ivy. He knew there was still a chance the prophecy was fake, that it was better to not get his hopes up, that he would likely never feel the Heaven's energies soak into his soul once more. That logic couldn't extinguish the small ember of hope that flared inside him.

"What did you mean when you said Michael's plans meant never seeing me or Freddy again?"

Gab fixed him with a hard look, "He's going to kill them all, Dev. He doesn't know who the supposed psychic is, and he won't run the risk of you being able to come home and take his place. He thinks you're getting too powerful, too close."

"Wait, kill who all?" Dev said shaking his head in confusion.

"The world, Dev. The humans." Gabe said with an inhuman tilt of his head. "He's done with this plane."

Dev fixed a dark look to the sky, as if glaring at his brother himself. "Then we need to get Ivy and act now."

He invited Gabe in, past the protective barrier that lined the compound and prepared himself for the worst. It wasn't much, these abandoned interconnecting buildings, but it was home. They had arrived knowing next to nothing about the Earthly world and had taken refuge here. It would never be the Heavens, but at least it was community and safety, warmth on a cold night. They had worked hard to make the previously condemned spaces livable, it hadn't been an easy job but the glamour Devlin had laid with Jas and Freddy's help had kept the mortals away and Michael's spies out. It was the best they could do and yet to Dev, it didn't feel like enough. Gabe had helped kick out most of these angels. So he wasn't surprised when Jasmine, one of the first to fall with him, hissed and immediately rushed Gabe when she saw him with him.

"What the hell are you doing Devlin! You bring *him* here? To our sanctuary?"

He sighed and caught her around the waist before she could hit Gabe, this was not going to be easy. They had all been made aware of Freddy's report, that he had spotted Gabe in the One Stop today, but Dev supposed it was one thing to hear about your abuser, another to see him in the flesh. Still, he believed in full-disclosure and had wanted them to all be as prepared as possible, though even Dev couldn't have predicted *this*, that Gabe had fallen.

"I know what he's done, Jasmine. Trust me, I was there. I haven't forgiven him, and I don't entirely trust him. But he is my brother and he has fallen. He sacrificed his wings for *us*. To warn us."

His bold declaration was met with a few mutters and looks of unease in the slow-forming group of angels in front of him, he released Jas.

"If Gabe is on our side, then he is welcome here. This is a sanctuary for the fallen and always will be. You know that, you helped me build it." Dev said pointedly to Jasmine before clearing his throat and glanced around, "As you know, I sent Frederick out to try and find the psychic, and his journey has taken him away from us for some time now."

The air itself seemed to almost crackle as he said his next words.

"Freddy wasn't sure he was following the right trail of energy, but today, I confirmed it. We've found the psychic."

Looks of disbelief and hope started to spread and Dev nodded and smiled, relieved to be giving them the news they had longed for. "Soon." he said, "You'll be home soon."

IV
IVY

ONCE she got home, Ivy paced around the entirety of her flat, which admittedly didn't take long. Considering her day, things couldn't have felt more abnormal. Interesting customers, hallucinations, and miraculous healing were not in her usual repertoire.

She sighed tiredly, her thoughts just going around in circles, it was definitely time for bed. She turned towards her bedroom just as someone knocked on the front door.

Letting her eyes roll as far back into her head as possible, she walked towards the door reluctantly, hoping that if she moved slowly enough, they would just go away. Sadly, another brisk knock sounded and she let out an irritated sigh. She placed her hand on the doorknob and was filled with a strong sense of foreboding and the urge to scream and run like hell.

Curious.

She opened the door warily and saw a Domino's pizza man. Hallelujah. The lord just knows sometimes. Unfortunately, she had not ordered this godsend.

She gave the bland looking pizza boy a look of sorrow as she broke the bad news, "Oh, sorry, I didn't order anything. Thanks though."

He just stared at her blankly with the pizza thrust out in front of him, blue eyes so pale they looked almost clear. An uncomfortable beat of silence passed, and she was officially creeped out as he continued to stare at her silently.

She laughed awkwardly as she started to close the door, the sound seemed too loud in her own ears amidst the quickening *thud* of her heart, "Well, thanks…"

With a sweep of air, huge motherfucking *wings* sprouted from his back that knocked her door inward. Ivy fell back onto her butt and let out a startled shriek, which he clearly didn't appreciate as he threw the pizza box at her head in retaliation, the pizza flew out of the box and hit the wall with the saddest sounding *squelch* she ever did hear.

Shaking with shock and rage she shouted, "You absolute *dick*. That was perfectly good pizza!"

Pizza quickly became the least of her problems as he pulled out a huge glowing sword (boy did she wish that was just a euphemism) and swiftly attempted to run her through with it. It was at this point that she became fairly certain she was hallucinating. Normally when things got punchy she could rely on her hair-trigger temper to get her out of a scrape, but all she felt now was cold fear.

She crawled backward on her fuzzy purple carpet, lamenting inwardly at what a pain her blood would be to get out of it for the landlord. What were the odds that she had escaped death once before only to be murdered now? A maniacal laugh escaped as she chanted, "You're not real" repeatedly. Right until the sword arced down towards her head and she let out a blood curdling scream.

Suddenly he, and thankfully it, burst into a spear of light and vanished with a pop. Revealing Freddy standing behind him with his own glowing sword.

"You killed him! What the fuck! Freddy?"

Freddy's sword vanished as quickly as it had appeared as he began poking his head into the few connecting rooms Ivy had in her flat. She had just hallucinated another angel and yet he was taking the time to be nosy?

"He's not dead, Ivy. Just in heaven." Freddy said, somewhat sarcastically.

"I've lost my damn mind," she panted and promptly passed out.

She awoke to Freddy's voice murmuring, presumably down the phone.

"She thinks she's crazy, Dev. She just bloody *sat there* while he almost took her out!" There was a pause and then he continued, "Of course I was keeping an eye on her, but I couldn't very well stalk the poor girl! That's how you get *arrested* for fuck sake."

She struggled to open her eyes, it felt like a truck had hit her, driven off and reversed over her again.

She froze at Freddy's next words though, "Look, you sent me to try and find the psychic, Dev, and I found her. I was guarding her until I knew for sure she was the one and it was safe to contact you, but after your stunt at the One Stop they were watching her too closely for me to do anything!" another pause and then, "Look, if I had been sure I would have called sooner, but all that matters now is that she's safe and I'll bring her to you."

Whoa. Hold the fuck up. Bring her to him? Suddenly, she realised it had gone quiet and struggled to relax her body again to feign unconsciousness. Footsteps moved closer to where she lay, and Freddy's arms scooped her up and began walking towards the front door. *Shit*, she thought and then in a desperate bid to be free, slammed her head up toward his nose with surprising accuracy and felt it crunch.

"*Fuck!*" Freddy shouted and promptly dropped her on the floor.

She scrambled up and attempted to run but he caught her by the hand before she'd gone more than a few steps.

"Seriously Ivy? You broke my damn *nose?* I save your goddamned life and you *break my fucking nose?*"

She felt a brief stab of guilt but quickly quashed it, he was trying to abduct her after all. He pulled his other hand away from his nose and swore at the blood on his hand. She rubbed the back of her head with her free hand, yeah, hadn't been her smartest idea.

"I'm not going to hurt you, Ivy. Neither will Dev. We've been looking for you for a long time."

She raised her brows at him. Right. 'Cos that didn't sound creepy at all.

"Me? Why would you be looking for me?" she asked, starting to creep towards the door but Freddy quickly grabbed her other hand and she squirmed to get him to let go.

He didn't let up for a second, "Goddamn it Ivy! I'm not going to hurt you! Listen to me! *Listen!* You are in danger – and it isn't from me!"

She eyed him doubtfully but stopped squirming after dimly recalling the – apparently very real – freaky dude with the huge instrument of death at the door. Maybe Freddy was onto something.

He sighed and scrubbed a hand across his face, "Look, let me take you to Dev and he'll explain everything I swear. What do you have to lose?"

"Um, my dignity, my life, my... sense of humour."

Freddy threw his hands in the air, "You'll be lucky to still have your head if you stay here." She must have still looked doubtful because he added, "That guy with the wings and sword? Don't look at me like that, yes I saw him and yes he was real." He said in answer to the wide eyed, disbelieving expression she was certain she now wore.

"They'll keep coming Ivy, they won't stop until you're dead. Come with me, and you'll be safe. Both Dev and I would die before anything happened to you."

She gave him a surprised look and he smiled in return, "You're important Ivy, we need you."

Appraising him slowly and not sensing any immediate danger, she reluctantly nodded, though she hadn't missed that he had said *need* and not *want*. Whatever they were up to, it was clear they were desperate.

He gave a relieved sigh, "Let's go."

Freddy bundled her into his truck quickly. They were getting stared at. Probably because he had dried blood on his face and she was still in her pink flannel pjs with her hair sticking up like she had just been electrocuted. They'd wasted no time leaving her apartment, when she'd tried to suggest changing into something a little less...deranged, Freddy had said: "Sure, make sure it'll look good in a casket."

She hadn't hesitated after that.

A drab looking woman with dishwater hair approached warily and looked at her like she was a dangerous animal, "Are you okay, sweetie? Do you know this man?"

She wanted desperately to laugh but thought it might come out sounding a little hysterical. What could she say really? Yeah, everything's chill, Freddy saved her from an angel trying to lop her head off? Somehow, she thought that might get her committed.

"Oh yeah, I'm fine, this here is *Freddy*. He's *real* nice to me, ma'am."

Freddy rolled his eyes at her tone and the woman looked a little unsure as to whether she was telling the truth. She gave the lady a reassuring smile but, if anything, the woman looked more disturbed at this, so she quickly stopped.

"It was nice to meet you, bye!"

Freddy shoved her into the truck, and she gave the woman a regal wave, snickering at Freddy's muffled curses about do-gooders as he pulled out of the car park.

"Aw relax, she was just trying to be nice!"

Freddy glowered and tugged anxiously at the golden ring in one nostril. "She was being nosey. It's not natural to be that friendly."

"Maybe she's an alien. Maybe *you're* an alien! Anyway," she said, reining in her thoughts, "you're always nosey, so isn't that a bit pot calling the kettle...?"

"That was for your own protection!" He huffed indignantly, and she grinned and shook her head.

"Ah yes, watching me take out my rubbish bins was a potentially life-threatening activity."

"Ivy, breathing could be a life-threatening activity for you." Freddy said pleasantly, seeming unbothered about the possibility of her imminent death.

She cast him a wary sideways look. If he had sounded a little less threatening just then she would have felt a lot happier. She wasn't sure she entirely trusted him yet and was on the lookout for any murder-y vibes, sarcasm notwithstanding.

"So where exactly are we going?" she wondered if they were going to, like, teleport somewhere. Another realm, maybe. Hey, she'd read Sarah J Maas — she knew how this shit worked.

"Compound on the outskirts of London."

Or not.

"You guys are freaking angels or some shit, and you're living in—"

Freddy narrowed his eyes at her as he interrupted, "Former angels, actually, and yes – if you have a problem with that, you're more than welcome to stay here and have your head cut off."

She rolled her eyes, geez Freddy was so uptight, "Wow Fred, snippy much?"

He glowered. She smirked.

"How long will the journey take?"

"If you don't stop yapping, you might not make it." Freddy said with an unnervingly pleasant smile.

Three death threats in as many minutes, it had to be a new record. "Ha, but seriously, how long?"

He shrugged noncommittally, "A few hours providing we don't run into any... complications."

Her neck cricked as she whipped her head around to look at him fully, "What do you mean, *complications?*"

"I mean, you almost getting shish-kabobbed-type complications. I thought I was pretty clear about the threat of imminent-death thing."

A siren sounded behind them and Freddy groaned as the officer waved them over. Freddy looked at her steadily, "Smooth your hair. You're a fucking mess."

She snorted and placed her hands on her heart, "Oh, Freddy, you know just what to say!"

He just rolled his eyes and scrubbed at the blood on his face.

There was a tap at the window and Freddy rolled it down to talk to the Officer on the other side.

"Everything okay?" Freddy asked, with an air of calm confidence that surprised her. The policeman, however, didn't look affected.

"We received a report from a concerned citizen about a young girl potentially being forced against her will into a truck fitting this description."

At this moment, his eyes landed on her. "Are you okay, Miss? Hurt? Did he force you to come with him?"

Freddy had gone very still beside her, so she gave them both her most unhinged smile, "Oh, I'm fine Officer, he wants me to come with him for the greater good."

Freddy shot her a look of ice and she smiled wider, "But honestly, everything's fine. Thank you."

The policeman's eyes were narrowed like he could sense something was off but couldn't quite figure out what.

Eventually he nodded, "Have a nice night then."

"You too, sir."

Freddy waited until he had driven off before swearing ferociously. "What the fuck was that?"

"You did technically force me, I was just being truthful. Lying is bad for the complexion." she grinned with a shrug.

Freddy's face had turned an odd shade of chartreuse which really did nothing for him and his brown eyes seemed to burn into her when he glared.

"You're fucking psychotic."

She blew him a kiss, "Not my fault you look deranged enough for that woman to be concerned."

He shook his head, put the car in gear and started off again, glancing into the rearview mirror to peer anxiously at his complexion when he thought she wasn't looking. She smothered a laugh with a cough, and he looked away quickly.

"Worst road trip ever." he grumbled but she could see a slight smile on his lips. She didn't think it was so bad.

V

IVY

AFTER the unexpected pull-over, the rest of the journey passed relatively quickly. The roads were mostly deserted, which was unsurprising considering it was nearing eleven at night. A slight drizzle had started, making a soft shushing sound against the window as it grew steadily heavier. Something in her eased at the sound, it felt like they were in their own bubble here in the car, like it was safe. She glanced at Freddy, he had been silent for a while now but sighed when he felt her eyes on his face for the umpteenth time.

"What?" he barked.

She shrugged. "Nothing."

He sighed again, cradling the wheel with one hand and rubbing the other over his eyes tiredly.

"What is it, Ivy?" he asked in a slightly softer voice.

She hesitated slightly, "I'm not saying I believe you – I'm ninety-percent sure this is some weird-ass dream and I'll wake up tomorrow safely tucked in bed. But, hypothetically speaking, if you actually were an angel and all this was real— "

"Which it is." Freddy interjected sardonically, fiddling absent-mindedly with his golden nose ring. It had to be a nervous tick, she'd noticed him doing it before and now wondered why. What was he so nervous to return home to?

She rolled her eyes. "Right. So... why are you here? I thought only bad angels fell."

Somehow, she didn't think angels took vacations, though she supposed she knew very little on the subject. For all she knew, they had annual holidays where they got together and did the conga. She could only hope Freddy wasn't one of those creepy angels you read about in teen fiction, going about creating evil Nephilim and shit, she already felt enough like a character from a Becca Fitzpatrick novel.

He gave a short laugh, "Are you asking me if I'm evil?"

She blushed slightly but gave an unaffected shrug, "Well, you can't be too careful nowadays."

He rolled his eyes, "I'm not evil, Ivy. Without going into too much detail because Dev will explain everything when we reach the compound, I don't think you'll understand. Some of it isn't my story to tell." His hands had clenched on the steering wheel and his normally warm brown eyes had turned cold.

"That means some of it is – you deserve to tell your parts of the story too, Freddy." she murmured softly, her hand nervously clenched and unclenched atop the scratchy grey material of the car seat.

His eyes flickered to her just once before facing the road again, his jaw tight, hands white-knuckled on the wheel.

"I didn't fall because I was *bad,* Ivy. It's...hard to explain. There are things even we don't know. We don't know of God, just Hades, we don't know how we came to be originally, only that we did. We're almost as clueless as you humans about our origins, the only one who could tell us much of anything is Hades and he rarely leaves his domain." Freddy paused to let all that sink in for a second, eyeing her warily before continuing.

"It's said that an angel created this world long-ago. It's one of the major three planes that has been kept up, expanded, and not lost to time. Their name has been lost to us over the years, we're long-lived but even we have our limits. Michael took over some twenty years ago in Earth time, molding this world into his ideal, with corruption running rampant. He grew mad with power. It was basically his way or the high-way, and he is very powerful, very strong. For angels, the better your creation, the greater indicator of power. As you can see, this is a pretty complex creation, so Michael taking over is a pretty big deal."

She just stared at him, unsure what to make of this, she had never been particularly religious, but she had hoped there was a meaning behind, well, *life*. "But why did you fall?"

Freddy snorted, "It wasn't so much a falling as being booted out," he said, rubbing his chest as if he could still feel the ghost of the pain.

"I protested Michael's treatment of some angels and Michael *really* doesn't like to be questioned. He and his brother, Gabriel," his lip curled at the name, "ripped out my wings and sent me spiraling through unfettered portal energy until I hit the Earth. Hard. Without any of the usual protections I'd relied on my wings for, I was pretty bad off."

"What did you do then?" she asked, unable to keep the concern from colouring her voice. *What are you doing?* A small part of her whispered, *you don't need to care about him. Just get the information you need.* She shook off that insatiable little voice and focused on Freddy.

Freddy sent her a small reassuring smile. "Then Dev came for me."

"He helped you?"

"Yeah, he helps all of us. Takes care of us, gave us a home, helped us train and become strong again. It was hard, losing my wings.

It uncenters you in a way I don't think I can even put into words. Devlin helped me find my centre again."

She sat back in her chair, unsure what to say this.

Finally, she settled on, "Are you happy?" She wasn't sure why she cared, didn't want to look at it too closely.

Freddy looked a little startled, as if nobody had ever asked before, which sent a little stabbing pain through her chest, damn it.

"Happy," he rolled the word over his tongue, stretching it out, tasting it before slowly nodding. "I guess I am. This is more my home than the Heavens ever were."

A bright smile spread over his face, transforming it and lighting his eyes, "I'm happy."

She grinned back. "You're doing great, sweetie. So, you and Gabriel... I don't suppose this would be the same Gabe who turned up in my shop the other day would it?"

Freddy's smile faded slightly, a frown beginning to pull at his lips. "The one and same," he said grimly.

"He didn't seem...evil to me? Maybe he's nicer now?" she said hopefully, because damn the guy had been attractive. It would be such a shame if he was one of the baddies.

Freddy gave a short laugh, "Gabe has never been *evil*. He just lacks the ability to say *no* to Michael in any capacity. He helped Michael kick his own brother out of Heaven. Gabe is like a sad little puppy. I've seen what you're like, looking after those strays you take in when you think the landlord won't notice... but sometimes strays bite."

She dutifully ignored his warning and focused on his info about Gabe and the others, she already knew plenty about the very real dangers in life and didn't appreciate the lecture. Honestly, it had been *one* dog. One! She was mildly disturbed that he even knew about it, stalker. Besides, he was forgetting one thing: she had let the stray go.

"Wait, do you mean—?"

Freddy nodded. "Yep, Dev, Michael and Gabe. All brothers. All powerful. Gabe just never had any backbone when it came to their oldest brother, unlike Dev. Gabe's silence became just as damning as Michael's over-lording in the end."

She shook her head, trying to picture the gorgeous guy flirting with her over the counter kicking someone out of Heaven. It just didn't fit.

"I can't see it."

Freddy laughed but there was no humour in it, "Trust me, I saw it first-hand. I knew him well and yet he didn't hesitate to throw me out like I was nothing."

Freddy's face had darkened again, and she felt bad for bringing it up.

"You're not nothing Freddy. You're a bit crazy, but that's to be expected as you seem to live in a world of it."

He offered her a smirk and shrugged, his dark brown curls brushing his lifted shoulders, "Seeing as you're now a part of this world, I guess that makes you crazy too."

Oh goody.

"We're almost there, try and get some sleep for the last bit of the journey. Trust me, you're going to need it."

VI

DEVLIN

HE had hung-up the phone pissed as hell, he felt oddly flushed, unsettled. If Freddy had been a few seconds later Ivy would have been missing her damn head. Dev's fists clenched involuntarily.

"What's got you so keyed up?" Gabe asked from where he was lounging on the worn leather sofa next to his bed.

Washed and in proper clothes, Gabe looked more like the brother Dev remembered and less lost and confused by the new world around him. It was like Dev's past had bled into his new life, tension sat heavy in his muscles and his jaw ached from clenching it. He was waiting for the other shoe to drop and Gabe looking more like his old self was unnerving. Gabe seemed a little quieter than Dev remembered, but he supposed having your wings ripped out wasn't an everyday occurrence. The fall alone could sometimes take days. Jasmine was watching Gabe with her crystal blue eyes narrowed, nostrils flared. A predator hunting prey.

"Nothing," Dev said, curt. Gabe's eyes assessed him, missing nothing.

"Is that so? Nothing, eh? I wasn't aware Ivy had changed her name." Gabe said with raised eyebrows and a smirk, Dev just shrugged back at him.

He wasn't entirely sure why he was so pissed at Freddy. It had been a close call, but it had worked out okay in the end and he'd even managed to get a little info on Ivy before she arrived. *She's stubborn, doesn't trust easily and is as likely to kiss you as punch you,* Freddy had said. Dev was an idiot. Partly for thinking he could win her over when she so clearly didn't trust anyone, but worse still, Dev couldn't help picturing that stubborn mouth and wicked tongue. The way she had brushed him off in that small shop was infuriating, her razor-edged smile said *come closer* but he didn't know if it was to kiss or kill.

He'd never really put much thought into the possibility of someone being able to see him for who he truly was, maybe he was... nervous. *No.* He cut those thoughts off with a start. If he ever wanted to go home, he needed her. That was all.

"Well in that case," Gabe started, swinging around and placing his sock covered feet on the laminate, "you won't mind if I call dibs? If she's nothing, it's not a problem, right? I mean, I've only met her the once properly, but she's quite attractive... I suppose I should at least try and enjoy myself before we all die a horrible fiery death, right?" he finished with a smirk, but Dev could see the flat look in his eyes.

Still, he had to fight down the insane urge to tell him to fuck off. Ivy wasn't his; he had no authority to say whether Gabe could 'have' her. Dev rolled his eyes and didn't bother to dignify Gabe with a response.

Besides, he couldn't see Gabe being Ivy's type, he was too... squeaky clean and she seemed a little rough around the edges. It caused him no end of delight when she had said she didn't think he looked like an angel.

You could say Dev was holding a slight grudge. In fairness, they had ripped out his wings and literally given him the boot from the only home he'd ever known. Not only that but aside from the few angels who chose to fall with him, Michael left them alone in an unfamiliar place. All because Dev wanted to stop the mass slaughter Michael was planning for this world, a plan he'd obviously taken up again. Once you had created new energy it wasn't like you could just disperse it, it *felt* and *existed* and *breathed*. Apparently, having all of his enemies grouped together in one place and actively looking for a way home had begun to worry Michael. Good. He *should* be worried.

Gabe was one of the people who chose to remain by Michael's side, making it a very, very long time since Dev had seen him last. It was still surprising that he was here – not that others hadn't fallen since the original fall, they had, and Dev looked after them here at the sanctuary. Devlin and his so-called demons. It was an inside joke by this point – sometimes you had to laugh, otherwise you'd scream. Jasmine had been one of the first angels to leap into the portal after him, her wings sliced off as Michael swung after her, ensuring they could never return. Where Dev's colouring was all dark hair, browned skin and green eyes, Gabe was soft lines with only an undercurrent of muscle. Gabe was lightness and honey. He looked every bit the angel he was, the resemblance between the two brothers practically non-existent.

Gabe was always Michael's favourite brother. Dev had questioned him too much, disagreed with him. Michael didn't like that. Devlin turned to Gabe and found himself suddenly swept up in a memory.

"You don't have to do this, Gabe." he pleaded.

Gabe frowned down at him, "Yes I do, Dev. You are entirely too mortal. You need to understand that they are nothing compared to us."

Sobbing, he cupped his younger brother's pale cheek, "Please, Gabe.

I'm your brother. I would never see you again."

For a split second, Gabe looked unsure. He looked into his eyes and Dev was so sure he was going to help him. But he didn't.

Instead, Gabe reached behind him, his eyes gleaming with tears. With Michael on his other side, he ripped Dev's wings from his back.

He roared in pain, Gabe's dusky brown feathers gently brushed Dev's face one last time.

"I'm sorry, brother." Gabe's foot connected with his chest and echoed in Dev's ears as he fell through clouds and lightning and stars. He sobbed and watched his tears turn to steam as the portal's energies began to burn. Dev stared at the world spinning around him and roared his promise that one day, Michael would know such pain.

Dev blinked away the memory and suddenly couldn't stand to look at Gabe's face. He turned to leave just as the door flew open and Freddy strolled in with Ivy in tow. Her frozen-blue eyes met his before moving over to Gabe and lingering. He didn't understand the look on her face and it troubled him, her brows were drawn together and she had her tongue messing with that damned lip ring again. She looked like she had something to say to Gabe and Dev was dying to find out what it was.

His shoulders slumped in resignation, now Ivy and Freddy were here Gabe wouldn't be going anywhere. He and Freddy used to be best friends...until Freddy openly disagreed with Michael and Gabe helped Michael pluck out his wings.

That sort of thing tended to put a dampener on a friendship. Freddy didn't even look in Gabe's direction and Dev watched his eyes darken in anger. His younger brother had never liked being ignored and he definitely wouldn't want Freddy to be the one to decide that they were done.

"Freddy?"

Freddy turned to look at Gabe with disinterest, "Oh, it's you." and sharply pivoted around to face Devlin, his back pointedly to Gabe.

Devlin fixed his eyes on Freddy, a burning sensation moved through him as his earlier panic returned. Blinked, and Freddy was against the wall held by the scruff of his shirt. Dev felt wild, his heart raced beneath his skin and his hands shook below Freddy's throat. What was he doing?

Freddy looked startled and he winced as Dev's fists scrunched in the material of his t-shirt. Ivy gasped and Dev knew that he must have seemed a blur, moving so quickly even he barely remembered it.

"What the fuck?" Gabe shouted and Dev loosened his grip slightly, the exclamation shaking something loose inside him. He didn't know what to do, he didn't know how to *let go*. Freddy's familiar brown eyes locked on Dev's in understanding and calm. Freddy placed a hand over Dev's and he at last let go with a shudder, almost dropping Freddy from the wall in his haste move away.

Ivy wrapped a pale hand around Dev's arm and tugged him away from Freddy, angling herself between them, "Are you out of your fucking mind? Get away from him. *Now.*"

He stared at her small hand, looking smaller and paler than it probably was compared to him. From what Freddy had told him, Ivy didn't trust, she didn't love, she didn't get involved. Dev wondered what Freddy had done to earn her loyalty. He had no time to ponder though as Jasmine was there in a flash, glaring at Ivy with a stare that Medusa would have envied. Ivy didn't even look at her, nor did she remove her hand. Dev turned back to Freddy and kept his gaze fixed on him.

"You were supposed to keep her safe," he said it low and deadly and Freddy looked at him with only a slight twinge of fear.

"I did. She's here, she's *safe*."

"For now! Now they know she knows about all this they'll become bolder. They won't give a shit about exposure, Freddy. They'll kill her, and you know it."

Freddy's face went red as he spat, "Me? *You're* the one who visited her at work. If it wasn't for you, she wouldn't have been on their radar at all!"

Dev gave a derisive snort. "You should have called me sooner. Why didn't you?"

"I *couldn't*." Freddy ground out, "I wasn't completely sure if it was her and before I had the chance to properly investigate, you came in and fucked everything up. I couldn't exactly go up to her and ask if she might *happen* to be a psychic! I would have been committed!"

Ivy interrupted, throwing her hands in the air as colour rose to her cheeks, "Enough! I'm here! Freddy saved me from the dude with the wings. Now, explain what's happening. Why was Freddy watching me? Who are you and why do you keep talking about psychics? Why were his intestines all over my floor," she asked pointing at Gabe, "and why do you want me here?"

She was breathing heavily by the time she finished talking, her eyes lit by an inner fire and her blonde hair seemed to float around her as she shook her head in agitation. She reached out as if to grab him with her other hand and Jasmine caught it, stepping into Ivy's space and pressing her back into the wall.

"Let her go. Now."

Jas' nostrils flared, "She could be dangerous, I don't trust her. You shouldn't either."

Dev rolled his eyes, "I think I can take her, Jasmine."

Before he could say anything more, Ivy twisted Jas' arm viciously as she writhed to get free to no avail.

"Is there anyone around here that's not crazy or prone to violence?" Ivy shouted and Jas reluctantly backed off.

"Not really no," Gabe said with a smirk. Dev grabbed Jasmine before she could try anything else.

"You'll fit right in," Freddy said with a slow grin, eyes following Jas closely and completely missing the hopeful look Gabe sent his way.

"Leave, Jas."

Jas nodded stiffly, giving Ivy one last threatening look as she left.

He sighed. "My apologies for Jasmine, she can be a little... overprotective."

Ivy narrowed her eyes at him, but he could see a glimmer of genuine fear in them before he continued.

"Firstly, none of that was a hallucination earlier. I'm an angel, Freddy here, is an angel and so are Gabe and Jasmine."

Ivy opened her full lips, to protest? He plowed on.

"His intestines were on your floor because he was chucked out of the Heavens around a week ago, minus his wings, and the fall is rough as fuck. Freddy was watching you because we've been looking for the psychic able to locate a portal and get us all home. Well, bar me." he smirked at her, "Say hello to the Devil, sweetheart. You're in for a hell of a ride." It was as if more and more terrible words kept pushing past his lips and he wanted to scream at himself in frustration because he was *fucking this all up*. Dev didn't know if it was Gabe's sudden arrival, that their chances of going home had finally risen, or if it was Ivy, somehow, but he felt untethered.

Ivy barked out a slightly hysterical sounding laugh, and he winced internally because this was not going the way he wanted it to *at all*. Before he could say anything else though her hand snuck out and he caught it seconds before it would have connected with his face. Heat travelled the length of his arm where their skin touched, and he quickly let go.

"How dare you," she seethed, apparently oblivious to what he felt slowly building. "Tell me what's really going on. Don't fucking bullshit me. You're no more the devil than I am the Easter bunny and now I'm even more sure that you're all insane."

Her blue eyes sparked with anger and her nostrils flared, he had to work hard to ignore the deep spark of attraction that pulled at him. She didn't think he was evil. Insane – but not evil. He hadn't realised how heavily that weight had been pressing on him until he felt it start to slide away. Hope reared its ugly head and made his heart thud out of pace in his chest.

He let his eyes stare deep into hers as he said, "I'm not going to tell you, Ivy. I'm going to show you."

Before she could say another word, he prowled closer, keeping his eyes on hers. She didn't back away. He lifted a hand and was shocked to see it tremble, saw her notice it too and quickly slid his fingers into her silky short hair. Devlin oh-so-slowly pressed his lips to hers and was rewarded with a gasp as he let their energies mingle, a sharp *zing* sparked through him, not unlike the way he felt around other angels. His thoughts scattered as her mouth pressed harder against his and

Devlin hastily recollected them. He gifted her the truth. A vision. The beginning.

VII

IVY

OH god, was he...? Oh god he was. Fuck. Her thoughts scrambled and then fled. Dev moved slowly closer, his eyes fixed intensely on her, his hand slid into her hair and she shivered at the heat from his palm. He fisted the strands lightly and she almost groaned. She should move away. He hadn't even kissed her yet and she was enjoying *this* more than any sex she'd ever had. It would be a mistake to let him kiss her and she knew from the way his eyes moved to her mouth that was what he was about to do. Knew it with every fibre of her being that was unbearably focused on him. She'd never felt this... aware of anyone before. Heat rushed through her, it was probably the worst idea she'd ever had, but she didn't move.

His lips pressed to hers, softly, as if tasting her. Mouth stroking slowly over hers, it felt like molten lava was coursing through her veins. Like her body wasn't her own, her mind blissfully, utterly still. Yet, she was *kissing* Devlin. Nothing about this was sensible or detached or smart. But right now she didn't care, not as long as his lips stayed on hers. Her thoughts drifted lazily, a strange calm descending. They'd have to add something cheesy to the door of the One Stop like 'Angels shop here' when she got back. If she got back.

Suddenly the calm faded and she could *see* things, just like in the shop when Devlin had pressed his lips to her hand. She could see Gabe, now recognising him as the angel with the dusky brown wings

54

and she could see Dev as he hurtled through the sky – propelled by the force of Gabe's foot, sobbing and burning. She could hear Michael cursing Dev and she saw the same swirling mass of blues and greens and deep purples open over and over as more angels fell. She could see a man, dressed in some weird carnival looking costume, staring Dev deep into the eyes as he told him about a psychic who would help bring them home. *All* of them.

They thought *she* was this mysterious psychic? And she'd been cosmically match-made by the universe to break Devlin's curse. She was regretting all the times she'd wished for an end to her boredom. This was...insane.

Suddenly she could see herself and she was falling too but the images zoomed by too fast, she couldn't *see* —

Suddenly, her numb lips lost their contact with Dev's as she was ripped away from him, her vision tunneling. She crumpled to the ground, too drained to stand.

"Ivy?" Freddy's voice called to her, but he seemed too far away.

"I've got her," a cool voice said, then hands were folding around her gently.

Sleep tight, my angel. Her mother whispered and Ivy fell into the awaiting blackness.

She woke with a start, gasping, hair flying in disarray. Dev was the only one there, worrying pinching his mouth while he stared at her. She gave a brief glance around and saw an unfamiliar room, similar to something you'd find in a hotel. Large double bed, bland beige walls and a door leading to what she could only presume to be the bathroom. So it wasn't all some freaky as fuck dream then.

He let out a sigh. "Good, you're awake. Look, I'm sorry. I didn't realise it would affect you that much."

He was looking at her anxiously, but she wasn't pissed at him, strangely enough. Perhaps that had something to with the fact that she could still feel the ghost of his lips on hers. She reached up and brushed them, thinking back to Dev and the visions he'd brought on. Michael seemed like the world's largest douche.

"Why did I pass out? And how do you know I'm definitely the psychic you're looking for? Freddy could be wrong."

She didn't fully understand what had happened, she needed an explanation if she was going to keep her cool. It's not every day some infuriatingly attractive guy pops up with his (literally) hot as hell brother and announces you're going to save the world. Devlin looked at her hesitantly, a world-away from the cocky front of...yesterday? Today? She honestly didn't have a clue.

"When I kissed you," he began carefully, the cocky smile returning to curve his lips when she blushed, "I was able to fuse our energies and open the pathways between your mind and mine, it takes years of practice and wouldn't have been possible if you were a regular mortal. Besides, Freddy rarely makes mistakes."

"It could happen," she said defensively, jutting her chin up defiantly.

"It could," Devlin allowed with a considering nod, "I know you're not thrilled about all of this but there hasn't been a mistake. As for why you passed out, I showed you the whole story, but I had to travel deep within your mind to do that. It can be confusing, being in an unfamiliar mind. I hit you with too much information at once. Your mind couldn't handle it and I couldn't find my way out again to stop. So, you passed out."

There was a small pause as she tried to absorb what he'd just said. Years of practice and even he hadn't been able to successfully use those powers - what chance did she have?

"Firstly," she paused and slapped him, mostly half-heartedly

He winced and scrubbed his jaw with his hand, "I probably deserve that, I shouldn't have kissed you."

"I'd appreciate forewarning next time." *Next time?* Jeez, how had *that* slipped out? "But I'm actually pissed that you had Freddy spying on me for a half year. Perverts."

"Er, well, I—"

"Relax. What's done is done, but I won't have that shit going on here. I'm entitled to my privacy if you want me to help you."

"Of course." Dev nodded firmly, as if relieved she wasn't slapping him again.

"Why did you show me all that anyway? I already saw a lot of it at the shop that day. Er, when are we exactly?" Ivy paused for a breath and caught a surprisingly sweet slight smile on Dev's lips. She avoided looking at them after that.

"You've been out about four hours."

"And you stayed that whole time?"

"Well, I did feel a bit responsible — it would be just my luck to finally find you only to fry your brains within five seconds of getting you here."

She couldn't stop the laugh that bubbled up because, well, it sounded like something *she* would say.

"Your brother seems like a douche." she said, quirking her mouth in an effort to contain any further laughter.

"Which one?" Dev asked dryly and damn if her lips didn't twitch. His hands absently played with the coverlet and she couldn't help noticing they were nice hands before quickly looking away. No lips, no hands, she amended. "I showed you what I did because you needed to know the full extent of the curse, of what's happened." Dev continued, oblivious. "Full disclosure, that's the deal. There will never be any lies between us."

That meant more to her than he could possibly know. "Do you really think I can help?"

Dev gave a shrug, "I hope so. We're going to have to train you up first though."

"I'm willing to try. I mean, it's not like I've got anything else penciled in my calendar right now." She couldn't promise any more than that she'd try, she wasn't one for love and mush – actively avoided it, even. She wasn't looking to be a hero, or make new friends. She just wanted to do what was right, and surely she had this gift for a reason? It would be a waste not to do anything with it – at the very least, they could show her how to use it, or maybe explain how she has it.

"How're you going to take on Michael? I mean, you're not even allowed 'up there' anymore right?" she asked with a slight frown.

Dev was quiet for a second before he answered. A flash of amusement crossed his face as she said 'up there', but fuck if she knew how it all worked. Dev's face darkened as he considered her question, and she suddenly felt nervous for his answer. Usually she was pretty on point with first impressions and she'd sensed that he was sweet under the bad-boy exterior.

"I'm going to repay the pain he brought upon every single one of us." He said at last.

Oh, cool. That didn't sound too... bloody.

"He ripped out my brothers' wings. *Gabe.* Me, I expected, but not Gabe." His face was tight with anger over the treatment of his brother and people, it was uncomfortably endearing that he thought of them first. That he saw their pain as above his. She wondered if he knew he was just as dear to his people as they were to him. She could tell just by the way Freddy had spoken of him, softly, admiringly.

"I'm going to rip out his wings as he did us, and he is going to fall," he smiled without any warmth, it was clear that he regretted what was to come. After all, Michael was his brother.

"There will be no end in sight for him, until he reaches Hades. The true Hades that is," he said with a wry grin and pointed look, as if embarrassed that he had told her he was the Devil.

"Yeah about that, you thought the best way to show me you weren't evil, or the devil was to tell me you were?"

Devlin's mouth opened and closed, clearly unsure what to say. Men. She would honestly never understand their logic.

"But Hades really exists? Obviously, you're not him, but... anyway, you never said how you're going to do any of that stuff to Michael when you can't even get into Heaven?"

He laughed sheepishly looking away from her, the tips of his ears blushing pink, "No, even my brother does not have the power to truly make me into something I am not." He gave her a sarcastic grin, "As for your other question, he said I couldn't stay, not that I couldn't visit, once we find the gateway that is. I can't get back without my wings, we need to find a portal. Only, they're quite difficult to locate. That's where you come in."

She shivered as their gazes locked.

Awkwardly clearing her throat, she looked away.

"So, the Devil exists?" she prompted.

Dev had a faraway look on his face as he answered, "Oh, he exists, he's just not me - despite my earlier melodrama." Dev's eyes lightened to a spring green as he arched his brows in amusement, "He is not the Devil as you know him though. He is the carer and keeper of the dead, usually keeps to himself... unless you're trying to steal one of his souls that is," he said with a grin and she was sure there was a story behind that remark, but she was a little afraid to ask.

"I'm a little confused about...well, everything. The things I saw in those visions were...I don't even have the words."

Dev looked at her consideringly, "The world doesn't work the way you think it does, give it time. There are different planes of being: the Heavens, the Universes and Earth. Michael took over the care for this planet once he gained enough power. The Heavens, yes, plural, are outside of this universe, outside all other universes and Michael rules there as a tyrant. He removes everyone who disagrees with him here, to Earth. We can travel those planes either via portal or with our wings, but since Michael ripped out the wings of everyone here..."

Her head whirled, "You need me to try and find a gateway."

He shrugged slightly, "Yes. I know it must all be overwhelming. Nobody really knows how we came into being originally, we just are. I had parents, just like you mortals." Ivy tried not to flinch, and pushed away the memories of her own family. "It's not so much that there is more than one Heaven," Dev continued, "rather that space as you know it, is relative. The Heavens and the Hells can expand as Hades sees fit. We reside in one part, the Heavens, and Hades in the other. If it helps, the closest humankind has come to a correct analogy is the Underworld. You can think of this plane as a sort of sub-hell if you like. It's fairly complicated to be honest, and quite probable that only Hades knows exactly how many planes there are."

"Right...well, if it's ruled over by Hades, why hasn't he stopped Michael?"

Dev's face darkened again, "Nobody really knows. I've had my run-ins with Hades before and it's odd that he would let Michael run amok. He likes his rules, that one, and he's entitled to have them seeing as he's the oldest being we know of."

Jeez. Sounded like they barely knew any more than she did.

"I don't know how to bring on the visions yet, until I can control them, I don't know how to help you find the gateway."

Dev's eyes widened slightly at the implication of her words, pupils dilating. She gulped, he may not be the devil, but it sure felt like dealing with him.

"Can you help? Show me how, I mean."

He slowly nodded, eyes fixed on hers, plush red lips between his teeth.

"We don't have to kiss," he confessed, "It was just the easiest way before. I had to make sure that I could get a connection with your mind without overwhelming it, not that that went according to plan though, I suppose."

She blinked as she realised what that really meant. Her mouth dropped open in horror. "Could you hear my thoughts?"

He nodded with a twist of his lips and she felt a stab of guilt as a tense silence filled the space between them.

"Oh." Was all she said. She could offer him nothing other than that. "Well, now you know I'm just as crazy as you all are," she said in an attempt to lighten the mood and was relieved when the tension broke.

Devlin grinned at her and agh, he had *dimples*. When life tests you it really doesn't pull any punches.

"So, visions," Dev said, interrupting the current inappropriate thoughts his dimples had inspired. God, she hoped that he couldn't still hear her thoughts.

He cleared his throat and licked his lips slightly, "It's mostly about concentration. I'll help with this one but you should probably try it by yourself too. Practise makes perfect," he said with a slight smirk. She nodded, and he came closer.

He sat down opposite her on the bed and she could feel the heat rolling off him from where she sat. She flicked her lip ring with her tongue nervously and immediately stopped because his eyes dropped to her mouth and watched her do it.

Fuck it. She leant in, their lips were a hairsbreadth apart and he rasped in a startled breath.

"What are you doing?" he murmured, eyes still transfixed to her lips. "I said we don't have to kiss to do this."

She leant forward and caught his bottom lip between her teeth and *tugged,* sucking lightly and feeling the silky texture beneath her tongue. His breath hissed out of him, and she gave a slight laugh.

"I know." she said, pulling back and smirking. "But where's the fun in that?"

His eyes caught a hold of hers as he bit his lower lip. Leaning in even closer, leaving her gasping for breath as his mouth drew closer still. It was more than fun. She needed to know if the way Dev had made her feel before was a fluke. It had felt like she was simultaneously at home in her skin and yet the sharp burst of desire had left her almost crawling out of it.

Dev kissed slowly, full of exquisite heat and she let out an involuntary groan. He gave a low laugh at the sound and she fisted her hands into his thick black locks in response.

"You're supposed to be concentrating," he whispered hot into her ear, "not making-out with me."

She laughed, "Right, because you weren't enjoying yourself."

She gave a pointed look to the way he had crushed her against him, the evidence of his *enjoyment* pressed solidly against her stomach.

He gave a shrug and smirked, "I might as well get something out of this."

She swatted at him – pig.

"Show me," she said and this time his kisses were lighter, more delicate, his hands buried in her hair. She pushed through the sensations zinging through her and focused on what she wanted to know. *Focus, Ivy,* Dev's voice murmured. At last, a vision rocked her.

She focused in on the image appearing and was startled to see herself sitting on a bed like this one, kissing...Gabe? What the fuck. Gabe was talking to her whilst kissing down her neck, "I can give you what you deserve, Ivy. Not him."

She wanted to slap him away. Why was she not slapping him away? Gah! She was kissing him back! Gabe was hot and all, but he was... not Devlin, was the first worrying thought that came to mind. Plus, according to Freddy, Gabe was not a good guy.

Gabe's kisses grew more intense and she was struck with the realisation that Dev could see this. They were still connected, literally at the lips. She needed to stop this, she thought as her thoughts were interrupted by her future-self moaning into Gabe's mouth. "Dev...."

Wait, what? Gabe pulled back and away with a dark laugh. "I guess that answers that then."

She watched her own face wince. Her lips, swollen from the force of his kisses, trembled.

"Gabe...I didn't mean..."Jeez. What the fuck had she just watched? There was nothing future-her could say to make what had happened better. He shook his head and pulled on his absent shirt.

Gabe glared at her, "Save it."

But his face was sad when he said his next words. "I could have given you the world."

The look of hurt was blatant on his face as he stormed from the room.

The vision cut out and she pulled away from a startled, slightly smug looking Dev.

"Well," she said, blushing. There was a lot to unpack there. Why would she make out with Gabe? She hoped that was some sort of weird vision Dev had created and not her future.

Dev's jaw was tight with irritation but a half-smile curved his lips. It was likely a real vision then, why else would he look so bothered? Fuck.

"Well, indeed," he pressed a searing kiss to her cheek and got up to leave.

"Dev?"

He turned around slowly and raised his brows in question.

"Thank you, for helping."

He gave a low chuckle, his warm eyes danced with mischief.

"Happy to *help* anytime."

VIII

DEVLIN

Jas found him quickly after leaving Ivy's room and judging by the glower on her face, she was pissed. Ivy had only been at the compound for less than a day and yet things seemed irrevocably changed, like the air itself was charged with the hope they all felt.

"I don't like this, Dev. It feels too easy." Jas had snagged him from the corridor and was now wearing a path in the beige carpet beside her bed. "What if it's a trap? I mean, we find both *her* and your traitorous little brother on the same day? Doesn't that seem a little odd to you?"

"Right now I'm not willing to look a gift horse in the mouth, Jas."

She threw her hands in the air in exasperation, a long sigh exploding from her, "What if this is all part of Michael's plan? I don't trust them. I don't want you to get hurt, especially with Gabe. He's a tricksy bastard and you know it."

Dev softened and moved forward to pull her to a stop and clasped her hand firmly in his, holding it to his chest. He knew exactly where this was coming from. They had all held out hope at first, that Gabe could change, that he would do the right thing. And they'd been wrong, over and over. "It'll be okay Jas, you don't need to worry about Gabe. I don't trust him either – I just don't see what other choice we have right now, this is the best chance we've got."

Jas tugged her hand from his grip and sank down onto the edge of the bed, "I don't trust that girl either. You can't lose sight of what's important Dev, plus she's basically useless until we train her."

"She's... gritty."

Jas' head snapped up and she looked at him in what could only be described as horror, eyes wide and mouth a tight straight line, "You like her," she said flatly.

"No, I just admire her. Did you know she slapped me across the face for kissing her?"

Jas rolled her eyes, "Is a slap to the face really all it takes Dev? I should have won your heart years ago."

Dev let a laugh escape, something he didn't get to do nearly often enough – he needed to be stoic, a leader, dependable. Not laughing and joking, it wasn't what the people here needed from him. But here with Jas, he could let himself relax a little.

Usually, Jas loved seeing him at ease, laughing and joking with her. Yet, for some reason the sound caused a crease to appear between her brows as she slumped forward. Here with her, he didn't have to worry about who might be watching. He'd felt a similar sense of surprising peace around Ivy. She was nothing like he had expected. "Just... be careful, please."

"Always. You know me, Devlin always-careful is practically my nickname around here."

Jasmine snorted, "Brat."

Devlin grinned back at her, unrepentant. Jas was a worrier, a very fierce bundle of nerves that would cut you as soon as hug you. Her red hair clued most people in to her volatile emotions but once you got to know her, nobody could be more loyal or protective.

"I can't believe you were ready to clobber Ivy earlier," he said with a shake of his head and a rueful grin.

Jas gave a delicate shrug, a surprising strength was hidden in her willowy form and Dev knew she could have done some damage if properly motivated. "I was only warning her and Gabe. He needs to remember who he's dealing with. He's still got residual energy from the Heavens but we've been training down here for years – it's like resistance training right? I can't wait to spar with him." A steely glint flashed in her grey eyes and a grin curled her red mouth, "I want to savour the look on his face when I kick his ass, repeatedly."

Dev laughed, "Now that I can't wait to see. We need to get Ivy up to fighting speed too."

The smile vanished from Jas' face at the reminder and she grimaced, "Ugh, she's a mortal Dev. There's no way she can hold her own against one of us."

"Maybe." Dev said slowly, mind whirring, "Although something odd did happen yesterday when I merged our energies, it felt the same as if I were to connect to the power inside any of you."

Jas shrugged, "Probably just whatever it is in her that makes her psychic or something."

"Yeah, I guess." Dev wasn't entirely convinced, but whatever it was Ivy could do, she was strong – that much was for sure. "Anyway," Dev said, turning towards the door, "I need to go and catch up with Freddy – I want to hear a full run-down of everything he observed guarding Ivy. Will you organise some extra patrols of the wards please? Can't be too careful now that Gabe is here."

Jas looked relieved as she released the hands she'd been twisting together and sprung up, "Sure. I'll sort that out now. Maybe Ezekiel or one of the others can help."

Devlin couldn't help the teasing smile that lifted the corners of his mouth, "I'm sure Ezekiel would do *anything* you asked him to."

Jas blushed a little but said nothing as they made their way towards the door. It was a well-known fact that Ezekiel had a thing for Jasmine, what Dev couldn't understand was why Jas didn't go for it.

"You know, you can cut down on patrol hours? Have a little time to yourself... or not?"

Jas rolled her eyes and tapped him sharply on the cheek twice, patronisingly, "Don't get involved Devlin, I can sort out my own love life."

Dev shrugged as they left the room and headed in opposite directions, "I make no promises!" he called out and saw Jas laugh before she rounded the corner, out of sight.

It took a while after Devlin had left for her to get her breathing back under control. She could still smell the heady, sweet and spicy scent of him in the room and that alone was distracting enough. There was a knock on the door and Ivy called tiredly for them to come in, wishing desperately that she was in her bed at home. She was admittedly half-hoping it would be Dev again. It wasn't, much to her simultaneous relief and disappointment.

It was Jasmine, the red-headed girl who had grabbed her like a complete psycho-bitch when Ivy had first arrived. 'Overprotective', Dev had called her. Ivy thought 'whack job' was a better fit, personally. Their eyes met, Jasmine's lithe form was lined with tension. Ivy got the sneaking suspicion Jasmine didn't like her much. Well, it was less of a suspicion than a cold truth. Jasmine had made her stance very clear when she announced to the room at large that Ivy wasn't to be trusted. Even though she'd barely been here five minutes *and* she was the one they were counting on to get them home. You'd think that would count for something, maybe a gift voucher or a fancy lunch... she'd never saved the collective arses of multiple people before, but there had to be some sort of protocol right? Maybe a little gratitude? Judging by the tight set of Jas' jaw and the hardness in her eyes, Ivy guessed not.

Jas took in her rumpled hair and still slightly reddened lips and laughed. Now, she didn't mean a nice 'let's-be-friends' laugh, no, this was more of a 'crazy-psycho-wants-to-cut you' laugh.

"Pathetic." Jasmine ground out from between clenched teeth.

Ivy felt her shoulders stiffen in response. Yep, it had definitely been the second kind.

"Your display back there? Yes, it was."

Jasmine only laughed again, her eyes were cold and focused on Ivy with a laser-like intensity, "Do you think he loves you? That you could ever be together? Devlin may *look* human but make no mistake. He's not."

"I don't know what would make you think that I—"

"Don't bullshit me." Jasmine said, a knowing smile twisted her face and Ivy itched to slap it off. Maybe mess her hair up a little too. Truthfully, she was interested to see where this was going. The crazy angel wouldn't try to take her out would she? What had her life become that this was something she had to think about? "You are nothing more than a ticket home to him. He doesn't *want* you. He *needs* you. If it weren't for his curse, you would not be here. He may act like he cares, but rest assured, you're not his *type*." Jasmine spat the words and Ivy restrained a flinch, not expecting the pure venom in the words.

Ivy looked at her, past the cold facade and clenched jaw, and suddenly she saw it. This time Ivy was the one who laughed.

"What is it, *Jas*? Are you worried that he prefers me? I've just met him. Get over yourself."

Ivy felt the sting of the slap before she'd even seen Jasmine move, but suddenly she was an inch from Ivy's face and her cheek was smarting from the force of the blow. It was shock more than fear that kept Ivy frozen, probably wise – she could be a little hot-headed, usually to her detriment.

"Consider that a warning." Jas said with a pleasant smile, all traces of hostility gone. "Just remember, *Ivy*, that when he says your name, every touch, every smile, every *kiss*, is just because he needs you. You serve *one* purpose. Once you've helped, you will be discarded, because you are nothing."

Jas walked out, leaving Ivy with a warm cheek and a cold feeling settling in her heart.

IX
IVY

FREDDY knocked on the door later that evening to tell her that there was food waiting in the canteen area. She called back that she'd be right out but the truth was, after Jasmine's little visit she'd been feeling reluctant to go back outside and face them all. Her legs had become tingly from walking back and forth in front of the door and her cheek still throbbed painfully. It had been a long time since she'd worried about what anyone thought, but for some reason, knowing that she *was* little more than the admission ticket they'd use to get back into the Heavens bothered her. She sighed and reached her hand towards the door handle for the thousandth time, she had to go out there – mostly because she was hungry and *nobody* wanted to see her when she was food-deprived. Her already-short fuse shrank to almost nothing and things could very easily become bloody.

She poked her head out the door and almost collided with Gabe's chest as he walked by.

He saw her and grinned, "Hey!" his eyes went to the still slightly pink cheek that was Jasmine's parting gift but didn't comment, though his smile slipped slightly.

She gave him a wary smile in return. "Hi."

"You coming for food?" he asked, slinging an arm around her shoulders and dragging her out from behind the door. What was it with angels and violating personal space?

She couldn't help a slight wince at the thought but nodded, "Yeah, if I don't eat soon, I'll get extra grumpy."

He chuckled and his whole face brightened, losing some of the coldness that seemed to be lurking in the shadows of his eyes, "Well, we wouldn't want that. Let's get some food in you."

Ivy sighed but the lure of dinner was too strong. What sort of food would they have? Freddy had mentioned a canteen through the door and in her head she was picturing some sort of school cafeteria. A smile flashed across her face as she imagined Dev, tall and muscled, holding a tiny lunch tray. A snort snuck out and Gabe tossed her a raised eyebrow as they continued walking down the corridor, she shook her head back. God, she hoped there would be something decent to eat though. They passed through some wooden double doors that were ridiculously heavy, she could barely swing them inwards. Gabe rolled his eyes as he watched her struggle and parted them with ease. The canteen was sleeker than she had imagined, but it was obvious they were making-do here. It was the least homely area of the compound she'd seen so far, with plain wooden tables and benches and horrible bright lights that hung from the ceiling, highlighting the cheap laminate flooring that creaked as they walked. A long table stretched against the beige back wall and seemed to hold an array of drinks and dishes: one meat, one vegetarian and one dessert. She grabbed a plate and helped herself to some of both, making a mental note to come back and check-out the tiramisu later. Gabe tugged her away from the table impatiently with one hand firmly in hers and she couldn't help but freeze as they turned. All eyes were on her. She swallowed past the lump in her throat as she returned those looks, letting a smirk flirt with her lips –

some seemed curious and some were unabashed side-eyes. Or maybe those were aimed at Gabe, whose hand she was squeezing like a lifeline. Ivy found Dev's eyes with an unerring accuracy that worried her, his focus was on the hand enfolded in Gabe's, a frown on his face. She made her shoulders relax and nonchalantly dropped Gabe's hand, he sent her a knowing look that she ignored. His eyes had also found Dev's and seen his displeasure. That wasn't why she had let go. Or at least, that's what she was telling herself. She spotted Freddy in amongst some other angels who weren't looking at her with open distrust – progress. Freddy looked up at her in surprise as she abandoned Gabe and made a beeline for him, setting her casserole wobbling dangerously. Freddy quickly grabbed her tray from her as she swung her legs over the bench and plopped down. A heat on the back of her neck let her know that Dev was still watching. Good. Let him look. It didn't matter to her anyway.

"Hey," a low voice said in her ear and she spun round to see an unfamiliar man with hair so blonde it was white, smiling at her from his seat on the bench at the table behind her. "I take it you're Ivy?"

She gave a slight nod and he smiled a bit wider, the whiteness of his teeth and hair cast a startling contrast to the deep darkness of his skin. He was narrow; slight shoulders and slim fingers on the hand he extended towards her.

"Drew. It's so great to finally meet you, I thought you helping us get home was the best part of this scenario but that was before I saw what a total smokeshow you are. If there's *anything* at all that you want I'd be happy to give it to you."

She raised her eyebrows at him as she swiftly retracted her hand. "Is that so?" she said, voice flat and face carefully blank. Could she not eat this questionable casserole in fucking peace? It had been a *day* and her temper was fraying at the edges.

He gave her a slow grin and raised his own, nearly translucent, brows at her. "Yes," he said, "I've heard a lot about you, and apparently you're not that choosy. Although even you could do better than pretty boy there."

Even her, huh? She followed the direction of Drew's eyes and saw Gabe, awkwardly sitting at a bench with meters of empty space on either side of him. A sharp stab of guilt throbbed in her gut, or maybe it was just hunger, she thought as she turned away from Gabe.

"You need to be careful who you associate with, running around with *him* isn't going to improve your rep any." Drew continued, oblivious to her rising anger. Freddy caught sight of the flush of colour staining her cheeks and did a double take, opening his mouth, eyes wide in alarm.

She responded before Freddy could say anything, afterall, there was only one person who had been sent to do reconnaissance work on her and he was sitting right beside her. What the fuck had he told Drew? Devlin? "Oh and I suppose you're just the one to help me get in with the right crowd?"

"There are *so* many places I'm good at getting into, if you want to meet me in ten I can show you. Or is just right here in the canteen okay for you?" Drew's full lips stretched into another grin and she fought to control her emotions. It wasn't working. Was this guy oblivious? Past the roaring in her head she dimly noted Freddy laying a restraining hand on her arm and wanted to rip it off and beat him across the head with it. *He* was the one who had to have been spreading this shit around and now he wanted her to remain calm?

A guy fucks a girl in the bathroom of a club and he's a lad. She does it once or twice and she's a slut? She was always careful, it was safe sex or no sex for her – but of course they didn't think about that, never mind the fact that she'd been on the pill since she was sixteen. Her pulse pounded dangerously in her ears.

Breathe, my angel, breathe. Her mother's voice floated through her head and Ivy relaxed her grip on her cutlery as she counted her breaths. It was a trick her mum had shown her. Ivy was prone to anger, getting in more fights than she could remember when she had been a teen. It had only grown worse since *that* night. She shook her head free of the voice before the other, darker, memories stirred to life.

She heard an odd spluttering noise and looked back around to see Drew dangling a couple of inches from the floor. He was held in place only by Dev's hand around his throat, who was glowering furiously at Drew. Good to know she wasn't the only one who had difficulty controlling her emotions. Devlin was... angry didn't seem like the right word. Hot? His jaw was clenched and the muscles in his arms flexed as he choked Drew, seemingly effortlessly. His green eyes had darkened and there was a slight flush of pink to his lips and cheeks that set her body thrumming. Fuck.

Should she stop him? She figured that was Jasmine's job, though she hadn't made a move before when Dev had gone after Freddy. Ivy felt a lot less sympathy about that now that she knew Freddy was, in fact, a dick. Ivy glanced at Freddy and was surprised to find him staring at Dev with his mouth hanging open. Was this not normal behaviour then? It wasn't like she'd experienced anything different since she'd arrived here. They were angels for fuck sake, you'd think they'd be above gossip and petty infighting. It wasn't her place to step-in, of that much she was sure. What if Jasmine was right, and Dev's reaction was just a ploy to get her to trust him? Was she being paranoid? She was pretty sure she was. Besides, she had seen Freddy's reaction and unless he was a ridiculously good actor, his shock was real.

Freddy at last leaped into motion, jumping up and placing a calming hand on Dev's shoulder, "Easy now, Devlin. Leave him be, Drew is not worth your time."

Devlin flexed his hand around Drew's throat before letting him fall to the ground in a flurry of long limbs. Dev's eyes blazed as he finally turned to her, "Are you okay?"

What, did he think he was her hero or something? She rolled her eyes at him as she stalked past to where Drew had sat-up, cocky smile back in place as he saw her coming his way. "See Devlin? No harm, no foul. I knew Ivy would be into it."

Her stomach growled loudly and her hands curled into fists, "You're right Drew, I'm *so* into this." Ivy offered him a hand and pulled him up from the floor, Drew let out a low laugh and slid a hand down her arm as he stood. Without missing a beat she clasped on to his wrist, twisted and slammed a fist into his nose when he stumbled. It was a move she had perfected at age fifteen when Lewis Richards had gotten handsy.

Her hand now hurt like a bitch, aching and throbbing, but she barely felt it through the rage that had risen up like an overwhelming tide of red. She dropped Drew's arm and spun towards Freddy, Devlin must have seen the murderous intent on her face because he was suddenly in front of her. Grabbing her by the arms, he held her in place with impressive strength as he blocked her way to Freddy. His hands were warm on her bare skin and she couldn't help the shudder that rolled through her at the gentle scrape of his callouses. Great, now she was mad, hungry *and* horny.

She furiously scolded herself and looked up at Dev, "I don't need you to fight my battles for me! I've already said I'll help you, so you don't need to try so hard. I'm not sorry I hit him and I'm pretty sure I owe Freddy a little hurting too, so *let me go.*"

Dev did so immediately. Freddy raised his hands in surrender, his eyes flicked to the table and she glanced over to see that her cutlery was a mangled mess dumped onto her dinner plate. She dragged her eyes away quickly, that hadn't been her had it? Her anger drained out of her until all she was left with was exhaustion. Her quota of weird for the day had been maxed out and now all she wanted was to sleep. Turning on her heel, she brushed past Devlin, ignoring Drew's groans.

"Ivy I—" he said in a low, confused voice.

"What?" she asked sharply. She didn't want to hear his excuses or his voice right now, didn't like the way her name in his mouth made her feel like she was both lost and found. She needed to get out of this room. Before she did something she knew she would regret.

"Wow, you weren't kidding when you said you got grumpy when you didn't eat." Gabe drawled with a grin as he strolled over. She flipped him off and moved to the food table, scooped up several pieces of tiramisu and a spoon and made to leave, ignoring the weight of Devlin's eyes on her skin.

"Ivy," Dev tried again, but she just turned and silenced him with a look. Concentrated hard on what she wanted him to see. *Full disclosure* he'd promised her before, well, she was giving that to him now and more. Then it happened. She made the connection. It came to her far easier now she had practised finding that little kernel of energy inside herself earlier in her room, grabbing onto that little something *other* over and over. Determined not to need Dev's help, or anyone's for that matter. Her anger at Jasmine had hummed in her veins, fueling and focusing her. Now it was only a slight struggle to find that kernel and use it to re-awaken the remnants of the connection between them, show him what he needed to see. What he needed to know she now understood.

"Just remember, Ivy, that when he says your name, every touch, every smile, every kiss, is just because he needs you. You serve one purpose, once you've helped, you will be discarded, because you are nothing."

She broke the connection, ignoring Dev's pale face and the hand he thrust through his hair.

"Tomorrow." Dev rasped out, clenching and unclenching his fists at his side.

"What about it?" she answered coldly.

"You're going to start training."

"Fine," she said. "Whatever you *need*."

Dev opened his mouth to respond but she was already out the door, clenching the spoon tightly so nobody could see the trembling of her hands.

X

IVY

WALKING into the training room of the compound felt like familiar territory. It was a large space filled with weights and punching bags, with matts hanging from one of the concrete walls. It smelled like sweat and her shoulders relaxed after stepping through the door. After everything that had happened to her, she had needed an outlet. An aggressive one. What could be better than learning self-defense? She still had a few dirty tricks that she used, perfected from days spent brawling as a teenager, but thanks to the classes she had kept up for two years she could also throw a clean punch. Sometimes she missed being in Reading, but she often didn't stay in one place for too long, didn't like to become too comfortable, or recognisable to the locals. Still, it had probably been the most comfortable place she'd lived since she'd lost everything that had ever meant anything to her.

Dev and Freddy were waiting for her in the middle of the room, both wearing similar outfits of loose vests and joggers. Someone had thoughtfully left her a baggy tee and pair of leggings on the floor outside her room, as well as a sports bra, she didn't question how they knew her size – Freddy had obviously been thorough. Bastard. The familiar burn of anger swept her up and she hissed out a long breath before relaxing her fists.

"You came," Dev said as they looked up and spotted her lingering by the door, as if the sound of her breath had alerted them. Maybe it had. She didn't yet know the extent of their abilities, or her own. Her mind had lingered on the crumpled cutlery, twisted up on her plate. It seemed beyond ridiculous that she had done that, like Freddy was suddenly going to whip out another set and say 'Ta-Da! Got you.' Only, he hadn't.

"I know you've got a little experience with self-defense, but I think you've still got a lot to learn. Freddy and I are going to help you with that." Ivy avoided looking directly at Dev. In that washed-out black vest top, nobody had the right to look that sexy. Instead, Ivy focused on her anger with Freddy, zeroing in on his stupidly cute brown curls and innocent eyes. He had the common sense to look slightly unnerved. Maybe he too was remembering her mangled cutlery from the night before.

Dev took her silence as assent and continued, "First thing you need to know is that we're faster than a mortal, stronger too. Our hearing is a little better than the average human but that's about the extent of our physical abilities. Without our wings, we're greatly reduced, slower and weaker. The only edge we have is that being without the energies of the Heavens for so long has made us stronger than those who remained at Michael's side. Think of it like resistance training."

Ivy gave a curt nod and the slight frown that had been building on Freddy's face deepened.

"Mentally, as you know, we have the ability to speak mind-to-mind, and to harness our energy into weapons."

"Like the sword that angel had, the one who was sent to... attack you." Freddy chipped in and she kept her flat gaze on him, he flinched away.

"So while it's harder to catch or hurt us, it's still possible with enough training." Dev said, clearing his throat lightly in the heavy silence that had descended.

"We hurt and bleed just like you," Freddy said.

She couldn't help the smirk that spilled across her lips, "Good to know."

Freddy threw his hands up into the air with a muttered curse and spun around towards one of the punching bags. He threw one punch, two, before swinging back around to face her. "What do you want from me Ivy? You're pissed I spied on you for a year? That I researched into your background? Well, tough shit. I was doing what I had to do, what I owed it to everyone here to do. You wouldn't understand that, though would you? You prefer to run away when things get tough."

She didn't bother to dignify the last with a response, she had her reasons and they would remain her own until she decided otherwise. "Fuck. You." She moved towards the door and suddenly he was in front of her, faster than she would have thought possible.

"Oh, running away *again,* Ivy? Colour me shocked."

Her eyes slid closed as she tried to take a calming breath. He wasn't worth her time, he wasn't, he wasn't, he wasn't. "I thought you were my friend," slipped out so quietly she almost couldn't believe it had come from her mouth. Silence. She opened her eyes to see Freddy's brown eyes soft, his face close to her own.

"What did I do to make you think otherwise?" He asked carefully, the lines in his face had eased and he tugged on his nose ring and then a curl nervously.

"Drew knew about my past. Some of it, anyway. You're the only person who knew anything about me." She knew hurt coloured her voice, wanted desperately to be able to hide it, but she was so damn tired.

Freddy pulled at another of the ringlets brushing the tops of his shoulders and gave a shrug, "Drew's a nosy bastard, he probably just overheard me talking to Devlin."

Relief flooded her senses, stronger than it had any right to be. She didn't want to care about Freddy, didn't want it to matter whether or not he had betrayed her trust. She willed her face into a cool, collected mask and gave a short nod in response.

Freddy watched her, eyes seeing too much and not enough and tipped his lips into a sad smile, "One day you're going to find there's nowhere else to run."

She gave him a small smirk and turned away, to where Dev stood watching them thoughtfully. He shrugged in response to her raised eyebrow. Too late she realised she'd broken her 'no looking at Devlin rule' and her eyes got caught somewhere about his hips as she eyed the joggers that hung just slightly too low. Freddy gave a pointed cough and she pulled her eyes away and bit her lip at the smirk on Dev's face. He knew exactly what he was doing to her. Fine. Two could play that game.

Ivy let a smile flirt with her mouth as she reached for the hem of her shirt and dropped it to the ground, leaving her only in the sports bra someone had found for her. Maybe Freddy wasn't as thorough as she had thought, something she was absurdly pleased about right this second as the slightly too-small fabric hugged her every curve. A muscle ticked in Devlin's jaw and Freddy glanced back and forth between them in obvious amusement, "Should I give you guys a second—?"

"No." They both demanded at the same time and Ivy fought back her grin and won.

Devlin beckoned Freddy forward, eyes never leaving hers, "Watch. Learn."

She couldn't hold back her eye roll, "Yes, Sensei."

They were the last words she uttered for a long while. Watching Devlin and Freddy spar was... mouthwatering. They were lightning quick and a fine sheen of sweat had broken out across their lithe bodies as they moved faster and faster. Freddy was marginally quicker than Dev, but Dev was sneakier – throwing in punches and feints Ivy would never have thought about. They were breathing hard and grinning like fools from the endorphin rush when they finally broke apart, slapping each other on the back as they moved towards her. Devlin whipped off his shirt in a fluid motion she didn't have time to brace herself for. Her mouth ran dry as she followed a droplet of sweat down his chest and over his stomach.

"So what did you learn?" Dev asked, and she didn't even have to look away from his chest to see how smug he looked, she could hear the satisfaction in his voice.

"You're sneaky. Freddy's fast."

She dared a glance up to his eyes and was instantly ensnared by their brilliant green, a flash of something – surprise? approval? – shone in his eyes for a moment as he considered her. Then a wide grin split his face, showing off the deep dimples in his cheeks and awakening a strange flutter low in her stomach. "You're a quick study," he said, still grinning.

"Very." She said before she could think twice about it. Had she sounded a little breathy? Dev's grin widened further. Fuck.

Definitely breathy.

"Now it's your turn." Dev said. She didn't move. Didn't trust herself to get within one meter of him, his strong body still shimmering with sweat. Definitely couldn't trust herself to let him put so much as a hand on her.

"Oh, I don't know. I was learning so much from watching you and Freddy."

Dev rolled his eyes but there was a knowing glint there that had her competitive side rearing its head, "You learn more by doing. Now, move your legs into position. I want you to punch me."

Her legs slid automatically into the fighting stance that had previously been drilled into her but she blinked at his next instruction. Normally, she might have jumped at the chance to punch someone consequence free but... "You want me to what?"

"Punch me." Dev said, making it sound as if he wanted to say something entirely different. Freddy looked distinctly uncomfortable and she couldn't hide the flush that spilled across her cheeks and down her chest.

"Won't that hurt?"

"Probably not," he said, arms folded tightly across his chest, making the muscles bunch in very interesting ways.

"Lord help me, *I'll* punch you." Freddy said and she let out a snort.

"Come on," Dev coaxed gently, so she balled up her fist and swung, pushing her whole body into the movement the way she had been taught. Dev caught the motion effortlessly in one hand.

"Now punch me like you mean it." Dev said and she was baffled, because she *didn't* mean it. For the first time in a long time, she'd found someone she didn't want to punch in the face. Was this love?

"Come on," Dev said again, "You've been torn away from everything you thought you knew, had someone who was your friend spying on you for months, been propositioned in front of the entire compound *and* been slapped by Jasmine. All within forty-eight hours. Are you really telling me you're not a little angry?"

Well, when he put it like that. "But none of that is your fault."

"Isn't it?" He asked, staring at her intently. "You were dragged into this because of me, Drew knew those things about you because of *me*. Jasmine... hurt you. Because of me."

He wasn't technically wrong, but she had never felt less angry in her life. "How do you even know about that? About Jasmine?"

"When you make a connection with someone mentally, you need to be a little more careful about how much you allow them to see."

Fuck.

"You don't have enough experience yet to know how to do that. I saw a lot more than you wanted me to, I'd bet. I saw your absolute rage, your helplessness, your guilt. What if it was your fault? What if Jess—"

She hit him.

Hadn't even intended to, didn't remember moving. It was like he had peeled away the first layer of her soul, leaving it to rot and crumble as it came into contact with the air and life around her. Like hearing Jess' name had made the world implode in her ears, echoing around her like a scream trapped in her heart. There were truths she hadn't admitted to herself, let alone anyone else. Her breaths heaved out of her in what sounded suspiciously like sobs but she felt nothing. Not as Devlin flew backwards, crashing into the concrete wall across the room. Still nothing as Freddy gripped her by the arm in shock before rushing to Dev's side. Dev who was already sitting up, a trickle of bright red blood smudged across his mouth, making his smile all the more feral as he stared at her. "There you are."

She had no words left in her. The light in Devlin's eyes faded as he took in the trembling of her body, the small bead of blood that had risen on her lip as she bit down to stop the cry that wanted to escape.

"Ivy," was all he said. She felt a breeze brush her face and suddenly his arms were around her. Warm, steady.

After a moment she pulled back. It was too much and not enough and she didn't want to listen to her body as it screamed out to be *closer, closer.* Her eyes met Dev's and his eyes darkened at whatever he saw on her face, leaning in, his mouth a whisper away from hers. Their lips brushed, once, twice. She pulled away, her body strung so tightly that the air itself hurt her skin.

Freddy had left at some point, soundlessly, or maybe she had just been too lost in Devlin to notice Freddy's absence.

Running away again?

She shuddered and pushed away the remnants of Freddy's accusation.

Breathe, my angel, breathe.

She breathed, and retreated, and ignored Devlin, still standing in the center of the room. Frozen, as if he could still feel the ghost of her in his arms.

XI

IVY

"Focus!" Freddy snapped, striking out at her.

It was their third training session that week and her body ached with every move she made, sitting on the toilet had become agony. Since she had arrived at the compound four weeks ago she had trained with Freddy three times a week, which was great, she had a lot of anger to work out. Mostly with herself. She had avoided Dev like the plague, which was admittedly hard when he ran the place. It was as if the universe was laughing at her, she found him in every corridor, stopping and talking to various angels. It had been awkward since she'd punched him across the room in a show of supernatural strength she had failed to replicate since, much to Freddy's annoyance. Devlin seemed to know the name of every single one of the hundred or so angels living at the compound and somehow knew exactly what they needed with an unfailing accuracy that blew her away. Not that she'd been paying special attention at all. Devlin gave the angels everything, holding no part of himself back in a way that she couldn't even fathom.

"I'm trying!" Ivy hissed through her teeth as she fell back and swung her leg around in what would have been an impressive blow had Freddy still been in front of her.

"You're holding back," Freddy accused, not even out of breath.

"Not on purpose," Ivy said with a pant as she braced her arms on her knees, "trust me, there's nothing I'd enjoy more right now than hitting you."

Freddy grinned cockily, bouncing lightly on his feet as he gestured her forward with two fingers.

Angels were damned fast and lethal fighters, in battle she would never hold her own. It was pretty clear to her that if she hadn't caught Drew off guard in the canteen she never would have landed that punch. She charged forward and Freddy laughed as he darted away, pushing her from behind. Her face hit the hard ground, scraping her chin, she rolled over as Freddy demonstrated what would have been a fatal strike. He wiped the sweat off his brow and she looked longingly at the lone tree in the courtyard. It was a surprisingly sunny day, rare for England, and Freddy was killing her out here.

She let loose her breath on a growl of frustration and rubbed tenderly at her grazed chin. Freddy well and truly wiped the floor with her each day, and he didn't have anything on the power of someone like Dev. Freddy also wasn't one for positive reinforcement.

"That was shit, Ivy."

She winced. "Really? And here I thought that my arse hitting the ground for the tenth time was a *good* sign." she said dryly.

"Technically it was your face this time," Freddy said with a grin as he offered her a hand up from the floor.

Someone slowly applauded from the sidelines. Ivy looked up, squinted her eyes against the glare of the sun, and saw Jasmine.

Jasmine stepped into the makeshift ring Freddy had set up in the courtyard. Ivy pulled on Freddy's hand and got back up onto her feet, sore muscles complaining as tension filled her body.

Furrowing his brows, Freddy called, "She's not ready to be

fighting anyone else yet, Jas."

Jasmine smiled in return. "Oh, come on, Freddy. I think she could stand to mix up her partners a bit, train with someone who won't go easy on her."

Freddy looked ready to protest again but stopped at Ivy's next words.

"No, Freddy, I think she's right," she gave Jasmine a smile, "Let's train."

It's on, bitch. It had been a frustrating few weeks and the prospect of paying Jasmine back some of the humiliation she had dealt Ivy was too tempting. Plus, it would be a nice change of pace to fight someone Ivy actually *wanted* to hit.

Her arms and feet positioned into the standard fighting stance Freddy had adjusted and made her perfect, she assessed Jasmine's stance. From the way she held herself, it was clear Jasmine was an experienced fighter. What had she been expecting? That Jasmine couldn't hold her own? *Shit.* It looked like this was going to be a painful experience, hopefully Ivy could get in a few good hits before Jasmine took her out. She wasn't stupid, she knew she was outmatched in speed, strength and experience, but in a battle of the mind, she was hoping she could win. So, in other words, she was actually very, *very,* stupid.

Freddy stood stiffly on the sidelines; refereeing the match and probably waiting to jump in to prevent Jasmine beating the shit out of her. Ivy gave Jasmine her sweetest smile and Freddy called the match into being. Jas smiled back, though it was more a baring of teeth, and advanced so quickly Ivy only managed to block her first blow before taking the next kick to the stomach hard. Freddy winced from the sidelines, looking like he was going to step in, she waved him off and straightened, ignoring the dull ache in her gut and forcing some air into her winded body. *Breathe, Ivy, just breathe.* This time she wasn't trying to fend off a wave of red, but center herself. All she needed was a second to think, to reenact what she had done to Dev in the canteen but with something more jarring... something that would prove that just because Ivy was human, she wasn't weak or less than them. Though it grew harder and harder to remember that with every punch Jas landed. Freddy had been practising with Ivy every afternoon once they finished sparring, since that day in the canteen and she could now show people only what she wanted them to see – rather than the whole contents of her brain, but she still had a lot to learn.

Was it cheating? Maybe.

But Jasmine was an angel, so Ivy would press what advantages she could.

Jasmine's fist caught Ivy's cheekbone and sent her sprawling away. Son of a bitch that had *hurt*. She'd have to add that to the long list of injuries she had acquired in the past few days. She dragged herself to her feet and gingerly pressed her hand to her cheek.

The red-headed angel grinned savagely, "Come now, Ivy, there isn't time to mill around in battle."

She sent Jasmine a calm smile, "You're right, Jasmine, there's not."

She leapt at the angel, hoping shock would keep Jasmine prone for a few seconds.

Ivy found herself dumped on the floor, coughing dust once more. Okay, that plan had sucked a little. Dragging herself up, they circled each other, Jasmine's footwork was flawless. Ivy spat her hair out of her mouth and wiped sweat out of her eyes, her fingers came away bloody from a cut she hadn't even known she had. Jasmine was beating her. Badly. Ivy had to make her sloppy, forget herself.

"Tell me, Jasmine, how long have you been in love with Devlin?"

Jasmine stilled momentarily before resuming her circling, she swiped at Ivy, catching her in the mouth. Jas smiled ferally as Ivy spat out blood.

"It's just odd." Ivy continued, ignoring the taste of metal coating her tongue, "You keep acting like the reason you and Dev aren't together is because I'm around but tell me, Jas, what about before?"

"Before?"

Jasmine's feet hesitated before taking their next step, seeing her opening Ivy pressed, "Well, Dev didn't seem to have any qualms about kissing someone he'd only just met, so I'm guessing you weren't together... oh! He doesn't know, does he?" Ivy let out a laugh, sauntering right up to a frozen Jas and pinching her cheek. "That is so... precious."

Jas seemed to forget all her training as she charged at Ivy like a bull and threw her down onto the floor. Jasmine's fist slammed into Ivy's face once, twice, and as Jas raised it again, Ivy lifted her head and they locked eyes.

Ivy immersed herself in every inch of the memory she needed, let it fill her lungs, her soul with its rot and shame and despair. Then she *pushed* and watched Jas stagger with the force of the vision. Falling to her knees, Jas stared unseeingly into the distance as Ivy stood up.

She played the memory like a film in Jasmine's mind, shutting down her own emotions as Jas began to shout, tears dripping slowly down her face. Ivy cut the memory off abruptly, she'd won the match and she was *done* with today. Jas sagged against the floor in relief, droplets of sweat covered her forehead as her eyelids fluttered.

Freddy ran over, accompanied by Gabe and a handful of others she hadn't noticed watching. "What did you *do*?"

Jas lay unmoving on the dusty ground.

Ivy looked at Freddy unfeelingly and he flinched at the coolness in her eyes, "She'll be fine."

At least, she *hoped* she'd be fine. Jas was a bitch, but she'd feel a little guilty if she drove her insane whilst sparring. Freddy looked at her blankly, and then gave a slow nod, still frowning at her worriedly, "Very smart, it's important to use all your resources when in battle."

Jas came-to with a gasp, her face paler than usual. Her eyes sought out Ivy's, face still wet with tears and her shoulders rounded with borrowed grief. Her voice cracked when she spoke. "Did they ever find them?" There was an edge of desperation in her voice that was familiar.

Ivy's hand shook and she squeezed it into a ball as she gave Jas a hard smile that tugged painfully at the fresh split in her lip, she didn't even feel the blood that slowly trickled down her chin, "No."

Then Jasmine truly did surprise her, "You should know that there will be no escape, they will burn for what they did. Hades will make sure of it." Her voice trembled and Ivy could see a familiar rage mirrored in Jas' eyes.

Ivy smiled at her, at last finding common ground with the angel, and it was a real smile this time.

"I hope they burn on Earth too."

She had made it back to her room without remembering the journey, her mind stuck in another time. Her hands shook as they reached for the doorknob, smeared with blood from the fight. Suddenly it was as if she were seeing double, hands coated in blood swam in front of her mind's eye. Her breaths rattled out, coming faster and faster, her eyes slid closed and mouth filled with saliva. All she could see were blue eyes staring up at her, so similar to her own. Cool, stiff, hands, limp against her skin. Ivy flung her eyes wide and tried desperately to focus on the dull, cracked blue paint of the door in front of her, the metal handle cool against her palm. It should have been grounding but her breaths didn't slow. The door swam in front of her as she grew dizzy. *Breathe, my angel, breathe.* A warm hand settled on her shoulder and yanked her back to the present, suddenly her breaths were filled with the warm, heady scent of Dev. He murmured her name but still sounded so far away. His hand slid from her shoulder to her waist, tugging her around to face him, cupping her cheek as he peered into her eyes. A tense pinched look marred his face as his lips formed her name. He gently ran a finger over one of the wounds on her face, barely brushing her skin with his fingertip but sending a bolt of heat through her. His thumb hovered over her split lip and she resisted the urge to nip at it as he slowly brought her back into her own body. *Drip, drip, drip.* Her lip was searing in pain as blood dropped onto the floor between them, she couldn't hide her flinch at the sound, as it threatened to pull her under once more. *Drip, drip, drip.*

Dev curled a hand around her freezing fingers, moving closer until his heat punched through her body and she breathed him in. Alive, so alive. Her still-trembling hands eased slightly, a draft kissed her face, cooling tears she couldn't remember having shed until

Devlin silently wiped them away.

"Ivy," he matched his breaths to hers, their breath mingling until her breathing was back under control again.

"It's okay." she said absently, thinking back to a different time, a different person she had said those words to.

"What happened?" his voice was tight as he assessed the collection of cuts and bruises all over her. "Who did this? Are you hurt?" There was something dangerous lurking in Dev's voice that she didn't want to analyse. His hands were steady as they tightened on hers.

"Me?" she laughed, a hollow sound without any joy. "No, not me."

His arms reached for her, but she pushed them away. She didn't need or want his comfort, not about this. *Drip, drip, drip.*

"Ivy, I just want to help. Let me in, please. Or let me get Freddy at least, just—" Dev blew out a heavy breath, worry pinching his mouth, "Just don't run away again."

She held his eyes as he looked at her steadily, his hand hesitantly reaching up to brush against her cheek. Breathing deep, she smelled the copper tang of her own blood and the memory crashed over her like a wave, so strong she pulled Dev along with her.

Drip, drip, drip. Ivy couldn't tell where the sound was coming from. She'd gotten home moments earlier, had insisted on going to Kayla's party and had left after being there a measly hour and a half. It had been absolutely dead, her mum had been right. She would have enjoyed staying home for family night way more. The front door clicked quietly closed behind her, she had hoped to sneak straight upstairs so she wouldn't have to look in Jess' eyes and explain that she had picked some party over spending time with her. Jess was ten and as far as younger sisters went, she wasn't bad. Constantly following Ivy around, begging to spend time with her, but Ivy found she didn't mind. In fact it was kind of... nice. Drip, drip, drip. Jess was her half-sister but it had never made any difference to them. Plus, it was fun to teach her swear words. Moving into the hall, something felt wrong. *The air was heavy, an odd musty smell filling it and Ivy paused with her foot on the bottom stair. Why was it so quiet? Normally during family night there would be laughter, music in the background while they played* Monopoly *or* Snakes and Ladders. *The house was eerily still.*

Drip, drip, drip.

"Mum? Dad?" Ivy called hesitantly as she rounded the bannister and approached the living room door. "Jess?"

She was listening intently and that was the only reason she heard it when her name was whispered. "Ivy..."

"Jess?" Ivy asked again, she stepped into the living room and gave a startled gasp. The carpet felt strange under her feet, spongey and crunchy at the same time. Warm liquid began to sink into her converse and she was grateful that the lights were off so she didn't have to see what it was. In the near-darkness she could make out the forms of her parents, one sitting at the dining room table in the corner of the room and the other lying on the floor near the doorway. Ivy walked over and stretched out a hand to her mother on the floor, she sharply pulled it back. Ice cold. Her mum's hand was starting to stiffen and a shudder worked its way through Ivy's body at the sight of her mother's unseeing eyes. A burning started in her chest, desperate for a way out, but there was nobody to fight. Not this time. Her breath came in pants and she nearly fell to her knees when that quiet whisper wafted through the room again.

Jess was on the floor, as if she had tumbled off her chair and was going to bounce up at any minute with a laugh. She didn't. Ivy hurried over to her and dropped down beside Jess' body, ignoring the way the blood on the floor soaked into the knees of her jeans, it felt hot against the coldness of her own skin. Dimly, she knew that was a bad sign. Shock. That was probably it.

Jess was warm still, just about. Her dark hair was stiff with blood and seemed to gleam purple in the street light filtering in from the window. Quiet tears sneaked down Ivy's face, trickling into her long hair as she reached for her sister.

Jess couldn't turn her head, she was too close to gone, the jagged line across her throat trailed off half-way, like whoever had done this had been interrupted and hadn't bothered to finish the job. The whites of Jess' blue eyes showed as they rolled towards her, wide with fear.

"Shhh," Ivy murmured trying to keep her voice steady, "It's okay. I promise it's going to be okay."

Jess relaxed ever so slightly, a sigh heaved out of her as her chest stopped moving. Ivy sobbed in full rattling breaths, unrelenting. That was how the first responders found her, alerted by neighbors to some strange noises coming from the Fayte residence. If Ivy had waited just ten minutes more, she wouldn't have seen the bodies. She also wouldn't have been able to say goodbye to Jess. Ivy didn't look at the scene around her when the police flicked on the lights. Didn't fight the hands that pulled her from her sister's body, didn't really see or hear anything as they cleaned the blood from her face and hands and asked her question after question. Ivy just quietly said the same response over and over, seeing but not seeing, "It's okay, It's okay,"

Numb.

Devlin's eyes were slow to open. Her breathing had evened out, like in showing him part of the deepest part of her she had eased the burden, cleansed herself. He squeezed her hand and then let go, a sharp pang lurched through her chest. Was that it then? She bared the still-healing wound of her heart to him and he'd had enough? Gotten all he wanted from her and was backing away now he really knew what lurked inside of her? She swallowed her emotions down deep, taking a soothing deep breath as she smoothed her face. Devlin watched the transformation with a blank expression until the smirk appeared on her lips, then his eyes glinted with challenge as he stepped forwards, pressing her back against her door.

His breath brushed over her mouth, tantalisingly close, as he murmured, "It wasn't your fault."

The breath froze in her chest, the smirk guttering on her face. "I could have saved them."

"You were seventeen, Ivy. *Seventeen*. It was a terrible thing, but you can't keep ripping your life apart because of it. It's not what they would have wanted." His eyelashes brushed against her cheek gently, igniting her anger at their delicacy as she roughly shoved him away.

"Well it's a shame they're not here to scold me." Ivy said smoothly but she didn't fight back when Dev's arms came down again and caged her on either side.

"Nobody else will be here either if you don't stop this."

She stared at him. Didn't he know? Didn't he understand that was exactly why it had to be this way? Because *they all left* and she couldn't take anyone else leaving. Dying.

"I could have saved them," she repeated flatly, she was going to lose it completely if she said any more.

"Ivy —"

"I *could* have!" She shouted, the words burning in her throat from the force of her cry, "I punched you across the room the other day! I crumpled solid metal cutlery like it was nothing! If I had just stayed home they would be alive and —"

"—and nothing." Dev said abruptly, "You only know how to throw a proper punch *because* they're gone. If they were still here you might never have known about your powers, your strength. And you *are* strong, Ivy. Much more so than just physically."

A tear spilled down her cheek and she knocked it aside quickly. She didn't feel strong. Maybe Dev was right, but it didn't change the what-ifs.

Devlin's eyes deepened to a dark green as they stared at one another. Her breathing hitched, though now for an altogether different reason, as she felt their closeness so acutely it echoed in her blood.

They moved at the same time. Ivy's hands fisted in his hair, Dev's lips crushed bruisingly tight against hers and she needed that. The roughness, the heat. His answering gasp to her heady moan was like wildfire zinging through her, setting her ablaze.

This was wrong, so wrong. She barely even knew him, not that it had mattered to her in the past. Sex was just sex. No emotions, no strings. Just pleasure and escape. The difference was she had opened up. Ivy broke away quickly, before she could think too hard on it, despite every nerve ending tingling, screaming at her to just *stay a little longer*. That it was *so right*. Dev's breath was shallow and his eyes were wide on hers, but he stepped back, giving her breathing room and she felt the absence of his heat immediately.

"Stop punishing yourself for the shitty thing someone else did. You don't have to run. Not from me." He added and heaved in a breath as he shoved his hands through his hair, taking a couple of steps back from her as if to stop himself moving closer.

Her head was hazy, full of his scent and the taste of his kisses. He reached out and let his hand drift through the ends of her hair almost absentmindedly, she shivered against the feather light touch and turned away. She glanced behind her before she stepped inside her room and gasped to find Dev practically nose-to-nose with her.

"When you're done running, you know where I'll be." he stepped back and pressed a searing kiss to her forehead. Her eyes closed involuntarily at the sensation and when she opened them again, he was gone.

XII

IVY

"This is shit." Ivy said after her fifth failed attempt at trying to bring on a vision. She had been practising all day, trying to work out how she was supposed to find the portal to the Heavens. So far, she'd had no luck.

Jasmine shrugged from where she sat, stretching out her long legs in front of her she said, "Take a break. You've been at it all day."

"I can't just take a break. We don't know how much time we have before Michael decides Earth is toast, every second counts."

Jas sighed deeply, the breath ruffling the ends of her hair. It was down for once and ran in heavy waves to her waist, it made her seem softer, more vulnerable. "You need to have a clear, calm mind to try and bring on the visions. I don't think sitting here and stressing is going to help – except to give you a headache." Jas said pointedly as Ivy rubbed her temples.

She and Jas had reached an unexpected understanding, maybe even a friendship. Ever since sparring in the courtyard a few days ago, Jas had been...different. Turning up at Ivy's door with a stack of reports and marching in like she owned the place, settling cross-legged on the floor much like she was now. It was like she had finally let down her guard, like Ivy had won her trust somehow by showing Jas the most wounded parts of herself. In a way, she supposed Jas knew her better than anyone now, save maybe Devlin. Ivy was glad, she much preferred the new, trusting, Jasmine to the one who had slapped the shit out of her.

Ivy groaned and let her head flop back against the edge of the bed as she wiggled her butt, numb from sitting on the floor for so long. "I just feel like I should have accomplished more by now. I've been here a whole month. And all I've seen so far is Drew flirt with everything that moves and an uncomfortably graphic vision where I got to take a shit with Freddy."

Oh and not to mention the random vision of her making out with Gabe. That Devlin witnessed. Awkward. Ivy opted to keep the last to herself, things were going so well between her and Jasmine, the last thing she needed was to make an enemy out of her again. Jas was protective over Dev, that much Ivy knew for sure, and she didn't think Jas would take it well if she thought Ivy was stringing him along. The truth was, Ivy didn't know what she felt about Dev. *When you're done running, you know where I'll be.*

But that was just the thing, with Dev, Ivy didn't want to run. Which meant she definitely should.

"I'm sorry." Jas said abruptly and Ivy blinked at her in surprise as Jas put down the papers she had been reading to stare at Ivy.

"What for? Unless you somehow planted that image of Freddy in my mind because —"

Jas rolled her eyes and flipped her long hair over her shoulder, "Not for that, idiot."

"Then what?"

Jas' hazel eyes flicked to the wall behind Ivy's head as she bit her lip, relinquishing it with a huff and looking Ivy dead in the eye, "For how I acted when I first arrived. I was..."

"Jealous? An angelic snob?" Ivy supplied with a quirk of her eyebrow.

Jas chuckled quietly and threw her hands in the air in exasperation, "I'm *trying* to apologise, you utter brat, so shut up and let me."

"Gee, you're doing a great job."

They both began to laugh. Ivy felt off-balance, unused to the warmth in her chest, the lightness of just... being.

"I really am sorry."

"For being a jealous angelic snob?" Ivy asked with a grin that widened when Jas smiled back.

"For being a jealous, angelic snob." Jas repeated solemnly before dissolving into laughter.

Jas began chatting idly and Ivy let a soft smile curve her mouth, relaxing fully for the first time all day as she listened to the sound of Jas' voice. Her eyes slid closed and her breathing deepened until the world fell away.

Heaven. She didn't think it would look quite like this. She looked up and met Dev's green eyes as he pulled her in close, his forehead resting against hers.

"Remember, as soon as things get crazy, just get yourself out. Okay? Don't wait for me, I can't stay here for long. The curse won't let me. When this is all over, I'll find you."

He kissed her once, fiercely, but his eyes were sad when he pulled away. What he really wanted was to stay here in heaven, where he belonged. Not return to Earth with her. Then a slow applaud began as Michael walked down a large white staircase, the contrast of his auburn wings startling against the paleness of the room.

"How touching." Michael said, the sneer on his face twisting and marring the otherwise surreal beauty of his face, "Don't you think so –

The vision ended as abruptly as it had begun, and she was aware that she was gasping for breath as Jasmine looked on worriedly, her hands resting lightly on Ivy's shoulders.

"What happened?" Jas asked quietly, once Ivy had caught her breath back.

Slowly, Ivy shook her head, her voice a soft rasp as she told Jas what she'd seen.

"So, we make it there," Ivy said, "but I don't know how. I was with Dev and we were in this huge room. It was completely white.... and Michael was there."

Jas nodded and Ivy could see her puzzling through what she'd said.

Jas looked at her steadily, "Thank you for helping us."

Wow, once Jas decided she liked someone, she was all warm fuzz.

"You're welcome." Ivy said softly. Despite it all, she felt like she should be doing more. "I'm just sorry I haven't been more of a help yet."

Jas shrugged, "You only discovered what you could do a month or so ago, cut yourself some slack. You need to relax, get some sleep or something."

"I'll sleep when I'm dead." Ivy said sweetly and Jas rolled her eyes. "Jas, Devlin's curse... if I don't fall in love with him, he can't stay in the Heavens right?"

Jas' eyes narrowed but she gave a curt nod.

"In my vision, Dev told me to leave when things started to get crazy, that he would find me on Earth because he couldn't stay in the Heavens. Jas... I think we make it there, but I don't fall in love with Devlin."

Jas looked equal parts relieved and worried, "You don't know that for sure."

"No, I don't. But the way he spoke to me, I don't know, he just seemed so certain that he couldn't stay."

"Well, we'll prepare ourselves for that possibility. Though Devlin can be ridiculously obtuse, you could dance naked in front of him and he probably wouldn't think you had more than a passing fondness for him. So we'll prepare, we'll try to find another way, but nothing is set in stone, Ivy."

Ivy wasn't sure which worried her more, the thought of falling in love with Dev or him being trapped on Earth forever.

"Would you stay for him? If he was truly unable to go back?"

Jas looked away from her, like she couldn't quite meet Ivy's eyes considering things would be easier on them all if Ivy *did* love Devlin, "I would follow him anywhere."

Ivy nodded, silent. She had thought as much. "For what it's worth, I'm sorry too."

Jas gave her a pained smile, eyes glittering suspiciously, "Don't be. You were right before, Devlin has never looked at me the way I —" Jas shook her head and stood abruptly, making her way to the door. "He is so good, Ivy. You should give him a chance. For his own sake," she said with a small pause, hand on the door knob, "and your own. We can't help who we love." Jas slipped out of the door quietly, clearly needing to escape. Jasmine was strong and Ivy couldn't help but admire that. She had told Ivy to give Dev a shot despite knowing it killed any chance Jas might have had with him. Ivy wasn't sure if she could have made the same choice. Jas was right, we couldn't help who we loved and it was for that reason that Ivy wished she could carve out her own traitorous heart. Weak, poisonous thing that it was.

Ivy shook her head free of the maudlin thoughts, using her power often left her feeling like this – drained and fragile and numb. Like she was both herself and not. She wouldn't be much use in a fight against other, highly trained, angels. She was strong sometimes, but she couldn't control it, and she didn't think the trick she'd pulled on Jas would work on a whole army.

So what could have changed by the time that vision took place? Why would she go with them to the Heavens? Surely Dev, practical as he was, would have recognised her as a liability in a fight? She needed to see more, nothing made sense and she didn't know what to *do*. Ivy slammed her fist against the floor, relishing the pain as it centered her, focused her thoughts.

Her eyes slid closed and a vision came to her, slowly piecing itself together but so hazy it made her feel nauseous. Something about this was different, not like the real-time images she'd been getting recently. This was faded somehow, foggy and echoey.

"Gabe..." A low voice murmured. Fuck. If she was having another make-out vision after spending so much time trying to focus she was going to scream. She needed to see something useful, not more soft-porn.

"OhshitGabe..."

The voice sounded deep and rough, a lot deeper than her own voice. Suddenly the thick fog of memory that swirled through the vision cleared and she stared at the figures entangled on a bed built large enough for wings.

Gabe groaned into Freddy's mouth as he tugged roughly on the messy curls that sprung up in every direction. They were sprawled atop silky looking sheets that shone bronze in the low-light, Gabe's hand clenched in them for a second before he reached for Freddy. Freddy bit Gabe's lip passionately and Gabe gasped as Freddy licked and sucked his way down the strong column of his throat. Hands slid slowly down Freddy's chest and lower still. Fuck. They had known each other as much more than friends. It was Freddy's right to tell her or not, but she couldn't help feeling a little twinge of hurt. He knew so much about her and yet she clearly barely knew him. Clothes were disappearing fast and frantically and oh, boy, she did not want to be here when they all came off. Wait. Angels got off in the Heavens just like humans did on Earth. Did that mean Dev had some angelic exes floating around out there somewhere? Ivy swore internally. It wasn't the time to chase that line of thought as a pair of loose trousers hit the ground and she tried to pull herself out of the vision, focusing on being anywhere but there.

It was clear to her that this was the past, from before Freddy fell, as this was definitely not her world. It felt different, something inside her recognising the energy in the air as foreign, lighter. Which meant that the real Freddy was in the compound somewhere while Ivy violated his privacy.

The other big giveaway was Freddy's wings. They were still intact and a gorgeous, light butterscotch colour that Gabe was currently stroking the length of with one trembling hand, a look of pure reverence on his face. One thing was for sure, she was seeing a hell of a lot more of Freddy than she had ever wanted to. Gabe growled into Freddy's mouth, caught his lip with his teeth and pulled. Freddy groaned out a breath and slid his hand down Gabe's muscled chest, Gabe's back arched under his touch and for some reason she couldn't look away. She didn't consider herself a voyeur but something about this was different, like watching raw energy crash against itself.

Freddy's hand moved lower and lower and she knew she had to get out. Shit, shit, shit. Gabe gave a wild gasp and she forced her eyes away. Wake up, Ivy. For fuck sake —

Her eyes flew open and she blinked against the harshness of the lamplight. God it was going to be hard to look Freddy in the eye for training tomorrow.

XIII

IVY

"You did good today." Freddy said, running a thin blue towel over his face before slinging it around his shoulders. "I know there's been a lot of talk recently about the fight you and Jas had, but just ignore it. It'll settle down eventually, they're just bored."

In all honesty, she hadn't heard much of the chatter, but she knew it was there. It was hard not to notice when people stopped talking when you came into a room, even harder to ignore the wary glances.

"It's fine," she said with a shrug and then started her cool-down stretches. Freddy joined her, moving his arm up so it was parallel to the ground as he bent one knee and stretched. She tried not to stare. It was hard not to think about what she had seen the night before in her vision when there was currently so much of Freddy on display. He had packed on a lot more muscle since he had been in Heaven, the dips and planes of his shoulders and chest stood out sharply, he had muscles in places she hadn't known were possible. It was easy to see why though, all he seemed to do was train. He spoke to people in the canteen, but she hadn't seen him hanging out with anyone in the corridors, always just striding purposefully from place to place.

"What?" Freddy asked with a raised eyebrow and she realised she'd been staring. He reached up and untied the curly ponytail that had been keeping his hair back from his face and a muscle danced in his bicep. She looked away hastily.

"Er, nothing, I was just wondering what you do for fun?" she said, blurting the first thing that came to mind that *wasn't* Freddy getting naked with Gabe.

"For fun?" He repeated tonelessly.

Ivy rolled her eyes, "Yes, *fun*. You can't just train all day."

Freddy shrugged, "It's different now I'm back here, when I was out looking for you I was free to do what I wanted. Here there are expectations; standards I need to uphold."

"Sure, but that doesn't mean you can't also let loose."

"That's pretty much exactly what it means."

She stretched her arms in front of her and then bent, keeping her eyes on the ground when she asked, "So there's nobody you're interested in?"

She dared a glance up and quickly looked away again. Freddy was staring at her in a way that definitely did not invite further questions, so she changed the topic.

"Did Jas tell you about my vision yesterday?"

"Yeah, she mentioned it. Visions of the future aren't set in stone, I'm not giving up yet."

Ivy sighed, "I can't believe I'm cooped up with a bunch of optimists."

Freddy grinned and retrieved his t-shirt from the floor, "I don't know, you didn't seem to mind being stuck with us when you had your tongue in Dev's mouth on day one."

Ivy swatted at him in mock outrage, "Well, he is very pretty."

Freddy nodded solemnly before bursting into laughter, she couldn't help but smile at the sound. He didn't laugh nearly often enough.

"I know you want to hate us." Freddy said as they walked down the corridor towards her room, "But I've seen the way you are around

Dev, hell, around Jas, even. This is where you belong."

"It was never a matter of belonging," she said and instantly regretted it. Freddy was like a dog with a bone, they'd had this same conversation over and over after training. He wanted her to care, she wanted him to leave it alone. So far, he hadn't taken her less-than-subtle hint. It was the first time she'd risen to his bait though.

"Then what is it? Every time you start to relax, something happens and your guard shoots right back up." Freddy caught her arm, pulling them to a stop not far from her door. His warm brown eyes were wide with sincerity and despite herself, she wanted to ease his mind.

She tugged absently on one of his ringlets and decided to indulge him, "As soon as we work out how to get you home, you'll all be gone."

His eyes lit with an understanding that made her squirm uncomfortably. He had looked into her past, he had to know about what had happened. It had wrecked her. She had been a kid, left alone in a world where the person who had killed her family still lived and breathed. She didn't want to ever feel pain like that again.

"You can't run just because you're scared," Freddy said softly, "you're stronger than that. You can be more than fear and bitterness and guilt. Besides, I won't leave you."

"But the Heavens —"

"Hold nothing of interest for me." Freddy said with a finality that left her with no doubt that Gabe had played a large role in that feeling. "I'm not going anywhere."

She swallowed past the lump in her throat and shoved Freddy lightly as she continued on to her door, "Damn right. You're going to win us this war, just flash all those muscles at Michael and he'll run in the other direction. Sheer intimidation."

"They *are* impressive," Freddy said smugly and tensed a bicep that she squeezed with a laugh.

"Overcompensating?" she said with a grin, never mind the fact that she *knew* he wasn't and oh god, she was thinking about it again.

"What is it?" Freddy asked her curiously, "That's the second time today you've looked at me funny."

"I'm just enamoured with you," Ivy said with a grin and blew him a kiss as he walked away. Freddy stuck two fingers up behind him and she grinned to herself as she walked into her room, some things never changed.

Her clothes hit the floor as she climbed into the shower, eager to be sweat-free again. There were a lot of downsides to living in several converted warehouses, the food was shit, the furniture was basic, but the water pressure was heavenly. She roughly towel-dried her short hair, quickly combing it into a side-part and climbed into a pair of soft grey joggers. She missed her clothes, her flat – a teensy part of her even missed the One Stop. But being without her wardrobe made her feel vulnerable. Clothes could be like armour, or, when used correctly, a weapon. At least she still had her combat boots, not that she got to wear them very much at the moment. Her eyes rested longingly on the space where the boots sat by the door, a light layer of dust had started to form on the toes. Trainers made-up the bulk of her footwear since she was training near enough every day, but they just didn't give the same weight behind a kick to the chest as her boots did. Letting out a long breath, Ivy turned away from the boots and settled cross-legged on her bed. It was time for answers.

She focused on the place she'd seen briefly in the vision, letting her shoulders relax and breathing turn deep. She cast her mind back and envisioned the white walls, the coolness of the air around her, the sweeping, long staircase. It was no use. She wasn't getting anything. Her eyes opened, and she swore. Loudly. Either this was another vision, or she truly had gone insane. She was in exactly the place she'd seen in her vision and it felt... well, *real*. Was she dead and in the Heavens somehow? Though, as Jas had explained to her a couple of days ago, all souls went to Hades. He would decide their fate after death based on how they lived their life. She looked around and decided to walk about a bit – what could it hurt? She was ninety-percent sure this was a vision. Probably.

A sound came from her left and she couldn't help the surprised squeak that escaped her as she spun around. There was no way she could mistake this being for a man, he looked different to the angels on Earth. His wings drooped, dull-grey feathers brushing against the floor, and his stooped back told her he must be ancient. The power that radiated out of him made the hair on her arms rise. He stared at her, grey eyes wide, clearly just as surprised to see her as she was him. His face was leathered and wrinkled, his eyes sunken, and for all his otherworldliness, he seemed tired. His voice sounded in her head, and she shuddered, unprepared for the unexpected intrusion. Jas had told her all angels had telepathic abilities of varying strength, it was largely how they chose to communicate during a battle to keep strategies hidden from the enemy, but she'd never expected to experience it herself. On Earth it was a hard skill to hone, the Earth plane's energies didn't agree with what it perceived as magic and so it was more draining.

Child, the angel said, his voice a weathered sigh, *I do not think you ought to be here.*

Her mouth opened to agree but he shot a warning look her way and she quickly closed it again.

You need to leave. It is not safe for you to speak here, there are those who would wish to do you harm. His voice thundered through her now, commanding, but she hesitated. She needed answers.

He shook his head at her and widened his eyes. *You must go, Child! Else* he *will find you here!*

The giant flapping of wings sounded off to her right as she closed her eyes and tried desperately to think about the compound.

She opened her eyes, but she was still in the Heavens. The grey winged angel fled, giving her one last frantic glance as he did so. Every nerve in her body screamed at her in awareness as the wings grew closer, she didn't want to even think about who or what they belonged to. She forced her eyes to close and concentrated on home. On comfort. This time she felt the transition as she moved from plane to plane and finally coalesced back where she wanted to be – home.

She opened one eye at a time, peeking around at her new surroundings. The sight of familiar grey walls and the shockingly-bright teal sofa she had picked out while drunk filled her with a ridiculous amount of happiness. Then she noticed the mountain of muscle lounging around on *her* bed through the open doorway to her room. Arsehole. He hadn't even stirred at her arrival. She snorted to herself quietly, what would he have sensed? A disturbance in the force? She was glad she amused herself, at least. Large, fluffy white wings hung off the edge of her double bed, surprisingly unruffled considering the way the angel was sprawled, face smushed against one of Ivy's pillows. Judging by the wings, she was guessing he was one of Michael's men and not someone Dev had sent to house-sit and water the plants – which to be honest, she would have appreciated. Her eyes ran over the large wings that were laid out across her bed as she moved further into the room. From afar they were awe inspiring, but up close? There were no words. They called to her, looking endlessly soft as if they were spun from the clouds themselves, and something inside her ached at the sight of them. She reached out a hand, to do what, she wasn't sure. The angel sat bolt upright, sword magically appearing in that way she still hadn't mastered despite all of Freddy's lectures about harnessing her 'energy'. How he expected her to have any energy at 7AM was beyond her. The angel moved so quickly he was a blur, standing in front of her in a blink with his sword pressed to her throat. It didn't hurt as much as she'd expected, so he couldn't be that powerful. Freddy's had been a lot hotter, both literally and figuratively. With the angel's sword threatening her, she did the only thing she could: screamed. It tore through her throat with a burn and the angel winced with a little jump, moving his sword just fractionally enough for her to leap away as he covered his ears. Her scream cut off with a wheeze and the angel gave her a disdainful look – clearly she was ruining his plans of a nice, quiet, murder.

She closed her eyes again and tried to do what she had done before by picturing the compound. She opened her eyes as something large flew at her head, she ducked and it just barely grazed her hair, smashing against the bedroom wall behind her. Ivy glanced down and saw a potted plant in pieces on the floor

"Do you bloody mind? I am *trying* to concentrate here!"

He looked so startled by her exclamation that he paused for a second, at least the bad guys had *some* manners trained into them. There weren't many of them who would wait for a second when you asked, like calling time-out in the middle of a game of Tag. Why couldn't she get out of here? Her power needed to work damn it, the angel had recovered from his shock and was striding purposefully towards her. *Dev. Take me to Dev,* she begged. The now familiar tingle of the move between planes sped through her body as the world turned black, colour bleeding in again slowly as she found herself staring into intensely green eyes.

She looked around and realised she'd managed to zap herself to Dev's room.

Dev had her cradled against him, his warmth soaking into her and she shivered lightly, "Ivy?" he asked, blinking blearily, "Everything okay?" he quirked his brows, looking bemusedly at her sprawled atop him and his white bedding.

She pulled away quickly, "Shit. Sorry."

She glanced around his room, avoiding his eyes, and saw the time. She'd somehow lost two whole hours. She scrambled unceremoniously up, her knees landing on either side of his hips. Her cheeks heated as Dev gave her a lazy grin.

"Oh, I wish I woke up like this all the time," he said with a soft laugh that slid over her skin, casting a faint flush over her.

She slapped his chest playfully and her cheeks burned hotter when he caught that hand, clasping it to his heart.

"Not that I mind, but why are you here? You know, in my bed and all?" his gaze searched hers and she could feel his heart beat under her palm. She hadn't thought there could be anything hotter than regular Dev. She was wrong. Half-asleep, voice-husky Dev was a thousand times sexier.

She cleared her throat and pretended not to notice his half-clothed state and adorable bed head as she answered.

"Well, I was thinking earlier. I had that vision when I was with Jas..." she winced, remembering what that vision entailed and hastily continued, "—um, yeah and I was just thinking that it seemed odd that I was with you in the Heavens too, right? So, I thought, maybe I'm not just supposed to show you to the gate. Maybe I somehow activate it?"

Dev's warm eyes assessed her with amusement as she continued to ramble on, a small smirk curving one side of his mouth and casting a deep dimple into his cheek that distracted her momentarily.

"I-I was thinking about the place I'd seen in my vision," she said, pulling herself out of her thoughts, "I thought it might hold some clues and I *needed* to know more but then suddenly I was there and—" she threw her free hand up in the air in confusion. She wasn't really sure what had happened, Freddy had told her the only way to travel through the planes was via portal or with wings. Neither of which she had.

Dev blinked slowly. "You were... there?"

She huffed exasperatedly and spoke slowly, barely reining in her irritation, "Yes, *Dev*. I was *there*. In Heaven, I presume. It was all white and there was some guy – oof!" she let out a breath as Dev, seemingly grasping what she was saying at last, sat bolt upright and half dumped her off the bed.

She glowered at him as he cast her a sheepish look and pulled her back up abruptly, their faces now just inches apart.

"You moved between planes? Are you okay?" he asked, voice low and husky, he ran a hand down her arm as if checking for injuries.

She licked her lips nervously as goosebumps sprung up under the trail of his fingers, "There was another guy – angel, there. He told me I should leave before the others got there. He saved me," she noted, somewhat surprised he had bothered.

Dev nodded thoughtfully, his nose just barely brushing against hers, "Perhaps you're not supposed to lead us to the gateway, maybe you *are* the gateway," he said looking at her in awe.

Great.

She let out a sigh, "So, I've gone from crappy Sat-Nav to a freaking *doorway?*"

Dev's lips twitched, and she bit her own to keep from huffing out a small laugh.

"Not so much a doorway, more like... a key. If we had our wings back, we would be able to travel between the planes at will, that's their primary function."

She did laugh that time, throwing her head back as she did. "You mean they're not just there to look pretty? Next you'll be telling me that you're the gatekeeper."

His brows rose in confusion and her smirk grew, "Really? You've never seen *Ghostbusters?*"

He shrugged, and her smile faded a little, remembering that he wasn't just some hot human guy and he probably didn't give a shit about *Ghostbusters* or any such human triviality – including her.

Well, that escalated quickly, thanks *brain*.

"Well, I've intruded for far too long. I'm sorry for waking you up," she said, scrambling off the bed and away from him.

His brows furrowed, "Ivy—"

"Goodnight, Dev."

She turned to hurry out of his room but paused at the low groan she heard just from behind the bed. She turned back to Dev in concern, but he wasn't looking at her. His eyes were on that same fucking angel that had tried to clobber her in her apartment. Dev shot her a questioning look and she winced and gave a little '*what can you do*' shrug and hair toss combo that she hoped he found cute. Judging by the look on his face – not so much.

"How did he even get in?" he whisper-shouted, she shrugged again.

"I may have missed out a few details."

At his incredulous look she shrugged, "I was in shock! So sue me. Before I came here, I landed at my flat first. He was there, he must've come along for the ride when I phased back here... Hey! This is a good thing! Now we know I can transport other people – though he does seem a little worse for wear."

The angel had stood, clearly having just regained consciousness, the tips of his wings brushed the ceiling as he tottered about dizzily.

Dev gave a low growl of irritation, "I'll have to check the barrier after this to make sure it's still working. I'm guessing that as you've been invited in and you were carrying him, he got past it."

She heaved a sigh and threw him an apologetic smile, "Sorry?"

But Dev wasn't paying attention anymore, his attention was now focused on the mostly recovered angel who had summoned his sword, it flickered in and out of reality as he swayed. It solidified into a bright beam of golden light that made her eyes hurt as he waved it about in Dev's general direction.

"Kal," Dev said, "It's been a long time, though I could have done with longer. What has Michael got you up to now? Cleaning his boots? Brushing out his feathers?"

Kal's features hardened with anger and it was clear there was no love-lost between the two.

"Devlin." The word was a snarl. "Things have changed. I'm not the footstool you remember and won't it be embarrassing when *I'm* the one to knock your ass out and drag your bitch back to Michael?"

She stared, agape, and she had thought he was polite before! What a dickwad. She picked up the closest thing and hurled it at him viciously, smirking when he ducked and the empty vase crashed to the floor.

"Turnabout's a bitch huh? Just like me." She smiled at him and he paled at the violence her face promised.

Dev gave a low chuckle. "Hell hath no fury," he remarked with a smirk.

Kal cursed at Devlin and rushed him. Dev looked unconcerned as he grabbed Kal by one of his beautiful snowy white wings while Kal struggled, attempting to shove his sword through Devlin's side. His wings were so white, they were almost blinding if you looked at them too long. A loud *crack* shattered the quiet as Dev bent Kal's wing at an odd angle. She could only watch in horror as it shuddered, several pure white feathers floating to the ground gently.

"You will not harm her, or me, or anyone else. Leave."

Kal raised his head and glared at Dev, bright white hair falling over a dark eye. He shoved away from Devlin, wincing when his broken wing brushed against the wall. Devlin turned away dismissively and Kal levelled a glare at Dev's back, eyes burning like dark coals in his pale face.

"Devlin!" She cried out as Kal raised his sword once more.

"I'll leave when you die!" Kal spat and lunged for Dev.

Devlin spun, graceful as a dancer and quickly gained the upper hand, darting away from Kal and knocking aside his punch. Dev was older and more powerful than Kal, even without his wings and weakened from the years on this plane away from Heaven's light. Their lithe bodies twisted as they fought, it was as beautiful as it was deadly. Both moving at a speed she could barely follow, Kal a fraction slower than Devlin on account of his broken wing, his short, silver hair tousled. It seemed as if neither would give up, until Kal flung his sword out. Not toward Devlin, but toward her.

Dev roared her name as he flung Kal to the floor with a savage kick to the chest. She dropped to the floor as the sword of light hurtled towards her, embedding itself in the wall next to where her head had been. With a flap of his still able wing, shining against the dimness of the room, Kal disappeared in a burst of light at the same time as his sword.

"Ivy!" Dev panted and dropped down beside her, "*Shit,* are you okay?" his voice was rough and sweat had dampened his hair into dark little curls around his temples. His eyes were wild, but his hand was gentle as it cradled her face, oddly, it stung a little.

Dev swore, "He cut you. Bastard." His eyes were fierce when they met hers, lips just a breath away.

"Ivy..." he whispered her name softly, like a prayer, before his lips pressed against hers, featherlight.

The heat from his mouth shot straight through her, a shudder wracked her body as she tried to hold herself back.

She pulled away first, breathing unevenly. Fuck it. "I want you."

His eyes were still closed but his lips turned up at her words, his hand moved down from her face, tracing a line of fire down her throat and between her breasts. "You can have me."

Devlin's lips hovered tantalisingly close to her own, she breached that distance to nip playfully at his bottom lip. Her toes curled at his slight groan but she pushed lightly against his chest, making him step back.

"Take off your shirt."

Green eyes pierced hers. "No."

Her mouth popped open, "No?"

Dev folded his arms across his chest, "You want me."

"I just said that didn't I?"

"And that's *all* you want?"

Her heart froze in her chest. *No.* "Yes."

"Then my answer is no." He reached past her and opened the door to his bedroom. "I'm not going to be another escape for you, like the rest of the guys you fuck. If you want that, fine. But that won't be us."

"*Us?*" She repeated, cold and hot all at the same time.

"Us." Dev said with a smirk, "When you're ready to admit that's what you want, I won't hold it against you."

"Don't hold your breath." She hissed and spun to face the door.

"Ivy?" he called.

Hesitating in the doorway she asked flatly, "What."

She could hear the grin in his voice when he replied and she cursed at herself for hesitating, knew he had noticed it too and didn't plan to let her forget it, "Next time you come to my room in the middle of the night... please don't bring anyone else."

She didn't look back, just closed the door softly behind her and did her best to ignore the soft laughter that followed her out, sending a shiver of heat down her spine.

XIV
DEVLIN

Ivy's late-night visit had affected him more than he cared to let on. He struggled to get back to sleep, instead tossing and turning, unable to get the sweet scent of her out of his head. Every time he closed his eyes, he was bombarded with images of her. The way her hair had felt like silk against his palm, how her laugh had sounded quoting *Ghostbusters*. He knew what she wanted from him, knew he wanted *more*.

Yet, she had hesitated before she left. Did it mean anything? He wasn't sure, and it was Ivy, she was even more bullheaded than Freddy, so he wasn't likely to find out.

He gave up on getting any more sleep and slipped out of bed, grabbing a hoodie from the drawer. The training room wasn't far from him and he could definitely stand to blow off a little steam. He hadn't been this worked up over a girl in... well, ever. He had never really had the chance to date or get to know anyone, not in the Heavens and definitely not on Earth, he'd had hookups but never anything serious. Had never really wanted anything serious, but Ivy had crawled under his skin and settled there. Her claws were in deep, logically he knew it could only end badly. He wore his heart on his sleeve far too often and Ivy didn't wear hers at all half the time. But there was a spark in her eyes, something challenging and heated that made him want to kiss her, all rational thought fleeing. She unravelled him and he didn't like it, he kept a tight leash on his temper but she pushed every one of his buttons and then came back for more.

Devlin shoved through the heavy wood doors to the training room and paused at the rhythmic *thwack* of hands hitting the punching bag.

"Do I need to beat someone up?" Devlin called out as he strolled into the room, Jasmine was attacking the punching bag with a ferocity that both impressed and shocked him.

"What? No. Why?" Jas asked, breathing hard as she caught the bag and moved to get a drink of water.

"Well did the bag say something to offend you? You were hitting it like there was no tomorrow."

"Just because *I* don't slack when I train doesn't mean there's something wrong." Jas said with a roll of her eyes. "You're up early. Trouble sleeping again?"

He nodded and began stretching to warm up.

"You seem to have had a lot of trouble since Ivy arrived." Jas said carefully and he shot her a wry look.

"Don't be coy, Jasmine. It doesn't suit you."

"Do you like her?"

"She drives me crazy."

"That's not a no."

Dev snorted and began throwing punches at the bag, "It doesn't matter. I know what she wants, I'm just not inclined to give it to her."

"And what is that?" Jas said cautiously, her face was pinched with anxiety and he sighed, catching the punching bag against his chest and holding it there.

"Me."

Jas' brows rose, "That doesn't sound so bad."

"That's *all* she wants, Jas."

She blinked at him in confusion before her eyes widened in understanding, "Did she say that?"

"Not in so many words," he replied with a shrug, "but it's what she meant. I might have been okay with no strings attached in the past, but not with her."

"Why?" Jas' voice was quiet and he took a step towards her but she stepped away to grab her towel.

"Because she makes me feel."

"Feel what?" Jas asked softly, her back turned to him.

Devlin paused, trying to find the right word to describe what it was that Ivy made him feel when he was around her. He knew exactly what he was scared of when it came to her, that she would probably never let her guard down long enough to trust him, "Alive."

Jas clenched her jaw but nodded, "Then you should go for it, Dev. Have something for yourself other than *this*," she said, gesturing around them and Dev knew she meant more than just the compound. But he shook his head and turned back to the punching bag.

"She made her choice, Jas. If she wants me, *really* wants me, then she knows where I am."

Jas looked like she wanted to say more but he needed to think about something other than *her*, even if for only a moment. "Spar with me."

Jas, to her credit, didn't hesitate. Just slid into stance and they began to fight, easy as breathing.

It felt like she had only been asleep for a few hours when someone shook her roughly awake.

"Wha—?" her hair was in her mouth and she choked on it for a second before peeling apart her eyes to see Jas glowering at her, dressed in workout gear. Ivy groaned and let her eyes close again, "It's my day off, go and spar with Freddy."

"Oh, I'm not here to spar. I've already been at it for *hours* with Devlin this morning."

Now *that* woke her up. Turned her down only to screw Jasmine? Classy.

She gave Jas a lazy smile, "Well, colour me surprised. You finally had the balls to fuck him then?" Colour stained Jas' cheeks and Ivy's smile grew, "Ah, better luck next time, love."

Jas shot her a glare that would have sent lesser women running but Ivy just laughed and patted the spot next to her in the bed. Jas' shoulders slumped and she sat awkwardly on the edge of the bed.

"It's harder than I thought, listening to him talk about you."

Ivy winced, "I'm sorry, I didn't realise he had been."

"He hasn't, not until tonight. What changed?"

"Nothing." Ivy said, unsure whether to feel relief or regret that Devlin wasn't thinking about her half as much as she seemed to be thinking about him. "Absolutely nothing and that's fine with me, but it's obviously not okay for him."

"Is it though?"

A frown tugged at Ivy's mouth, it was too early for deep conversations like this. She glanced at her phone and bit back a growl, "Jasmine. Do you know what time it is?"

"A little after dawn. Don't change the subject, you're lying to yourself, and to him."

"A little after —" Ivy spluttered, no wonder it had felt like she'd barely had any sleep!

"I know things have been hard for you, but they've been just as hard for Devlin. You don't know how much he goes through to seem strong for them, to get them home. He feels responsible, you know."

Ivy did know. She could see it in the way he spoke to the others, the way he shouldered every burden and refused to let anyone else bear the weight.

"He said," Jas continued through Ivy's silence, "that you make him feel."

"Feel what?" Anger? Lust?

"Alive."

The word whispered through her and settled somewhere close to her heart. *Alive.* It was exactly how being around Devlin had always made her feel, she just hadn't been able to put a name to it until then. Not that it mattered. She'd offered him what she could and it hadn't been enough. She'd been quiet for too long and Jas stood with a huff and turned with her hands on her hips.

"I just don't know what else to say to you, Ivy. All I've heard since you arrived is how *strong* you are, but I don't see strength. I see a coward and a liar."

Amused, Ivy stretched languidly before sitting up slowly, "Is that so?"

"I told you before that you should give Devlin a chance, I did that for *him* as much as you, because he deserves to be happy. He deserves to come home with us. Who would that make me if I didn't even try and put aside my own feelings to help him? I guess you wouldn't understand that though, you don't care about anyone except yourself." Jas' eyes were like fire, her hands were trembling as if she could barely believe the things she was voicing aloud, the insecurities, the fears.

"That's not true." Ivy said calmly, a small ember of anger slowly began to burn in her stomach, lighting her veins and making her dizzy with each word escaping Jas' mouth.

"They would have been disappointed." Jas said, Ivy's heart froze in her chest, breaths no longer reaching her lungs. "You won't let yourself care because of what happened to them, because of what could happen to any of us. The killer is still out there, what if he was targeting you? What if he comes after someone else? But that's bullshit and you know it. We're stronger than any mortal ever could be."

Ivy's hands slowly curled into fists and Jas' voice seemed to echo strangely in the room as a red haze filled her vision.

"Better they had died, than to see the mess you've made of your life."

Ivy had never been able to move as quickly as the angels until that moment, the duvet flared out after her, falling to the floor as if in slow motion as her hand closed around Jas' throat.

"How dare you." The words came out in a snarl, forced up past the lump in her throat. The first lines of regret started to settle into Jasmine's face as Ivy slammed her against the wall by her bedroom door, the plaster shook and dust trickled onto the carpet. She didn't care. All she could see was red. Blood on the floor, on her hands, in Jess' hair.

"Go ahead." Jas rasped, resolve tightening her jaw even as she began to turn pink. "If I'm wrong then deny it."

Ivy couldn't. What could she say? That she wasn't a coward? That her parents wouldn't be ashamed to see what she'd done with the life she'd been fortunate enough to keep when they had lost their own?

"Ivy," a voice said and she looked to the now open bedroom door. Freddy stood there, concern pooling in his warm eyes, "Let her go."

For a second she couldn't remember how. Then her hand flexed and Jasmine slid against the wall before catching herself. A white handprint stood out starkly on her throat and Ivy couldn't stop the brief stab of guilt that flared.

"I don't know what the fuck just happened here, but I think you'd better leave." Freddy said to Jasmine, arms folded across his chest, "You two just made half the compound shake."

Jas looked up at her and Ivy's anger reignited. The familiar haze of red tugged at her, though she wasn't sure who she was really angry at – Jasmine or herself.

An odd look crossed Jas' face as she stared at Ivy but she simply shook her head and turned to leave, "It doesn't have to be this way. You've been cowardly, but that doesn't mean you have to be a coward."

Freddy bristled but Ivy waved a hand at him, armour once more in place, "I think that's a bit rich considering you've been in love with Devlin for years and never once told him the truth – but *I'm* the coward?" Ivy knew she was. That didn't mean she had to give Jas the satisfaction of knowing she'd hurt her.

Jas glanced over her shoulder as she left the room, "Sometimes there's more strength in staying silent when you know that speaking up will only hurt the ones you love."

Jas left and Freddy stalked after her, poking his head around the door frame and glaring at her all the way down the corridor. "What a sanctimonious bitch."

A reluctant smile twitched her lips but she shrugged and sat down heavily on her bed, "She wasn't wrong. I am a coward. A selfish coward."

"A little bit of cowardice never hurt anyone," Freddy offered as he sprawled out on the bed beside her, curls bouncing as he brushed them out of his face lazily.

Ivy laughed, "That's not even slightly true, Fred."

"Still," Freddy smirked, "fuck 'em. Long as you love me, right?"

She sighed and laid back down next to him, pulling the duvet up off the floor and under their chins, "How could I not."

"I knew I would win you over. What did it? My muscles? My impeccable sense of humour?"

"Your penis." Ivy said with an absent wave of her hand.

"My — what?"

"It's a story for another time."

"Or, you know, maybe it's a story for *right now.*"

Ivy looked at Freddy, his eyes were wide but his lip was twitching, she burst into laughter, "You look ridiculous right now."

"Me? I'm not the one who was choking Jas out wearing only bed-head and tweety bird boxers, now *that* was a heck of a scene to walk into." He gave a low chuckle and Ivy's smile faded.

"I shouldn't have said what I did to Jas."

"So apologise." Freddy said, as if it were really that simple. "I'm betting she said some things she shouldn't have too."

"Maybe." Ivy sighed and curled close to Freddy, resting her head on his chest. "You're too muscley to be comfy."

"Go to sleep, Ivy."

"Will you stay?"

"I'll stay."

XV
IVY

FREDDY had been gone when she woke up again, having slept away the afternoon and well into the evening. She didn't blame him, he was the sort that needed to keep moving. She knew what that felt like, the need to run, to escape, to just be out of your own head. She felt like that now. Her stomach growled loudly in the dark room and she sighed and checked the time on her phone, it was too late to grab dinner. If she wanted something, she would have to make it herself. It was funny how easy it was to become used to having food made for you, she'd gotten lazy. Despite everything, she was building a comfortable life here with — *everyone*, she thought, catching her thoughts before they could drift to a certain green-eyed devil. It was a shame it couldn't last.

She shoved her legs into the closest pair of joggers on the floor and didn't bother with a bra as she chucked on a hoodie and screwed up her hair. Tonight, she needed to quiet the overwhelming thoughts in her head, just for a moment.

Ivy started in the direction of the canteen and, she realised belatedly, Devlin's room. It wasn't likely she would run into him was it? She smoothed down her slightly greasy hair with a wince before whipping her hand back down to her side angrily. What did she care what Dev thought? With a huff she reached up and dug her hands into her hair, mussing it so it stuck up in odd clumps escaping her ponytail and felt a brief flare of vindication before her shoulders slumped. God, what was she doing?

The doors to the canteen looked tall and alien in the dark, sending a skitter of unease down her spine. She rolled her eyes at herself as she pushed through them without slowing and promptly shrieked when a loud bang and muffled curse made her jump. Her mother had always said she was drawn to trouble like a magnet and now more than ever, it seemed she had been right.

A shadowy figure crouched next to a box of spilled plastic cups and she approached warily, hoping it wasn't Drew, or worse – Jas. The figure moved into a patch of light flowing from the open kitchen door, still cursing, clearly they'd been trying to raid the kitchen just like her. Whoever it was stumbled and sat down hard on their arse. She let out a startled laugh as their face hit the light.

"Gabe?"

He blinked his bloodshot honeyed eyes blearily at her, took a hearty swig from the whiskey bottle he loosely gripped in one hand and slurred her name drunkenly.

"Ivy," he tried to focus on her, eyes squinting in the dim light and managed to stand only to stumble again, falling into her side. Breath heavy with booze blew in her face as he peered at her, "You look *ravishing* tonight, love."

She rolled her eyes, knowing she looked thoroughly mad with her hair sticking out like she'd stuck her finger in a socket. "What're you doing out here, Gabe?" she looked him over and noted the dark circles under his eyes and the stubble along his jaw.

He gave her a shrug that lacked its usual elegance, "Drinking. Thinking." He paused to sit down on top of one of the round tables closest to them, before flopping backwards and laying down, almost upending the bottle. Ivy hastily snatched it away, ignoring Gabe's protest as she took a swig. Tonight she felt... reckless. The need to act, to run, to fight or fuck burned inside her.

She settled down on the table, Gabe's knee warm against her leg. "I prefer the whiskey to the vodka," he said at last, breaking the silence that had comfortably descended as she sipped and he stared up at the ceiling.

She gave a low chuckle, "Nasty stuff, vodka. Where did you find the stash?"

He shot her a lazy grin not unlike his brothers', the light from the kitchen highlighting the lines of his proud jaw and nose, "It wasn't exactly hidden. Or at least, that's what I'm going to tell Dev if he catches me."

She shook her head. "You're going to need a better excuse than that. Besides, it's Freddy you need to worry about, not Devlin."

Gabe's face twisted and he reached up to rub at a small slash on his chin, just a shade paler than his usually honeyed skin tone, she had a terrible feeling she knew where he'd got that scar. Ivy held up her hand as he opened his mouth, "I won't hear a word about it. Whatever happened between you is *just* between you. Got it?"

Gabe pouted, the fullness of his lips making him look ridiculous, so she ignored him and had another swig.

"Ugh." Gabe said, throwing a hand over his eyes dramatically, "I feel terrible."

"You'll feel worse tomorrow," Ivy said cheerfully and Gabe smacked her on the arm. "Just wait til the hangover kicks in."

"Well, I suppose that only happens when you stop drinking,

right?" Gabe asked and she watched dumbfounded as he produced another bottle of booze from somewhere and began drinking it.

She winced, "Yeah there's no way Dev's not going to notice two bottles missing."

"Four," Gabe slurred, "I had the vodka remember? And something called a schnapps before you got here. Now *that* was nasty." He gave a delicate shudder and a laugh spilled out of her before she could stop it.

"Agreed. I don't touch the stuff, the only thing worse is Absinthe."

Gabe opened his eyes, intrigued, and she began to tell him about a night she'd spent drinking absinthe, it was a short story. She didn't remember most of it.

Gabe chortled, "I can't believe you punched the bouncer."

"Well, it was that or give up the traffic cone and I'd become fond of it."

Gabe laughed again and she found herself laughing with him, uncontrollably. She laid back against the table too and stuck her legs in the air.

"What are you doing?" Gabe asked, an innocent sort of curiosity in his voice.

"Feels nice." She took another sip from the bottle, dribbling some of it down her chin accidentally, pouring downwards was... hard.

There was a moment of silence and then Gabe stuck his legs in the air too.

"Huh." He said in a high pitched voice.

"Told you."

They started laughing again and once they'd started they couldn't stop. She was breathless as she waved frantically at him, barely even noticing when one of the bottles wobbled dangerously on the edge of the table. Ivy kicked her legs around, gasping for air and wiped the tears from her cheeks as she turned and found their faces only inches apart. She glanced away hastily, "Ugh, I'm starting to sober up."

"Already?" Gabe asked.

"Fast metabolism." She explained, reaching for the bottle again. It had been a long time since she'd had whiskey, it didn't keep her drunk for as long as absinthe, but that stuff was the devil's juice and she was happy to go without.

"Angels too," Gabe said, "If I don't keep it up I'll be sober in an hour or so."

"Well, we wouldn't want that now would we?" Ivy said with a smirk and clinked her bottle against his. "I'm almost out, direct me to the infamous stash."

Gabe waved her off and stood, "I've got it." He said and then promptly knocked her empty bottle to the floor with an errant foot. They both froze at the loud sound of smashing glass, but when nobody came to investigate, relaxed.

"I feel like a kid sneaking about their parent's house," she said and with the happy buzz of alcohol the thought didn't even sting.

"Sorry," Gabe grinned and headed into the kitchen, she was relieved he didn't have dimples. She didn't want to be reminded of his brother right then.

Fuck. She was thinking about him again.

"Whiskey!" Ivy called and Gabe strolled out of the doorway, his hair gleaming red in the light.

"*Gabe,*" he said with a smirk, "not Whiskey."

It was a dumb joke but she laughed like it was the funniest thing she'd ever heard.

"I don't think I've ever heard you laugh so much before."

"Well, there's not been much to laugh about."

Gabe nodded as if he understood exactly what she meant, and maybe he did. The angels weren't exactly thrilled to have him there. "Sometimes, I miss him you know. Michael, I mean."

At her startled look, he just shrugged and took a hearty swig of whiskey before continuing.

"He wasn't always... like he is now."

"An areshole, you mean." His grin was slightly crooked, she noted dimly, and he had a freckle above his lip that she hadn't really noticed before.

"He loves me, in his own way. I know one day he'll forgive me." Gabe said in a mostly incoherent mumble as he sipped from the bottle once more, eyes distant, lashes seeming inexplicably wet. Her brain was turning to mush from the whiskey, and that was just fine. Just the way she liked it, usually.

They sipped in silence until her brain caught up with the conversation. "Forgive you for what?" she asked, only a beat late.

His shoulders slumped, head bowed, he seemed...defeated. Gabe had finished his bottle so she passed him hers, managing to slosh it over her hand only a little. She licked the liquor from her fingers and smirked when he followed her tongue with his eyes. She flicked her lip ring with her tongue for good measure and stopped teasing him.

"I'm betraying him." he whispered, shaking himself out of the reverie she'd managed to put him in, "I know it's the right thing but I don't know... maybe we'll never be the same." His eyes were unfocused when they met hers, the gold flecks in his eyes swirling.

She hadn't realised how close they were sitting.

She counted every freckle across his nose with a brush of her finger and laughed without really knowing why. The buzz of the whiskey numbed her, she'd forgotten how nice it was *not* to worry or overthink. Even if it was just for a few minutes. She needed this. She needed fun and meaningless, not Devlin – she pulled her thoughts away from that dangerous territory as Gabe leaned in closer. So close she could count each of his eyelashes, he reached out a hand and stroked down the length of her hair, it felt wrong. Where were Dev's callouses? Her eyes flew open though she hadn't realised they'd closed.

"Ivy..." Gabe said, breath ragged as he pressed his soft, full lips to hers in a barely-there kiss. Guilt hit her straight away and she pulled back.

"This wasn't what I saw." She mumbled to herself and saw Gabe's brows furrow in confusion. She couldn't do this to Freddy. Fuck, why did she have to have the worst impulse control? She couldn't even really blame this on the booze, she was known for making rash decisions. Or maybe she could, she decided as she stood up and swayed, almost falling to the ground. A warm hand caught her firmly and pulled her up. She looked up to thank Gabe and felt the words freeze in her mouth as she drank in the sight of green eyes, who knew people could dimple when they were mad?

"Devlin!" She tried to say, but it came out more as a slurry squeak.

His eyes moved past her to where Gabe still lounged atop the table, looking perfectly calm with his head cushioned in one hand.

"You came to join the party! I wondered when the fun-police would appear." Gabe said with a laugh that she didn't join in with, a sick feeling was moving through her chest that had nothing to do with the alcohol. How much had Devlin seen? Had he watched her pull back from Gabe's kiss?

"I thought the bottle breaking would have sent you running, but apparently not. What, have you got some sort of bat signal installed for when Ivy gets frisky? Because you should know, Freddy was the one leaving her bed this afternoon, not me."

Devlin's eyes were burning so bright they seemed to almost glow and she was irritatingly turned on by the muscle ticking in his jaw. Why him? Why couldn't she have felt that way about... well, not Gabe, he apparently was just using her to hurt both Dev and Freddy by the looks of things. Strangely enough, she found she didn't care.

Devlin turned his back on Gabe, pausing only long enough to say, "Get that cleaned up," with a nod to the broken bottle on the floor. He tugged on her arm and she began stumbling out across the canteen after him. Her stomach growled and she realised she'd never even had the food she'd gone there for. No wonder she'd been making such awful decisions, never kiss a man on an empty stomach, that was her motto.

"What sort of motto is that?" Dev asked, looking amused in spite of himself and she realised she'd spoken aloud.

"Er, a sensible one?" she asked before plopping down on the floor just outside the doors to the canteen. "Do these doors look spooky to you?"

Dev bit his lip, he looked impossibly tall from where she sat and she gave a squeal as he bent down and heaved her up and over his shoulder, granting her an impressive view of his backside.

"Don't puke down my back." Was all he said.

"I can—"*hic* "—hold my liquor."

A soft laugh rumbled through him, she never would have known if it hadn't vibrated through her chest pleasantly.

"Devlin?"

"Ivy?"

"Jas said I'm a coward."

Silence. She swallowed thickly.

"Do you think that too?" She asked quietly, her heart beating a frenzied staccato in her chest.

He didn't reply and the moment passed in what would have been an awkward silence if not for the fact that she was rip-roaringly drunk. It was then that she noticed they were going in the wrong direction.

"Hey! Where are you taking me? You're not kicking me out are you? Gabe had most of the whiskey, I just had the one!"

"Bottle," Devlin muttered under his breath, "My room was closer. Besides, I don't trust you not to cause trouble in the time it would have taken you to get back to your own room."

His room. Alone. With Devlin. And his butt.

His grip tightened on her legs and she cursed, realising she'd be speaking aloud again.

"My butt," he said in a tightly controlled voice that she suspected was masking laughter, "will behave itself, I assure you. The same cannot be said for you, however."

Devlin placed her on the ground, his hands steadying her shoulders as she swayed. She looked up and felt a bolt of desire arc through her, his eyes danced in amusement. Bastard. He knew how much she wanted him. Dev read the look on her face perfectly and grinned, flashing those infuriating dimples and she clenched her fists to keep from reaching for him. He reached behind him and opened his door, gesturing her in first and she swore softly as she brushed against his chest walking in. A low chuckle chased her inside and she paused by a chest of drawers, looking everywhere but at the bed as she felt Devlin move past her.

"I won't bite."

She looked up and felt everything in her go still as she took him in, shirtless under the zip-up hoodie he had discarded, the bed sheets rumpled, the dangerous grin on his face that said *not unless you want me to.*

She didn't move and his smile faded slightly, "Get in bed, Ivy. It's late and I've already been dragged out once tonight at the behest of the neighbours."

He looked away, not meeting her eyes as he spoke and instead messed with the duvet before climbing onto the bed. Interesting. A truth maybe, but not *the* truth.

She walked over to the edge of the bed, feeling around for it in the near dark with her hands until she brushed against warm skin and jerked back. Devlin let out an annoyed breath before grabbing her around the waist quicker than she could move and chucking her down against the pillows.

"Sleep." He said.

"But—"

"Sleep," he repeated, more gently.

She closed her eyes and obeyed.

XVI

IVY

Sweat poured down her face, dripping into her eyes and she distractedly blinked it away. Her fists hit the training dummy in front of her with a resounding *thwack* that no longer sent pain spiraling down her arm like it had the first time she'd done this. She was frustrated. It was the second time in as many days that she'd gone to bed with a guy and woken up to find them gone. That was usually *her* move and she didn't like being on the other side of it.

"You're getting better."

She near enough jumped out of her damn skin, not realizing anyone had snuck in. A humorless laugh slipped out of her as she turned to meet Gabe's tawny eyes. "I'm nowhere near good enough yet to take on one of you though, and we all know it."

Gabe scrubbed his hand along the slight stubble on his jaw as he looked at her.

"I shouldn't have kissed you last night. I'm sorry. I was being a dick, dragging you into my pettiness with Devlin and Freddy, but I was actually having a good time before that."

She was surprised, figuring she'd seen the real Gabe yesterday evening and that he hadn't given a shit about her. Ivy shrugged, "No hard feelings."

He gave her a vulnerable, hopeful look under his long lashes, "Friends?"

She rolled her eyes but smiled slightly, "Well I did share my whiskey with you last night and I don't do that with just anyone." Backing away from the punching bag, she rolled her shoulders and released a deep breath, "I'm supposed to be practicing how to use my powers."

"Under whose orders?"

"Freddy's."

"In that case I daren't distract you." Gabe started to leave but paused when she called out.

"Do you... want to help?"

Gabe looked at her warily, "Well, that depends. What exactly *are* your powers? You're not going to set me on fire or something are you?"

"As amusing as that would be..." she said and then phased behind him, tapping Gabe on the shoulder and winking at his gaping face, "No. That's not what my power is."

"This is how we're going to get home?" Gabe asked, eyes wide.

"Stop looking at me like I've grown a third boob, it's just plane hopping, no biggie." It was actually a big biggie, and Gabe knew it, judging by the hesitant look on his face.

Ivy pouted and stretched out a hand, "C'mon, friends don't let friends teleport alone and I need to practice with another person."

He sighed but placed his hand in hers, giving a short yelp as she moved them from one side of the room to the other and then paused, breathing hard. "It's a lot trickier carrying someone else."

"It's going to be hard for you to transport us all to the Heavens then." Gabe said with a faraway look on his face.

"Or," she countered, "I just need more practice."

He nodded thoughtfully, "Well, let's just stick to transporting within the compound for the moment before we try anything inter-dimensional," he said with a little laugh.

She nodded, a wry grin twisting her lips. "Sounds safe."

Gabe didn't look too reassured by the way her voice caught; she couldn't say she was either.

They spent the rest of the day hopping from room to room, usually scaring some poor unsuspecting angel shitless, which made Gabe howl with laughter each time. Around about their twelfth hop, she decided she needed to sit down, before she fell down. Gabe grinned at her as they flashed into the cafeteria, almost on top of Ezekiel, a tall angel with skin so dark it was almost blue.

He flashed very white teeth at them in a grimace and swore, "Damn, Ivy, you gotta stop doing that!"

She grinned at him tiredly and reached for the chair behind her, plopping down into it with a sigh of relief.

"Sorry, Zeke."

He waved her off with one hand and walked away to join some of the guys he usually ate with at another table.

Gabe sat opposite her, excitement lit his eyes as he gave her a wide grin. "That was freaking amazing! We should see how many hops you can do with two people tagging along. Maybe Jas?"

She nodded distractedly, too tired to protest his choice of accomplices. Truth was, Gabe had been right. There was a bit of a difference between carrying one or two people and an entire compound of angels. Obviously, she was going to have to do more than one trip. Maybe it would be less tiring to shift planes altogether rather than these short hops all in the same dimension. Did she even have to go? Could she just transport them all with the power of her mind? She focused on Gabe and imagined him landing in the bin on the other side of the room. Gabe gave her a funny look when her eyes crossed, and she eventually gave up, giving him an innocent smile in return. Clearly phasing someone without touching them was harder than them tagging along as she phased, especially when she was already tired.

"Do you think I should slow down? I'm pretty tired, I don't want to burn myself out."

Gabe waved a hand dismissively, "Definitely not, we should keep going. Your body is just adjusting to your powers is all, burnout is pretty rare and hardly ever fatal."

She nodded, relieved and Gabe smiled at her brightly.

"Let's switch it up a bit, try something a bit less... physical." Gabe suggested, though from the slight leer on his lips she could guess that was generally not his preference.

She rolled her eyes, "Okay, like what?"

He gave her a grin, completely devoid of the earlier douchery and she blinked in surprise at the sudden change.

"Well, we know you can send thoughts, visions, etc. You've done it to both Jas, Dev and Freddy now correct?" Ivy nodded and Gabe continued on, "But can you receive thoughts too?"

"Well, I did bump into an angel once and he spoke to me telepathically."

Gabe shook his head, "That's different, the angel must have wanted you to hear him if he was speaking to you. But with a little practice, you should be able to touch the minds of anyone here, maybe even control them." She didn't much like the sound of that and opened her mouth to tell him so but he plowed on. "So let's concentrate on honing that skill. I want you to clear your mind, concentrate, listen to the thoughts of the people around you."

She did as he said, keeping her mind blank and blah, blah, blah. She sighed – it wasn't working, she was tired and hungry and becoming increasingly cranky.

"I can't hear anything, Gabe, this is pointless!"

He rolled his eyes, "You've been trying for approximately two minutes, Ivy. Try again."

She clenched her fists but tried to clear her mind. At first there was nothing, but then there was... everything.

She groaned, her eyes rolled in her head and landed on Gabe who was watching her with something like concern and mild curiosity. His mouth formed her name in slow motion, the buzz of voices in her head grew louder and her whole body was made of sound, she couldn't tell where their thoughts began and hers ended. Her heartbeat quickened, and it felt as if fire licked up her skin, heat burning through her veins, boiling her blood.

Something stung her cheek, breaking whatever trance she'd fallen into, and she gasped as a glorious hush washed over her. She sagged against a cool surface and blearily opened her eyes to see Jas hovering over her, looking unsure as to whether she should slap her again.

"Goddamnit Jas," Ivy rasped, "I thought we were past the slapping stage."

"You almost roasted your synapses! What were you thinking?" The last was directed at Gabe with a glare.

"I didn't think she'd be able to tap into all of them at once," he said with a shrug, levelling his gold eyes on Ivy apologetically and offering her a hand up from the floor.

"You're lucky I came along when I did and saw what was happening," Jas said, still in stern teacher-mode, "You could have died, Ivy."

Ivy's hair was damp with sweat that was rapidly cooling, and her tongue felt thick in her mouth. "Yes, well, that *would* be inconvenient for you now wouldn't it?"

"Ivy—" Jas said, taking a step toward her but Ivy waved her off.

She stood reluctantly and winced, "I'm just being melodramatic. I'm done for the day." She said with a nod to Gabe. "I'm going to go and shower, I'll see you guys later," she mumbled and then dragged her leaden, aching feet to the door.

Fuck this. Why was she dragging her sorry arse around when she could just – there. Back in her room, quick as a flash and... yep, she was going to puke now.

She moved in the general direction of the bathroom but threw up before she got there. Luckily, she hadn't had any lunch yet and had only had time for coffee this morning so there wasn't much damage. She felt like utter shit and her mouth tasted like something had died in it. There was a soft knock on her door and she winced as the sound split through her head.

"Ivy?"

Oh god. That was Dev's voice. He couldn't see her like this. She looked like she'd gone on a month long, alcohol fueled bender – and it had only been the one night!

"Go away," she groaned, stumbling into the bathroom, lunging to avoid the small puddle of sick on the floor. A bath. That's what she needed. She wasn't sure she could stand long enough for a shower. She ran the hot water and ignored the second, louder, knock on her door.

"Ivy, please. Let me in. I just want to make sure you're okay."

Now that? That pissed her off.

Anger fueling her aching joints, she stalked over to the door, neatly dodging her puke pile, and flung it open. Dev's eyes widened when he got a look at her and she inwardly winced, wishing she had at least taken the time to check if there was puke on her chin before opening the door.

"Okay? No, Dev. I'm not *okay*. None of this is okay! I can do things I didn't think were possible and I can hear things I don't want to hear! My body hurts all over, I look like shit and honestly, I just want to be left alone right now. So just go."

His eyes were gentle but they held a challenge as they took in the circles under her eyes and defiant tilt to her chin. Despite everything, it felt good to let go. To not keep everything bottled up inside and to instead scream *FUCK YOU* to the universe. He pushed the door open wider and stepped closer to her, forcing her to take a step back.

"I'm not going anywhere, Ivy."

She blinked tears of frustration out of her eyes, she would *not* cry damn it. "I don't want you here, Dev. Go."

A muscle in his jaw ticked and a brief flicker of hurt lit his eyes, making her instantly regret her words. The truth was, she'd pushed people away for so long that she didn't know how to say *yes, stay, please please stay.*

He stepped closer and leaned in, "No."

She let out an inhuman growl and thrust out her arm to push him from the room, even as her heart felt like it might burst with relief, he caught her hand in his and did the same again when she tried with her other arm.

"Enough," he said, his voice gruff as he released an arm, gripping them both with only one of his and pulled her against him, wrapping an arm gently around her waist. "Stop," he said softly, leaning his head against her hair.

She sagged against him, a few stray tears sneaking free.

"Come on," he said gently, and led her to the bathroom. He poured some bubble-bath into the bath she'd left running and then set about mopping up her sick while she looked on dully, feeling only a small burn of embarrassment.

When he was done, he turned off the taps and moved to where she was standing at the sink. She eyed the bath longingly, finished rinsing her mouth of the puke taste and took off her sweat-stiff clothes. Dev turned around hastily, and she couldn't help the ghost of a small smirk at that. She stepped into the hot water and let out a moan, it was bliss to her aching muscles. The bubbles were so thick they covered every inch of her, but Dev's eyes were still heated when he turned around.

"Better?"

She nodded, and he sat beside her, lathered up his hands and slowly worked her shoulders. Oh my god, the man had magic hands.

When her muscles had all turned to jelly and she felt suitably clean and like less of a hot mess, she stepped out into the towel Dev had waiting for her. She let a small laugh escape amid her shivers because he had his eyes closed even as he wrapped the towel around her.

"Thank you," she said and caught her breath at the touch of his bare hand on her skin.

His arms tightened on the towel around her and his lashes fluttered slightly before they opened to reveal his eyes.

"Sorry," he said with an apologetic smile, "hard to see what I'm doing with my eyes closed."

"I didn't mind."

Devlin kept quiet, pressing a barely-there kiss to her forehead. She sighed into his warmth and slowly breathed him in, pulse slowing and headache easing slightly. She moved closer and let her head loll onto his shoulder, soaking his shirt. If he minded, he didn't say. He dragged his fingers lightly down her sides, barely touching her, he pressed slightly harder and she groaned quietly as he seemed to hit all the sore points in her back and ease the pain.

"Wha-What are you doing?" she rasped unevenly.

His voice was husky when he replied, "Drying you."

She started, realizing his hands had been on the towel the whole time, smoothing up and down, catching stray water droplets as they ran down her skin. She wished he would catch them with his tongue.

"You're projecting." Dev whispered softly in her ear, nipping gently at the lobe and catching it lightly with his tongue. His voice startled her out of her thoughts. Projecting?

"What?" she asked distractedly.

He let out a low chuckle that sent shivers over her skin as his breath tickled her, "I mean, not that I mind. I would love to have my mouth on you..."

Her face heated. Ah. Projecting. She got it now.

"Sorry," she said, embarrassed, her mind obviously too tired to shield any of her thoughts.

He pulled away from her, his face a little flushed.

"For what?" he looked genuinely confused and she blushed because hell, she didn't want to spell it out for him. "It's okay to want something *more* for yourself, Ivy."

There was that word again. *More.* She knew what he was asking. She looked up at him hesitantly and met his eyes, "Do you want something, Dev?" Her breath came slightly quicker as he leaned down and pressed his lips to hers in a kiss so full of want it made her gasp, heat beginning to pool at her center. He pulled away and stared deep into her eyes.

"I want you, Ivy."

He stepped impossibly closer, his hands cradling her face as she murmured his name, urging him on. She ran her own over his shoulders and down his chest as he pressed his lips to hers firmly and she was drowning in the sensation of his lips, his hands.

He pulled away, looking slightly flushed and said, "Are you sure?"

She looked at him steadily and slowly let her towel drop, it ghosted down her thighs and fell to the floor.

"I've never been more sure about anything."

He slid his warm fingers into her still wet hair and pulled her mouth to his, stroking her tongue lightly with his own. She groaned into his mouth and heard his breathing quicken in response. His hand caressed her bare side and gripped her hips as he pulled her closer, her still damp breasts pressed flush to his chest, nipples tightening as he reached up and stroked one peaked tip. She gasped, heat coursing through her and following the path of his hands as they traced her curves and stroked up her spine.

"Ivy..."

"Mhm?"

"If we don't stop now... we won't," his eyes were heavy with desire as they searched hers.

"Who said anything about stopping?"

He cursed quietly, but it sounded more like a plea, and reclaimed her mouth with his own, tongue twining expertly with hers as he gracefully swept her up and carried her to her bed. The towel became entangled with her legs as she tried to wrap them around his waist. Dev chuckled slightly, the low sound reverberating through her as he disentangled them, giving her room to push more of herself against him.

His eyes closed involuntarily at the sensation and she grinned, sitting up and tugging off his damp shirt.

"You're wearing *far* too many clothes," she panted, pulling them off one by one, dizzy at the sight of all his golden skin on display. She paused for a moment to admire the sheer gorgeousness that was Dev.

The hard, heavy length of him strained against the dark grey of his boxers and she reached out with a fingertip and traced his impressive length, leaning in and mouthing the shape through the material. Smirking at his answering gasp.

He gently pushed, and she found herself flat on her back as his large hands smoothed down her body. His head dipped and she moaned as he trailed kisses over her stomach and across her thighs. His hands worked the bundle of nerves at the apex of her thighs as his mouth slid closer to where she desperately wanted him to be, she bit back her moan but gave in when his mouth finally closed over her. Her hips shifted helplessly, his tongue stroking until her muscles quivered and she cried out.

"Dev," she panted as his fingers slid back into her wetness.

He kissed back up her body and curled her leg over his hip as he kissed her, sliding against and then into her gently and then harder as she moaned. He murmured her name into her mouth, their lips slamming together as they reached fever pitch, lost to wordless gasps as they fell over the edge together.

He smoothed her hair away from her face, his dark lashes tickling her cheek as he leaned in and kissed her.

"Sleep." Dev whispered his voice soft and husky, the same but so different to the night before. She curled up next to him as he stroked her hair and let her eyes slide shut.

"Stay," she murmured.

He smiled against her cheek, "I'll always stay, Ivy."

XVII
IVY

WHEN she awoke, Devlin was still there. At some point during the night he had curled his body around hers, protecting her even in his sleep. He looked softer somehow, face relaxed, hair curling around his ears. She smiled as he let out a gentle snore and stroked the day-old stubble on his cheek.

His eyes opened blearily and then widened adorably after remembering where he was.

He sat up abruptly and vainly attempted to flatten down his bedhead, "Ah, good morning?"

She let out a small laugh and stretched. She knew she probably looked wretched, but she was so comfy she didn't really care. Dev sent a heated stare her way and she grinned, "Good to know I'm not out of your system yet, Devlin."

His face turned serious as his eyes roved her face, "I don't think you ever will be."

She blushed and decided to change the topic, "I have no idea what time it is."

He relaxed slightly, apparently deciding she had no regrets and wasn't about to kick him out of bed.

He gave her a small grin, "I lost track of time around 3AM when you started snoring your head off, at which point the hours seemed to drag on and on..."

She gasped in mock horror and flung a hand to her chest. She did not snore! A fact that she repeated aloud and Dev just laughed.

"Well, your 'not snoring' kept me up half the night."

"Well, you seemed to be doing just fine this morning, sleeping beauty," she said with her eyebrows raised. He gave her a gruff look which turned into a slightly more mischievous one as he leapt at her, she let out a squeak, bracing herself for a... hug?

He laughed at the look of shock on her face and waggled his brows as he pulled her closer.

"I was your valiant knight in shining armor last night *and* I put up with your snoring, I think I deserve a token of your affection milady."

She looked up at him and snorted, "Well, I'm afraid good sir, that I gave my last handkerchief to Freddy, so you're out of luck."

He gave her a rueful look that made her roll her eyes, "Freddy huh, not Gabe...?"

She slapped at his chest and gave him a fierce look that made his own eyes seem to burn hotter.

"*No.* Not Gabe."

Dev gave her an entirely all too pleased, very male look as he grinned and said, "Good."

She rolled her eyes and fake coughed, "Sorry—can't—breathe... too much testosterone..."

Dev burst out laughing, startling her and she found herself grinning goofily back, entirely too flustered with the dimples that had once again appeared. They were flirting, she realised with a start. They were snuggling and laughing and talking and she... *liked* it.

Unsure how to deal with this new development, she closed her eyes and rolled onto her side, away from Dev. This only succeeded in getting him to spoon her, however. Which was altogether more distracting than the hug had been.

Suddenly, the door burst inwards, and Freddy threw his hands in the air. "I've been looking for you everywhere Devlin!"

"What's wrong?" Dev asked, serious once more and she couldn't help but mourn the disappearance of the carefree Devlin for just a moment.

"Some of Michael's men broke in and grabbed Gabriel. We're trying to hold them off in the canteen but there's a fuck-ton of them, I think they're trying to take him."

Devlin's face showed no emotion except grim determination, "I should have known Michael wouldn't let Gabe walk away that easily. Go and grab everyone you can, raise the alarm if you have to, it'll be worth potentially alerting the mortals if it means we can save lives."

Freddy nodded and ran back out of the door, a sword of light already burning in his hand and a moment later an alarm pierced the air.

"I need you to stay here."

"I can't do that. I can fight, I feel fine today, maybe I can use my powers —"

"You're not ready and I won't lose you. You nearly burned yourself out yesterday."

"Gabe said my body was just adjusting, that nobody ever really burned out."

Devlin paused tugging on socks she was pretty sure were hers, "He said that?" She nodded and an unreadable look crossed his face.

"What is it?"

"Something doesn't feel right." Dev said shortly.

"Look I'm sorry about Gabe, it—"

"It's not that," Dev said with a wave of his hand as he at last gave up on the socks and stood, tugging on a pair of joggers. "I just don't know why Gabe would have said that to you. Burnout is really common and can be fatal, especially for new angels who don't know what they're doing."

"Well, maybe he thought it would be different for me because I'm mortal?"

"Maybe," Dev murmured. "I don't know what's going on, but something is off and I don't want you out there."

"Well luckily, you're not the boss of me," she said and shifted in front of him to face the door, pulling on joggers and a t-shirt as quickly as she could.

Wow. Should she stick her tongue out too? Dev cast her a wry look but sighed in defeat, clearly sensing she would just do what she wanted anyway.

"Fine. But you stay back, don't put yourself in danger unnecessarily."

She stared at him incredulously, "Do you even know me?"

Dev rolled his eyes and strolled out the door, clad in nothing but his joggers and bare feet, conjuring his own sword as he walked. Show off.

She stopped at the door, a thought crossing her mind. Dev glanced back at her with a raised eyebrow and looked both relieved and suspicious when she waved him on.

Just how much could she do with her gift? Yesterday she had tuned into the minds of everyone in the damn compound and true, it had almost killed her. But she was better prepared now. For what, she wasn't sure, but she had to try something. *If* she could reach the minds of Michael's angels, maybe she could incapacitate them the same way she had done to Jas. Maybe she wasn't completely useless after all, maybe... she could help?

She concentrated, feeling the presence of the angelic minds outside singing at her and tethered herself to them, catching brief glimpses of conversation, telepathic chatter. If she could somehow link their minds together tighter, maybe she could phase them all out of this plane in one go.

She slid into the mind of one of Michael's men and recognised the angel he was squaring off with as Tariel, a friendly blonde angel. Despite his small size, he was ferocious. This she knew firsthand after sparring with him and Freddy. She exhaled slowly, watching Tariel slice at the angel and slid her mind against his before following his connection to another of Michael's angels and pulling them tighter. She searched until she found another mind, and another, tethering them together until she had them all.

Ivy panted as sweat ran in rivulets down her body, this was harder than she had thought but it was going well so far.

Stop, she thought and felt the angels pause as one in consideration. Then they rebelled, their thoughts clashing into her creating a loud hum of noise that filled her senses as they fought against her hold, it was enough to drive someone mad. She squeezed their minds tighter with sheer will and desperation, holding them in her own mind and crying out as she pictured the smooth clean walls of the place in Heaven she had seen once before and thrusting them through the dimensions.

Ivy groaned and Freddy ran in as she finally relinquished the minds of Michael's men. They burned as bright as flames, calling to her from across the planes, fading as she sank gratefully into the darkness climbing the edges of her vision.

He didn't know why Ivy had stayed behind, all that mattered was that she was safe and he could concentrate on the fight without worrying about her. Devlin jumped into the fray, thrusting his sword through one of Michael's angels and trying to avoid eye contact, didn't want that moment of recognition as he stabbed someone he knew, someone he might have once loved.

The most worrying thing about the attack was how they had gotten in. The compound was protected by a powerful boundary spell; nobody could come in unless invited.

A traitor. All of Devlin's instincts screamed *not right,* he was missing something. Something important.

He felt a sword slice at his arm and hissed at the cool burn. He spun round and found himself faced with one of Michael's right-hand men, Ashford.

His eyes were as cold as chips of ice when they met Dev's, he sneered, "You won't know what's coming until it's too late. You'll get what you deserve, you'll all—" he was abruptly cut off with a shudder as he disappeared in a pulse of white light.

Dev stopped and looked around to see the same thing happening to all of the invading angels. They had frozen in place, waging some sort of internal battle as they shuddered and some screamed, before disappearing in small flashes of light.

Ivy.

He ran out of the canteen, not caring whether the last of the angels had disappeared yet and found Ivy's door wide open. His heart beat loud in his ears but he relaxed slightly when he saw Freddy kneeling beside her on the bed, he knew Freddy wouldn't let anything happen to her. Freddy cast him a worried look and Dev felt his breath catch as Freddy pressed Ivy's wrist, searching for her pulse. A sigh of relief left him when Freddy nodded and Ivy's eyelashes fluttered.

"Stupid girl." Freddy said affectionately, stroking her hair back from her face.

"God damn it, Ivy. What did you *do?*" he said sharply, but there was no venom in his voice. Not after he saw her prone form lying on the bed. She gave a weak laugh that was completely at odds with her fiery personality and he winced at the sound. She looked so small, fragile, her face entirely too pale and drawn.

"I'm okay, just weak. I need food... and sleep. Lots of sleep," she said, yawning her way through the last of her words.

He mustered up half a smile, "That can be arranged. I need to go and check on the others first though."

Ivy nodded and he felt a brief stab of guilt as he remembered running out of the canteen, the battle had been over but he had still picked her over them. He couldn't say he regretted it though as he moved closer to perch on the side of the bed and took her cool hand in his.

"Next time you're going to do something stupid at least tell me first."

Ivy shrugged and mumbled something he couldn't hear.

"What?"

"I said," she mumbled, raising her voice slightly, "I didn't know it was going to be stupid 'til I did it."

He rolled his eyes but snapped to attention when Jasmine appeared at the door, slightly breathless, her eyes wide and face pale as she took in the room.

"Is she—"

"I'm fine. Who knew angels were such fussy mother hens?"

Jas huffed out a relieved laugh before turning to Devlin, her face becoming serious once more.

"How bad is it?" Dev asked her quietly, trying not to disturb Ivy, whose eyes had drifted shut again. They flew open at his quiet murmur and focused on them.

"Not good. We weren't as prepared as we should have been, fortunately we had only a few injuries, they disappeared before they could do too much damage. But Dev, they took Gabriel."

"They took him? Why?" Would Gabe be glad to be back with Michael? He hadn't exactly received a warm welcome here with them, but he had only himself to blame. Devlin had accepted the loss of his brother a long time ago, but that didn't mean he wanted Gabe behind enemy lines being subjected to Hades-knew what. Jas shrugged and that same niggly feeling tickled the back of Dev's brain. "What of the wards? Any clue as to how they were able to get past them?"

Jas bit her lip and delivered the news he had been expecting, but the words still came as a blow. "They're intact. Somebody had to have let them in."

"Why would someone do that?" Ivy asked and Dev shook his head.

"I have no idea," he said, but he had a terrible feeling they were going to find out.

XVIII

DEV

HE stretched his free arm and looked longingly at the one trapped beneath Ivy's head. She had been exhausted when Freddy and Jasmine had finally left. There had been an odd tension between her and Jasmine that had eased when Jasmine had given Ivy a hesitant smile before leaving. Devlin wasn't sure what exactly he felt for Ivy, just that she was important to him, and so was Jasmine. Honestly, he was just glad they weren't at eachothers throats anymore, though he supposed there was still time. Ivy had dozed off for a few hours before waking and scarfing down some of the food Freddy had left outside for her and then moved onto fulfilling other hungers. He wasn't entirely sure where she had found the energy to do to him half the things she had. It had been a long time coming, he supposed. As much as she had hated it, he knew she had burned for him. Had seen it in her eyes every time they sparred and in the goosebumps that rose to the surface whenever he brushed her skin. Devlin had duties to attend to, people that needed him, especially after yesterday's fight – but he hadn't been able to leave her. Not when she had come so close to death not once, but twice. It likely made him a terrible person, especially as everyone here had chosen him, put their faith in him, but he would have let it all burn to see her safe. Ivy mumbled in her sleep, lashes fluttering as her nose scrunched up in an adorable frown that she probably thought was intimidating.

It was incredible really, how someone so small and...soft, could be responsible for saving them all. They had only known each other for just over a month but already he felt a connection to her he had never felt before. A quiet ease, a steady flame. With her, he wasn't Devlin the Fallen, he was just Dev and there was a power in that. Being able to choose who he wanted to be.

His jaw clenched as he recalled the numb look in her eyes earlier, at everything she had suffered since being uprooted and brought here. She was made for more than this, she deserved better. Ivy deserved someone who would run her bubble baths every time she wanted one and kiss her bruises. He couldn't be that for her.

"Now *you're* projecting." A quiet voice murmured, startling him.

He gazed at her face and now open eyes and traced her lips with a finger. She kissed it before she spoke again, "I can take care of myself Dev, I don't need anyone to kiss my bruises or run my baths."

He furrowed his brow as he kissed along her clenched fists, "You shouldn't have to take care of yourself. You shouldn't be involved in this, you're too—"

"Too what, Dev? Soft? Vulnerable? Weak?"

"—important, Ivy."

She looked at him steadily, sleepy eyes soft and vulnerable, "You're wrong. I wasn't *uprooted*, I've never belonged anywhere like I do here. Here I'm needed. I think this is exactly what I was made to do, to find you and Freddy and Jas, and help you. Even kicking and screaming along the way. I would do it all over again to find you."

He fixed his eyes on hers, smoothing her brow with his fingers. He sighed and rolled forward until his body completely covered hers and buried his face in her hair.

"Words of sentimentality from Ivy Fayte, hell must be freezing over."

She laughed and rolled him over gently, straddling his body. "You lot have ruined me," she said with a wicked grin, punctuating her words with hard kisses that sent the blood rushing directly to his groin.

He shuddered under her touch and kissed her back just as ferociously, nipping at her lip when she attempted to talk again.

"No more talking." Of course, she didn't listen and in typical Ivy fashion, attempted to mumble around his lips. "Fine. If you can still form a coherent sentence while we kiss then I'll just have to occupy you another way."

He rolled her body until it was beneath his, twining their hands together as he kissed down her neck softly, nipping at the hollow of her throat. He let his hands ghost across her curves as he pulled the baggy tee she was wearing up and over her head, throwing it aside impatiently and kissed lower down. Her breath hitched in her throat and words finally seemed to fail her as he teased a breast to its peak with his tongue, teasing the other with his hand before moving lower.

Her hands caught in his hair as she whispered his name, growing louder as he found the sweet spot between her thighs, her hips unabashedly riding his mouth as she shouted his name like a prayer. He raised his head to look at her and marveled at the sight before him. Ivy's hands relaxed their grip on the pillow behind her as her hips sank back down onto the bed, her skin was lightly flushed and her lips red and swollen from their kisses. He gently pressed a kiss to them and smiled against her mouth, pulling her against his chest. Perhaps he didn't need to go home to once more belong.

XIX
IVY

THERE was a tension in the air over the next few days that had nothing to do with the attack from Micahel's angels and everything to do with what was going to happen next. Everyone in the compound had been waiting for far too long for this moment and now that it was almost here, emotions were running high. She had been practicing her phasing every spare moment, under Freddy's watchful eye so she didn't get close to burning out again. Gabe had been right about something at least, her body *had* needed to adjust, she was taking on triple the amount of food than before to compensate for the energy she was burning. Freddy had taken to filling her pockets with energy bars for her to eat in between hops.

Things were weird, she felt unsettled. The easy peace she had begun to find with Devlin and the others had been interrupted. Gabe was gone and it was hard for her to reconcile the person she knew with the person he had been before, was he their traitor? If not, should they have been fighting harder to get him back? She knew Devlin was worried about her, but she was more worried about what was going to happen when they reached the Heavens. The incoming fight, Devlin's curse. All of it weighed on her mind. They hadn't spoken about any of it though, just trained all day and lost themselves in each other every night.

A small smile curved her lips as she thought about it. If anyone had told her a month ago that she'd be living in a compound full of angels that would become her friends, she would have laughed herself hoarse. The world worked in mysterious ways, it seemed.

They were having an emergency meeting to decide what they were going to do now that Michael had made a move and they finally knew how to get back to the Heavens. While she was glad to set things in motion, she was equally nervous about the part she had to play. An awful lot of this was resting on her. The person she had been before she got here would have run, and a large part of her still wanted to do so, but she was working to be better. Jas had been right, and Ivy wanted to live her life the way her parents would have been proud of. Freddy fell into step beside her as she made her way to the canteen.

"What do you think he's going to decide to do?" she asked Freddy as they drew close to the doors.

Freddy looked grim, his mouth in a tense line and even his hair seemed less bouncy than usual. "I think he's going to want to go after Gabe."

Ivy considered this as they pushed through the doors. Devlin hadn't seemed overly concerned by Gabe's capture, but maybe he'd just been putting on a good show? The thought bothered her, she didn't want him to feel like he needed to pretend around her. God knows she'd laid it all bare for him. Several times. A smirk tried to rise to the surface but she pushed it back, now was so not the time.

Dev glanced up from the table he occupied as if feeling her eyes on him, his mouth quirked up into a smile that she couldn't help returning. Freddy snorted from beside her and she fixed him with a glare, "What?"

"Nothing!" Freddy said, raising his hands innocently, "You two couldn't be more obvious."

"I didn't realise there was anything to hide." Ivy said, "We're all grown ups here, what's a little sex between friends?" Freddy shot her an amused glance and a laugh stuttered out of her before she could clap her hand over her mouth, "That's not what I meant you filthy, *filthy*, bastard."

Freddy just grinned and claimed a seat opposite Jasmine, Devlin glanced between the two of them with raised brows. She fanned her slightly flushed cheeks and waved him off, there was no way she was repeating that.

"Out with it, Devlin." Freddy demanded before Dev could open his mouth.

"Wait, isn't anyone else coming?" she asked looking around, the canteen was empty but for them.

Dev shook his head, "The people here trust that I'll make the right decision, especially with Jas and Freddy here sharing their input. Besides, only the people in this room know what we do – that someone here betrayed us."

Jasmine sighed, "How do you know it wasn't Gabriel?"

Dev rubbed at his eyes tiredly, it was clear this was a conversation they'd had several times. "Maybe it was, but it never hurts to be careful. Until we know for sure, we proceed with caution."

Freddy's expression hadn't changed while they had discussed Gabe but she couldn't help wondering whether all this talk of betrayal was reopening old wounds for him. He cooly raised an eyebrow at her when he noticed her staring and she gave him a worried smile.

"So what *is* the plan?" Freddy asked, looking away from Ivy uncomfortably.

"It's clearly not safe here anymore, the haven we created has been violated. I say we bring the fight to Michael. There's no sense in us waiting around, especially if Gabe is the traitor – who knows what information he's already given up?" Jasmine was all business but Ivy could see the faint dark circles under Jas' eyes, things had been less tense between them since the other night but Ivy still needed to fix things.

"I agree," Devlin said with a nod. "The only question is whether you're ready Ivy."

She opened her mouth to speak but was cut off by Freddy, "Even if Ivy is ready, you want us to just charge in there with no strategy? We need more allies Dev. Michael has us outnumbered, even if we have the advantage from training on Earth."

"Maybe," Ivy said, threatening Freddy with a glare when he looked set to interrupt her again, "we can find allies among Michael's angels." All three of them looked at her blankly and she rolled her eyes, "Michael rules through fear, not loyalty like Devlin, right?. If given the opportunity, maybe some of his angels will fight for us."

"Double cross him, you mean." Freddy said thoughtfully before giving her a curling grin, "I love the way your mind works."

"Thank you," she said, with a pleased smile.

"Having more allies and reducing Michael's numbers would be a huge boon to us," Devlin said slowly, "but how do we reach out to them? Some of them may be too scared to double cross Michael. If we fail, that's a death sentence for them."

"True, but they're never going to get an opportunity like this again if you fail." Jas pointed out, brow furrowed in thought.

"Why don't I do it?" Ivy said suddenly, "I was able to move all of Michael's angels to the Heavens using their telepathic links to one another, but I could still feel their minds calling to me from across the planes. If you guys know who might be sympathetic to our cause, then maybe I can connect with them in the Heavens."

"That... could work." Devlin said reluctantly. "But what happened last time —"

"Won't happen again," she said with a confidence she didn't feel. "I've got more control now, besides I'll just be talking to them, not transporting anyone. We need this."

"So, when do you want to do this?" Freddy asked, sounding like he was planning a party rather than going to war.

Dev's eyes searched her face, as if looking for any hesitation or worry before nodding slightly, "Two days," he said decisively. "Enough time for Ivy to contact everyone we might need and to rest up so she's at full strength to take us across."

Two days to get ready. In two days they might all be dead. Was there really any way to prepare yourself for that? She'd already lost everyone she had ever loved once before, she'd be damned if it was going to happen again. If there was anything she could do to buy them a fighting chance, she would do it. Without remorse or regret. She'd found understanding and maybe even peace with the people in this compound and some overgrown pigeon wasn't going to fuck all of that up.

They were running out of time. Devlin could feel it trickling through his fingers like sand, grasping and never quite slowing it down. He had wanted more time with Ivy, hadn't yet had his fill of her laugh or the way she tasted on his tongue. He wanted more time for his people, for them not to have to fight in this war of his brother's making. Cursing Michael's name for the hundredth time, Devlin made his way down the corridor. He'd been running about all day after the meeting, speaking to his people, coordinating last-minute training, helping Ivy contact some of Michael's angels. Hopefully getting a taste of Ivy's power would help persuade them to fight on their side. He'd started organising a clean-up crew too, for better or worse it was unlikely they would be coming back here, aside from Devlin maybe.They were going to leave the wards up but without maintenance a stray mortal could end up wandering in. Everything was going well between him and Ivy, whatever their attraction was, it hadn't been borne of his curse or even out of necessity. Just heat and want and maybe even friendship. But was it love? He didn't think so. Maybe once they'd taken back control of the Heavens they could find out what had happened to Hades and he could remove Devlin's curse instead.

Devlin had been avoiding thinking about what would happen if they won. Either way, Dev lost. Lose the family he had chosen, and who had chosen him, or lose both his brothers – regardless of the pain they had caused him in the past. It was still possible that Gabe wasn't their traitor, Dev could only hope that any lingering affection Michael had for their younger brother would stay his hand. Curse his soft heart, but he didn't want to be the one to destroy Michael. Sometimes fate didn't care what you wanted. His brother's reign had come to an end, Devlin hoped he still had his heart by the end of it.

Jas walked past him, offering him a grim smile as she chatted to Ezekiel.

"Jas, could I have word?" Dev asked with a slight smile and nod to Zeke who grinned back broadly.

"Sure, what's wrong?" she asked as they moved slightly further down the corridor.

"Aside from everything, nothing. I just wanted to ask how the extra practices were going and see whether you could check in on Ivy to see how she's getting on with her phasing?"

Her hazel eyes squinted as she looked at him shrewdly, "The practices are going well, everyone is in good condition it's just a matter of the numbers now. As for Ivy, I'm happy to help, but why don't you check on her?"

He scrubbed his hand through his hair and blew out a long breath. He felt... guilty. He had responsibilities and he couldn't be seen slipping up this close to the battle they'd spent so long preparing for. More than that, he didn't want the last few days they had together to feel like a goodbye.

"Things between Ivy and I are just... I don't know what's going to happen tomorrow Jas, and when I look at her, I *want*. I can't look her in the eye, knowing it might be the last time I do."

Jasmine placed a gentle hand on his arm, her face understanding, "If the worst happens Dev, you'll kick yourself for not spending all the time you could with her. You do so much for us. Everyone is grateful, nobody begrudges you your happiness. Especially as we all know..."

"I won't be able to stay if we win."

"We'll find a way." Jas said firmly, "It's time to do something for yourself, we've got this covered. I'll run the practices and Freddy will coordinate clean-up. You go see Ivy. You deserve this, Dev. You both do."

Dev felt something in him ease as he loosed a breath, "You're right. Thanks Jas, I don't know what I'd do without you."

He gave her a swift kiss on the cheek and went to find Ivy, leaving Jas with a sad smile on her face as he walked away.

XX

IVY

Dev was AWOL. He had been ignoring her ever since the meeting and she had no clue why. Had she spoken out of turn? She didn't think Devlin was the type to care about rank but maybe she shouldn't have said anything in that meeting, maybe she was there as a courtesy only. Except, that was ridiculous and what she'd come up with could make all the difference in the fight to come – if there was one thing Devlin cared about it was helping his people. Every time she had seen him in the corridors or walking through the courtyard he had been too deep in conversation to notice her, which was offensive frankly, some stupid internal Dev-dar always told her when he was near. Or, he turned tail when he caught sight of her. They had spent the past few days enjoying eachothers company and bodies, but maybe that was all it was to him. That was fine, of course, she had never wanted her heart to get involved. Yet... *he* was the one who had pushed for more! Every time she inevitably got stuck thinking about Devlin her head went right to this place, looping around over and over. *Just face it,* a snide voice said, *he's just not that into you.* She told that stupid voice to fuck off. She rounded the corner with a huff, cursing men and their stupid cute butts.

"Ivy!" Freddy's voice rang out from behind her, she slowed her pace and he quickly caught up to her.

"Hey, what's up?"

"Just checking in, you know, making sure you didn't fry your brain today."

"Brain is intact, thank you for checking. Have you seen Devlin?"

"No, sorry. Not since this afternoon. Trouble in paradise?"

"Not yet," she said with a grin, "We don't arrive until tomorrow."

Freddy rolled his eyes, "Well, don't be too hard on him. He's been running around all over the place getting everyone ready for tomorrow. Oh and kind of preparing to save one of his brothers and kill the other one." Ah, yes. She supposed there was that.

"Fine. I can't promise anything, but I'll try." Freddy let out a relieved breath and she wrapped an arm around his waist.

"Hey, you okay?"

He shrugged, "Yeah, no. I honestly don't know how I feel right now."

"I know you and Gabe were... close, this must be hard, the not-knowing."

Freddy stiffened and looked at her warily, "I was talking about preparing to fight to the death. What were *you* talking about?"

Shit. Freddy didn't know that she knew about him and Gabe. Fuck. Luckily, they were interrupted by Dev rounding a corner and calling her name before she could respond. Freddy gave her the stink eye and she tried to look innocent.

"Hey, Fred, everything going okay?"

Freddy gave her one last questioning look before backing away, "Yeah, everything's fine. See you guys later."

"So," she said as they fell into step together, "what's up?" Things had never felt tense between them before but now everything felt off.

Dev sighed and bit his lip, "Things feel weird. I don't know what's going to happen tomorrow and I hate it, at least here I'm in control."

Ivy nodded slowly, "True, but control won't do you much good if Michael collapses this world. At some point you have to let loose, some things are uncontrollable."

He let out a short laugh, "I know, you are the most stubborn, *willful* person I've ever met."

She grinned, "You love it."

It felt like a new tension filled the air at the mention of the *L* word. Dev stopped outside her door and spun to face her. "Ivy... about tomorrow—"

She pressed a finger to his lips, cutting him off. She didn't want to think about the *what-ifs,* or even about tomorrow at all. Just one more selfish-time, she wanted to focus on the here and now, on the heat and passion they'd unexpectedly found.

A spark of heat lit in his eyes as she stepped closer, "I want you."

It was what would always pass as more for them.

"I want you too." Devlin said, his voice a little hoarse as she closed the distance between them, stretching up on her toes to ghost her lips across his once, twice. With a groan, his hands caught her by the waist, lifting her up and into him as Devlin pressed her against her door. Ivy moaned and slid her hands into his hair, pulse roaring in her ears even as she flicked her gaze to either end of the corridor warily. Dev rocked his hips against her and her eyes fluttered closed on a sharp inhalation, *this* was what she needed. Not a goodbye.

More her heart demanded, and she obliged, needing to feel bare skin under her hands, her mouth. She pressed hot kisses to his neck, revelling in every gasp as she inhaled his scent, committing it to memory, because who knew what tomorrow would bring —

No. Ivy cut that thought off abruptly, pulling away from Devlin and saw his eyes were as wild as hers, his lips red and swollen.

"More?" he asked roughly and she nodded. "Say it."

"More," she whispered as his hand cupped her breast through her shirt, trailing down her body to slip under the waistband of her joggers while his other hand worked at his fly.

"More?" he asked as he slid a finger inside her, curling it when she cried out, throwing herself forward to muffle the sound into his shirt. Dev soothed her aching core with practised strokes as he kissed her. "Tell me."

"More," she moaned when his lips left hers, gasping wildly when she felt him at her entrance, hot as he rubbed against her. His hips moved torturously slowly, teasing her in deep circular strokes until she yanked him closer, pulling him in deep.

Devlin groaned her name, hips moving helplessly, the wood cracking dangerously behind her as his hands braced in the doorway to her room.

He dropped his head to watch where they moved together, a shudder wracking him, and a louder crack ran through the wood as he moved against her harder. He looked up and his eyes met hers. Ivy's breath caught in her chest, he was *stunning,* lips parted and hair rumpled, eyes burning into her. Who would have thought that tightly-controlled Devlin would lose it with her, fucking her against the wall as she told him over and over, *more, more, more.*

When they were spent, Devlin cradled her to him before gently helping her legs to the floor, where they proceeded to tremble as they surveyed the damage done to the door.

"It could have been worse," Ivy said, waving away flakes of wood and paint that drifted errantly through the air, some landing on

Dev's shirt. "I admit, I'm impressed. I thought you'd at least take me inside, fucking against the wall is a very *me* move."

Dev smirked, cheeks lightly flushed as he stepped closer and gave her a long, lingering kiss. "You undo me."

The words sent an unexpected thrill through her but she just grinned, "C'mon let's get inside before we scandalise the neighbours further."

Dev nodded, serious once more, "We have work to do."

"You mean you didn't just come here to thoroughly ravish me?"

There was that smirk again, "No. That was just a bonus. We've got a few more people to contact before we leave soon."

She nodded, and they entered her room in a peaceful silence. Quieting her thoughts was hard, especially when all she could smell and taste was Devlin, on her skin, on her tongue. He settled himself on her bed and she couldn't help but think it felt right, he looked so natural sitting there at her side. Like he'd always been there and always would be.

"Are you ready?" he asked and she nodded. Despite everything, she would be sad to leave the compound. You never know who or what was going to come into your life and make you a better person, but Ivy knew that no matter what, she was leaving here forever changed.

Entering Dev's mind was now as familiar to her as her own, snatches of thought called to her but she pushed it all aside and let him direct her to what she needed to see, reaching out to the angels he showed her. Finding their unique flame across the planes and following the trail back to them, delivering the same message over and over, '*help us, join us.*'

An hour passed, and she needed a break.

"I think we're about done now." Dev said, and she nodded. "Listen, Ivy—"

"Don't. I don't want some half-arsed goodbye. We're going to be fine."

It was silent for a minute before Dev spoke again, "You are so fierce and so strong but once we've made it there, I don't want you to stay. I want you to come back here, where you'll be safe."

"Dev, that's not..."

"Listen to me. You're not ready. You may have these powers, but you're human, Ivy. If they try to hurt you, they will probably succeed, and I don't know what I'd do if that happened. I need to focus on my people, on freeing Gabe, like it or not you'll just distract me."

She recoiled, she never wanted to be that for him – a burden, a liability. She never wanted him to feel like he had to choose between her and helping the people he was sworn to – people who had put their faith and trust in him. But she wasn't helpless, she could fight and she was strong. Stronger now than she'd ever been. As if she had needed to break anew a thousand times to become fiercer, tempered. A weapon in her own right. Ivy phased before her thoughts had fully formed, appearing behind him and placing her hand against his back. "That's how quick it would be for me to kill you, Devlin. If you think for a second that I wouldn't do it, to save you or Freddy or Jas, then you're a fool. *You made me care.* There is *nothing* that I wouldn't do to protect that. Don't underestimate me, Devlin."

His hands fisted at his sides, "I'm saying this *because* I care. You can't use your powers that many times in a row Ivy, at some point you're going to get tired. How long will you stay alive when that happens?"

"I'm done with this conversation."

He caught her arm, "I'm just trying to keep you safe."

"I don't need you to keep me safe. I need you to trust me."

His eyes darkened as he ran his hand through his hair, "And I need *you* to trust *me*."

She realised with a start that she did trust him. Didn't know when it had happened or when the people here had begun to mean as much to her as they did to Devlin, but this felt like home in a way she had never experienced before. She knew that no matter what, the people here would have her back, and she would have theirs. They had trained together and laughed together, tomorrow they would likely die together. But if she could save even one of those lives by fighting with them then it didn't matter what Devlin said. Besides, what made him think that she'd be able to get back onto this plane after shifting so many people already? They hadn't practiced that, wanting to conserve her energy for the day. She would do what she needed to and he would do the same, but she couldn't let one of their last nights together end like this.

A long sigh eased out of her as she let the fight drain out of her body. "Whatever you want, Dev."

"You," he said. "Just you."

XXI

IVY

THE canteen was tense two days later as the group of angels huddled together, preparing for battle. Anticipation hung in the air, setting her teeth on edge. Only she, Dev, Jas and Freddy knew about the possibility of some of Michael's angels joining their side and she could see some of their group looking around, measuring their number. They were only about a hundred or so strong, but they were fierce and lethal fighters. She had trained with a lot of them and knew that at the very least, Michael's men were going to be hurting by the end of the day.

"Hey," Freddy said from behind her, making her jump. "Are you well rested? Did you have some food and stuff?"

He had been hovering over her since their conversation in the hall the other day, like he was worried she was going to run.

"Freddy, for the millionth time, stop fussing! I'm fine. Take care of yourself, don't worry about me. Have you seen Dev?" She scanned the room a third time but still couldn't see his familiar form in the crowd.

"I think he and Jas went to get weapons."

She blinked at him, "I thought you guys just magically conjured those up?"

Freddy snickered, "Well yeah, but if we get tired we don't want to waste our energy on maintaining our swords."

"Then what's the point in them?"

"They're non-lethal on the Earthly plane, they just send Michael's men back to where they came from. Less hassle than a body."

"But today..."

Freddy's face hardened, "Today is not the day for mercy. No matter the weapon we use, we will strike hard and fast and without regret."

Some of the nearby angels heard his words and nodded

"Ivy," Freddy began in a much softer voice.

"Fred, c'mon. What is it with everyone recently? First Dev, now you? Don't do this. We'll both be fine."

He smirked at her and rolled his eyes, "I was just going to say you have bacon in your teeth."

"Oh."

"Yeah."

Just then she spotted Dev at the other end of the room and waved him over, running her tongue over her teeth while staring suspiciously at Freddy.

"Hey. Have you got everything?"

Fuck. This was it. Moment of truth.

"We're ready, are you?"

"Almost," she said, leaning into him and pressing her mouth solidly against his. He gave a sharp breath of surprise against her mouth.

"There," she said, pulling away, "Now I'm ready."

Freddy grinned, "Do we all have to kiss you to be ready, Dev?"

Dev snorted, she laughed and said, "You wish, Freddy."

Freddy gave her a horrified look and she poked out her tongue.

"If you three are quite done?" Jas remarked, eyebrows raised.

"Nowhere near," Dev said in a low voice just for her, her cheeks flushed and Freddy pretended to gag.

Jas cleared her throat but quieted when Dev turned to the small crowd that surrounded them. A hush fell and she shivered at the weight of the stares on her skin. Despite what she had said to Freddy, there was a very real chance they wouldn't all walk away from this. Her chest tightened as she tried to keep her breathing steady. She would find her way through it, regardless of what happened next, but she still sent up a soft plea for them to all make it through this in one piece. It was time to fight – or die trying.

"Today we go to fight, for our home, for each other and for the home we made here on Earth." Devlin began, "Michael has betrayed each and every one of us. *He* was the one to cast the first blow, *he* is the one who left us here alone and bleeding and *we do not forget!* As we fell, so shall he. Hades save his soul."

Eyes gleamed with tears and determination, but none left Devlin's face as he pressed two fingers to his lips and bowed. "You have been my family, my comfort and my home for so many years. It is an honour to fight beside you and, should we fail, to fall at your side."

Devlin turned to her, eyes shining in what might have been fear or gratitude, she wasn't sure, "Are you ready?"

She gave a small, jerky nod and held out her hands. Devlin grasped her right and Jasmine her left as the angels all held onto each other. A hand, a scrap of clothing, until nobody was left alone or untethered. Together, until the end. She closed her eyes and pictured the same white space she'd found herself in several days ago and *pushed*. The power drain was instantaneous as the world blurred around them and she slammed into the ground of the Heavens.

"Ivy! Ivy, are you okay?" Jas' voice was sharp in her ears and Ivy pulled herself unevenly to her feet, wiping away the blood that had started to trickle from her nose. The warm, soothing energy of the Heavens seeped into her and she felt herself relax, despite knowing what was to come.

Her eyes found Dev and she gave him a weak smile, "Honey, you're home."

His eyes lit on her with concern, moving to stand beside her and ran his hand down her arm while he studied her intensely. "Are you alright?" his voice was quiet, and his mouth was turned down as he assessed her.

"I'm fine, I just need a minute is all. Did I manage to bring everyone over?"

Dev nodded, and she looked around distractedly as he spoke in a clear commanding voice, "Michael probably knows we're here by now, brace yourselves."

Her energies curled against the Heavens as if greeting an old friend, rubbing against each other playfully. Using her abilities to get here had left a mark on the air and it wouldn't be long until Michael noticed, he had to have been expecting them to come — there was nothing else they *could* do.

Heaven.

She didn't think it would look quite like this. She looked up and met Dev's green eyes, he pulled her in close, his forehead resting against hers.

"Remember, as soon as things get crazy, just get yourself out. Okay? Don't wait for me, I can't stay here anyway. The curse won't let me. I'll see you when this is all over." He kissed her once, fiercely, but his eyes were sad when he pulled away. What he really wanted to do was stay here in heaven, where he belonged. Not return to Earth with her. Then a slow applaud began as Michael walked down a large white staircase, the contrast of his auburn wings startling against the paleness of the room.

"How touching." he said, the sneer on his face twisting his otherwise surreal beauty. "Don't you think so, Gabe?"

No. There was no way but – there was Gabriel. Walking behind Michael in absolutely pristine condition, dusky brown wings once again gracing his person.

Gabe looked at them standing together and smirked, "I wouldn't dwell on her affection too much brother, we both know how much of it she hands out."

Her eyes went to Dev, how would he meet this latest blow? He hadn't trusted Gabriel, but he had *hoped*, and somehow that was worse. The shock on his face was immediately replaced with anger.

"I should have known. How many times did we wait for you to change, to think for yourself – and yet, again I am left looking more the fool for it. For what we once had I'll ask you one final time, but after this I'm *done* giving you second chances Gabriel. Do the right thing. Join us now, or lose me forever and may Hades save your soul."

Michael began a slow laugh that made her skin crawl as he looked at Dev with pity and triumph. She longed to wipe that smug smile off his face. With a crowbar.

"Oh my brother, don't you see? I didn't *force* Gabriel to do anything. He's quite the genius really – killed the prophet who told you how to get rid of your curse, but not before forcing him to use his gift to catch a glimpse of what our lovely psychic would look like. After that, it was quite easy to orchestrate the 'fall' so that Gabe would wind up in her little shop." Michael's face turned to hers with a sneer as he looked her up and down dismissively, "Gabe gambled that you would try and come back up here once you'd found *her* Devlin, there was no way you could let down your precious angels. So we figured, why not have a little fun? We even had a little bet going, didn't we, Gabriel? Unfortunately, you surpassed my expectations dear, I thought for sure that Gabriel would be able to bed you."

Her head span trying to process all this new information and being called a slut twice in as many minutes.

"But – Gabe's wings! He said he came to warn us..." Ivy said, and Michael belly laughed at her words.

"A ruse and a glamour. Why would I kill off the humans when I have such good fun torturing them? But I'm afraid the fun has come to a close and it's time you are dealt with, as I should have done a long time ago." Michael snapped his fingers and his angels appeared behind him. Fuck. There were so many, at least double their numbers.

Dev turned to her blindingly fast, "Leave, now." He didn't stop to see if she would comply as he turned back to Michael and stalked towards him. She only pulled out her own sword as the sea of Michael's angels rose up before her. At least fifty of Michael's angels turned on their comrades as the fight began and a wave of relief washed through her as she realised their plan had worked, some of the angels she and Dev had contacted were fighting with them and they had surprise on their side. Dev had made it over to Michael in record time and the two were fighting furiously, just a blur of wings and steel.

Blood quickly marred the white floor in drips and arcs, feathers scattered between the carnage as wings were shredded and angels fell.

She ducked as someone threw a sword in her general direction. Her eyes darted around trying to find the culprit and saw an empty-handed Kal charging at her, clearly with a score to settle. One of his wings drooped slightly, a remnant of the fight between him and Dev, and his eyes burned with anger as they locked on hers. She ran to meet him head on, ducking under his sword and kicking out at his injured wing. The rage and pain that had consumed her for years roared out of her in a wave of brute force as she sliced her sword deeply across his calf. Kal roared with pain and knocked her back with a kick to the stomach, leaving her breathless. He struck out, sloppy with pain and she darted to the left to avoid his fist, slamming her own into his face and sending a spray of blood flying.

"Bitch." He growled.

"I think we already covered this," she said, and swung her sword in a high arc, slicing deeply into his chest. Kal fell. Ivy didn't pause to consider what she had just done, instead she spotted Jas in the corner fending off three of Michael's angels and headed in that direction. She had hurt Kal. Probably killed him, but she would do it all over again to protect the people she... cared about.

Ivy narrowed her focus to the space beside Jas and reappeared next to her just in time to catch a sword that would have hit Jas in the chest. Ivy wasn't yet at full strength, it was like her power was slumbering inside her instead of reacting when she reached for it. It would have to be enough.

"Great timing." Jas said wryly and Ivy grinned, turning to face her opponent.

She hefted the sword, her palm had started to sweat around the hilt and small flecks of blood stained her arms. The angel she was fighting swung his sword at her and Ivy tarried it with a thrust of her hand, projecting an image of her sword slicing to the right of the angels' head while she struck to his left. Her sword cut through him easily as he swung at air and she gagged as blood ran to the hilt of her sword. Angels may be something other than human, but they still bled like one.

It was then that she noticed Gabe stood off to one side, sword hanging loosely in his hand as he observed the battle. Heat lit her veins and she instantly found herself in front of him.

"You son of a bitch," she panted, "How could you do this to him? We trusted you! *I trusted you.*"

"Ivy —" he started but she quickly cut him off.

"No! Tell me, were you trying to kill me that day I almost burned out?" She raised her sword between them, the awful thought had occurred to her some time ago but she hadn't wanted to believe it.

Gabe winced, "You can't fight me. You know I'll win."

She swung towards him before he could move, slicing his chest shallowly before retreating, "Tell me! Look me in the eye and *tell me* what you tried to do to me."

"Fine! Yes, it's true. I did try to kill you, because I wanted to avoid *this*." Gabe said, gesturing to the bloodshed surrounding them. "Think what you want of me, Ivy, but I never wanted this to happen. My brother left a long time ago, I can't undo that and neither can he. Coming here was a mistake, he has sent you all to your deaths."

"He didn't leave you."

"What?"

"Devlin *didn't leave you*. You left him." Rage was boiling inside her, she couldn't stop seeing that pale hopeless look on Devlin's face as Gabe had walked down the stairs. "You ripped off his wings and abandoned him. So don't try and pull this high and mighty shit. *You* are the villain here." She moved her sword quicker than she thought possible, rage and pain fuelling her every move, until her sword tip lay against his throat. "Give me one good reason why I shouldn't end you right here."

Gabe went pale, "I can't."

She pressed a little harder but froze as Gabe crumpled to the floor, unconscious. Eyes wide, she stared at Freddy who had appeared behind Gabe. He was bleeding from a shallow cut on his arm but otherwise seemed fine.

"What are you doing!"

"Preventing *you* from doing something you would have regret. He doesn't deserve death." Freddy said calmly, "He will be dealt with when this is over." he dragged Gabe to one side, out of the worst of the fighting.

"Are you sure that's why you saved him?" The words escaped her before she had time to think about them. Freddy froze with his back to her before spinning around and staring at her.

"Yes," he said at last, "I'm sure." Then he was gone, vanishing into a throng of heavy fighting and engaging another of Michael's angels.

She looked around slowly, more than half of Michael's angels had fallen or surrendered despite them having the advantage of numbers. Devlin had clearly trained his angels well.

Something cool pressed against her throat and she froze, dimly recalling Jas' words that there wasn't time to stand around during battle.

"What do you think, brother? Decapitation? Disembowelment? Sword through the heart? Any preferences, sweet Ivy?" Michael whispered the last, lips brushing the outside of her ear when she heard him gasp, his guard dropped slightly as he clutched his shoulder.

"Move, Ivy!" Jas shouted, and Ivy phased free of Michael's grasp to see Jas face-off with him. Devlin struggled to his feet and her heart froze in her chest as she saw the blood pouring from the wound in his side.

Michael was bleeding lightly where Jas had managed to stab his shoulder but he seemed more amused than concerned, a faint smile curled his lips as he watched them. "Ah, little Jasmine. Still running around after my brother? It's a shame really, I quite liked you. You were always so fiery."

Jas snarled, and her sword moved like a stream of silver through the air, clashing against Michael's. He was laughing as he blocked yet another of her attacks, carelessly swiping at her sword hand and knocking the weapon free. Ivy scrambled to reach for it but froze with it clasped in her hand as Michael's sword plunged down, straight through Jas' chest. Devlin gave a hoarse yell that sounded as if it had been ripped from his chest and Michael chuckled. Too quickly for her eyes to follow, Jasmine's head fell with a wet thump, landing next to Ivy.

She screamed, swearing unintelligibly as she reached for Jas like she could fix the damage. Dev lunged for Michael only to be held back by two of his angels.

"You bastard!" Ivy sobbed, teeth chattering and struggling to see through her streaming eyes as she scrambled to her feet. This wasn't what she needed. There would be time to grieve Jas later, right now she needed to be the old Ivy. The girl who could push any emotion down.

Michael grasped her hair and thrust her head back, pushing her down onto her knees. She didn't feel it. Didn't even gasp at the familiar feeling of warm blood soaking her trousers as she knelt. Michael peered into her eyes, smiling in feral delight.

"Oh, this one will be hard to break I think. Maybe I'll keep her Devlin, what fun we could have."

Ivy didn't flinch, just spat in Michael's face and let a grin that was more teeth than smile twist her face. He blinked and reached for Jas' limp hand, wiping the spit away and flinging it back to the floor.

"Did you really think it would be that easy? I trapped Hades himself," Michael said with a smirk, "One little human won't—"

Ivy slammed Jas' forgotten sword with all her strength into Michael's calf and dove out of the way when his grip slackened.

Retrieving her own sword from the ground, she spun to face Michael. She closed her eyes, her mind as empty as her heart, and focused on Michael's thoughts. They sung at her, an icy flame, she blew past his mental barriers easily. He swung towards her and she stepped aside, countering each move he made as he thought about it. His sword sliced for her neck and she weaved as it plunged towards her, she stepped forward and ducked under his arm. Kicking his damaged leg, Ivy thrust her elbow into his partially-healed shoulder and let her sword press against his throat, drawing tiny beads of blood. She pressed against his damaged shoulder until his sword clanged to the ground.

She leaned in towards him until their noses nearly brushed,

"Why create me? Why create a key to save Dev and usurp you?"

Michael looked at her with bemusement, "Oh, Ivy. Why on Earth *would* I do that? I like my fun but that would be convoluted, even for me. Had it occurred to you that perhaps I didn't?"

She blinked, startled. "If you didn't, then who did?"

Michael shrugged, "Hades knows," he said flippantly, "But it wasn't me."

She could hear the grunts and wet sounds of flesh meeting sword behind her, presumably as Dev broke free of his captors. He ran to them and levelled his own sword at Michael.

"Funny really," Dev said, "You say you've trapped Hades... that means there's probably very little control on his plane right now and I happen to know several angels," he paused, his eyes landing on Jas' still form, "that would be very happy to see you there, especially without the usual rules in place maintaining order."

Michael's face paled, Dev continued, "I guess you know what happens now."

Michael, surprisingly, smiled. "Ah, yes. I can guess what you might have had planned. That is, if the portal to Hades had not been previously sealed by me... and without Hades to force it open on his side, well, I don't think you have any way of getting me there alive."

Dev's face tightened, "I would prefer not to have to kill you, it's true. There's been too much death already today. You deserve whatever those poor souls have in mind for you and if there's no other way, dead will get you to Hades' realm just as easily as any portal."

Dev raised his sword to Michael's chest and Ivy quickly caught his arm. He'd lost one brother to betrayal tonight. She couldn't let him kill the other.

Ivy turned to Dev, her hand sliding to cup his around his sword and lower it a fraction. "I will take care of Michael, but I need you to do something for me."

Dev looked hesitant but nodded.

"Don't follow me."

She kissed Devlin and grabbed for Michael's hand, focusing on his memories of Hades.

"What—" Michael said but she pressed the blade of her sword deeper into his throat.

The planes started to shift and she caught Devlin's eye one last time, allowing her pain to resurface but something else too. Something she'd realised when she had seen him on the ground, blood pooling around him.

"I love you, Devlin."

His face paled with realization. "Ivy! Wait!"

XXII

DEV

IT had been six months since he'd last seen Ivy. Now here he was, standing at her door, feeling curiously... empty. He'd gone over and over this moment in his head the past few days while he tried to figure out what he'd say - hell, what *she'd* say. Would she be happy to see him? Hug him? More? Only one way to find out. He squared his shoulders and rapped on the pale green surface of her door. Shuffling sounded, and he tried not to laugh when he heard a bang and muffled cursing from inside.

It flew open unceremoniously and left a short, frazzled, blonde woman standing in the doorway. She seemed to make the space around her glow and for a second, he couldn't do anything but stare. Her voice cut through his unexpected reverie.

"Dev?" Her blue eyes were wide and her voice breathless, but she didn't approach him and that sent a spear of some kind of emotion searing through his chest.

"Hey," he said lamely. Hey? *Hey?* After the days spent imagining this moment, *that* was all he could come up with?

Ivy seemed to agree as her brow furrowed and she asked, "Hey? What's wrong? Why are you here? *How* are you here?"

He ignored her questions and gestured behind her. "Can I come in? Kind of a long journey."

Without waiting for a response, he moved closer and to his

disappointment she moved back and away from him.

Ivy huffed but closed the door behind him, "I mean it Dev, why are you here?"

Well, that certainly wasn't the warm welcome he had been hoping for.

"If I said I just wanted to see you, would you believe me?"

"No," she replied. "It's been six months Devlin, I figured if you were coming back it would've happened by now."

So, she was pissed because he was *late*?

"Look, I didn't think you'd want to see me, seeing as you ran off with Michael and then never came back—"

"I was doing what was *best* for you. You needed to be there and the other worlds aren't where I belong—"

"Well, I belong wherever you are."

Ivy fell silent at that and he blew out a strained breath and thrust his fingers through his hair.

"I wouldn't have come and bothered you unless I had any other option, but I don't. I need your help." A flicker of something that looked like hurt briefly crossed her face before fading.

"Help with what?"

He hesitated, "We need to get the portal to Hades up and running again, it seems that Michael wasn't lying. Hades is missing and things are sneaking through the gaps in the planes that shouldn't be, the Underworld is spiraling out of control. We need to find out where he's gone and help him reassert control before the less savory souls escape onto a nicer plane. The chaos from the Underworld could affect all of us."

"How am I supposed to help with that?"

"Well, the issue we're facing is that Hades is too far to journey for any of the angels left with us that have wings. Their inner power is small, which is why Michael never bothered to remove their wings – even this trip to Earth was costly for them, and the portal can't be fixed from this side."

"You mean...?"

"We need to go to the Underworld. We know you can definitely shift there and back, you're the only shot we've got."

"Great. So, once we're there, then what?"

Well, that wasn't a no, though she looked less than enthusiastic. Actually, she looked pretty great. Beautiful, even. "I don't suppose you'd leave if I asked you to?"

"Probably not."

"That's what I figured, so you'll stay with us and help."

"Us?"

As if he were waiting for the perfect moment, someone else knocked on Ivy's door. She frowned but opened it. A look of delight instantly spread across her face as she swept Freddy up in a hug.

He guessed the chilly reception was reserved just for him, then.

"Freddy? You're coming with us?"

Freddy mumbled something incoherent into the shoulder Ivy currently had him smushed into.

Dev gave a loud sigh, "Did you have to make such a dramatic entrance?"

Freddy extricated himself from Ivy and just gave a noncommittal shrug, as if to say, *sorry not sorry*.

"So, when do we leave?" Ivy asked, seeming much more eager now that she knew Freddy was also coming. Dev tried his best to quash the pang in his heart and his rising jealousy, *he* wasn't the one that had run off and not come back.

"As soon as you're ready to give us a lift," Freddy said with a grin that spelled trouble.

Ivy nodded absently, "Okay, well, I'll pee and then I guess I'm ready."

Dev looked her pajamas up and down.

"You might want to put on something a little more sturdy, the Underworld is not a soft and fuzzy place, this is going to be dangerous."

Ivy looked down at her fluffy PJs and sighed, then turned around and headed to her bedroom.

"Won't be a sec then," she called.

Ten minutes later, Ivy was appropriately dressed in cargo pants, a t-shirt, fleece and sturdy boots, and they were ready to go.

"Do I need to bring snacks?" Ivy asked, "I heard you can't eat stuff down there because you get trapped and shit?"

Dev tried not to laugh at the serious expression on her face.

"You can bring snacks if you want," he said, it was probably preferable, he'd never known anyone else who got as hangry as Ivy. She looked relieved at his answer, knowing Ivy she'd probably already stashed them somewhere.

"Okay boys, buckle up and grab a hand." Ivy said, closing her eyes. The world started to whirl around them when he faintly heard someone calling Ivy's name. They materialized hard, smacking into the ground. Ivy was on her hands and knees clearly trying not to vomit.

"I don't know why that was so hard," She gasped, "There was only the three of us."

"Um, actually..." Freddy said, nudging an unconscious male on the floor with his foot.

"*Shit.*" Ivy said. "Jeff."

"Who's Jeff?" Freddy asked, and Dev was glad he hadn't had to be the one to ask, he was worried how it might have come out. Probably jealous. Possibly sad. The second option would have been worse.

"Er, well, he's my new neighbour."

"Damn, he took my apartment?"

"Yeah. He's a lot less nosy than you, though."

Freddy stuck out his tongue and Ivy opened her mouth to respond when a roar shook the sand that surrounded them, ripples of gold swept out and glimmered in the sun. Dev had a sinking feeling he knew just where they were. Hot sun beat down on them and it was only going to get hotter, there was nothing around them except sand dunes, waves of heat wafting off them in the midday sun.

"Maybe we should talk about this later." Dev suggested dryly. Ivy was peering around them, an adorable line puckering the space between her eyes as she scrunched her nose in distaste.

"Where the fuck are we?" She demanded, "This looks different to where I came in before."

Always with that mouth... "How can someone so innocent looking have such a foul mouth?" Dev smirked and Freddy rolled his eyes.

"Hades have *mercy*, we do not have time for you two to moon over each other. We need to get out of here, now. If I'm not mistaken, those don't really seem like friendly demons racing towards us over there and I'm guessing the other inhabitants of the sands didn't just go on holiday."

Ivy and Dev turned to look, her face went ashen and Dev curled his hands into fists as he saw what approached.

"Definitely not where I landed before," Ivy whispered hoarsely.

The creatures that were approaching were like a wave of darkness spilling out over the endless sands, the only clue that this was not ordinary darkness was the glow of red eyes interspersed throughout its furls.

"Where did you drop Michael anyway?" Freddy asked and Devlin's breath caught, unsure if he wanted to know what fate had befallen his eldest brother.

"Into the darkness." Was Ivy's only reply as she wiped a bead of sweat from her brow. Dev knew how she felt. The only thing worse than the heat of the Sun Sands was the freezing cold nights.

"They're the Guardians of the Sun Sands," Freddy said, "Maybe they think we're damned souls running amok."

"Well, Devlin did once tell me he was the devil."

Devlin glowered at her for the reminder, "So what do we do?" he asked as the first tendrils of darkness began to breach the closest dune.

"We run." Freddy said, eyes glinting in the reflection of the dark.

Jeff still hadn't stirred, so Devlin slung him up and over a shoulder as they turned and began to run in no particular direction except *away*.

Ivy was gasping not before long. Sweat continued to run down her face, leaving a trail in the sand.

"You didn't keep up with your training," Freddy accused, eyes narrowing on Ivy's jelly legs. Ivy panted and flipped him off.

"Yeah, well, I didn't think I'd be running through the Underworld anytime soon."

It was clear Ivy was flagging, he nodded to Freddy who reached to snatch Ivy up in his arms with more care than Dev had admittedly shown *Jeff*, whoever he was. Before Freddy could heave her up, the darkness was on them. Thin tendrils wrapping around them, slicing through any skin on show. Dev hissed as a particularly bold shadow slashed at his forearm, blood dripped into the sand, sizzling against the heat of the grains and sending an iron tang up into the air. As one, the glowing eyes all turned to him, abandoning Freddy who was huddled over Ivy as they sighted bigger prey, smelled the power in his blood.

Dev had heard stories about the Guardians of the Sun Sand. To be condemned to this desert was a fate reserved for only the most foul souls. The endless sun, hotter than anything on the Earthly plane, could peel the flesh from your bones but during the night was when the Guardians came out to play. The fact that they were out now, in broad daylight only showed how bad things had become here. They needed to find Hades. Fast.

The shadows wafted closer, trailing darkness as they moved towards him, eerily silent as they prowled over the sand. Not a grain stirred. Faintly, he could hear Ivy shouting. The sun was being shut out. A blessed relief, were it not for the all-encompassing dark. Dev faced the glowing eyes, setting Jeff down on the sand and shielding him with his body.

"That's right," he murmured softly as they drew closer, as the darkness became more complete and the only light radiated from their eyes, "more power in me for you to drain than in them. Come on," he coaxed lightly, "you know you want to."

The first shadow leaped, lighter than air and faster than even Dev's eyes could track. He could do nothing as the darkness bled into him, as the air became heavy with the scent of his blood. He knew from past experience in the Underworld that the Guardians would most likely leave the others alone. Everything in this plane *hungered* and once they got what they wanted, they usually left. They would drain him of power, fixate on him. On the kill.

Dev knew he'd guessed correctly when the sunlight began to warm his empty body once more. Ivy was screaming. He tried to open his eyes, tried to go to her. *She needs you. Stand up.* His limbs were so heavy, or were they light? Or had the darkness ripped them from him in their eagerness to reach for the power inside?

"Dev!" Ivy panted his name through a sob, "Oh god, Freddy, there's so much blood."

"He shielded Jeff, barely a scratch on him."

"Freddy, what do we do? We need help. Can you heal him?"

Freddy's silence spoke volumes and Dev could feel Ivy's hands form into fists in the heavy dampness of his shirt. Then she began to scream and swear and beg. He had thought that watching her face off with Michael would be the worst thing he would have to endure, seeing her caught in his brother's arms, facing certain death. But hearing her scream as if her very soul was being rendered in two made the barely-beating thing in his chest break.

Dev could hear Freddy frantically shushing her, he knew as well as Dev that they would be attracting things far more deadly than the Guardians otherwise. That was if they weren't already on their way, drawn by the overwhelming pull of Dev's blood.

"No. *No.* Get off of me, Freddy! I am not leaving him. *I am not leaving him, get your hands off me!*" Ivy roared the last, calling out for someone to please help them and Dev knew that even if he never saw her again, he could die happy knowing that maybe she did still love him just a little bit after all.

XXIII
IVY

ONE moment she was screaming at Freddy. The next, the world was shifting around them as if she were using her powers but she'd done nothing. Except, something was different. After transporting three people she was usually wiped out, often a little nauseous, but she felt fine. In fact, she felt invigorated. They hit the ground hard, if Dev wasn't in such critical condition – she would not think of him as dead – then she might have laughed as Freddy's head clunked off a stalactite when they reappeared. There was still time. There had to be. She'd only just got him back and now she was losing him all over again. True, she had done the ditching, but it had been half a year! He turned up on her doorstep and asked for a favour? No declarations of love or even thanks that she dropped his arsehole of a brother into hell for him, just a 'hey' and 'can you give us a lift?'

So, Dev couldn't be dead. They needed to have *words*.

"You can't die. I'm pissed at you." Ivy muttered as she looked around for where Dev might have landed. She froze as Jeff thunked down beside her and then an almighty *splash* split the silence. *Shit.*

Dev had landed in a large, luminescent pool. Face down. *Of course, why would she be able to catch a freaking break?* She quickly leaped into the water after him, but he was already coughing, rolling onto his back and heaving the water out of his lungs. God, she hoped it wasn't poisonous. It looked fine, whatever was making it glow seemed to be contained to the pool as the water Dev was spewing looked normal. She looked down as something brushed her hip and gave a loud shriek that echoed around them wetly. It was a fish, small and slim with scales that gleamed silver and seemed to be casting out light. The pool was filled with them, making it seem to glow as they floated idly around Ivy's feet. She waded through the water to Dev's side, she was completely graceless, her arms flapping out in the air as she splashed through. God, at this rate she would end up accidentally drowning him. She gave up walking and began swimming towards him, reaching him in moments and pulling his head towards her chest as she supported his body on her knees.

Dev's thick dark hair was plastered to his head, bringing the sharpness of his cheeks into sharp relief. The deep slices that had marred the creamy flesh of his throat had begun to close, as well as the deep claw marks in his forearms. He had been absolutely covered in scratches, bites and other marks when the darkness had finally parted. The Guardians of the Sun Sands had mauled him half-to-death and then left. Seemingly disinterested after they'd literally made a meal out of Dev. She watched as the water lapped at a deep cut across his jaw and it slowly faded. His eyelids fluttered and his hand spasmed in the water.

"Dev?"

He groaned and opened his eyes forcefully, as if prising them open took tremendous effort, they roved frantically until they settled on her.

"Ivy." His voice was a sigh of relief. Typical, he'd been the one dying and yet he was worried about her.

"You protected Jeff." She didn't say it as a question, but he answered anyway, with his eyes sliding closed again now he knew she was alright.

"He's important to you."

Jeff was... Jeff. He was hopelessly good, probably too good for the likes of her. They'd been on a couple of dates but things just weren't the same, apparently Dev had ruined other men for her. His list of flaws only grew. Ivy heaved a sigh, and brushed Dev's hair back from his eyes.

"C'mon, let's get you dried off." She began to gently pull him back towards the edge of the pool, which wasn't as easy as it sounded. Dev was *heavy,* even in water. She was panting by the time they reached the edge. Dev had been dozing as she dragged him – while he had healed outwardly from whatever properties the water possessed, it was clear he was still drained.

"Thanks for your help, Fred."

Freddy's back was to the pool but he spun around at the sound of her voice, looking a little guilty, and helped haul Devlin out of the water and lower him to the ground to rest.

"Yeah, I was a little busy, pet."

Busy? Ivy raised her eyebrow but peered around him to see what he'd been doing while she was helping Dev. A very freaked out Jeff met her gaze.

"Ivy! Where the hell are we? One second we're in your apartment and the next we're in a cave! And *why* am I finding sand in places that sand *really shouldn't be*?"

She winced, she could try and ease Jeff into this but frankly, it was better he acclimated quickly, "We're in the Underworld. I sort of have magical powers."

"Sort of?"

"Well, definitely."

"Oh god. It's happening isn't it. I've finally gone mad. This is all some crazy fever dream—"

Freddy slapped him lightly, "Freaking out won't do you any good now. Hello, by the way, I'm Freddy. That's Dev. He saved your life. You're welcome."

This was clearly the wrong thing to say, Jeff went completely ashen and began pacing the short length of the wall opposite the pool, muttering to himself. His feet wore tracks into the sandy floor and Ivy bent down for a closer look, finally having time to take in her surroundings a little more now nobody was trying to kill them and Dev wasn't dying. The sand here seemed softer, not like the Sun Sands which had been hard as glass and scorching hot. She ran her hands through it absentmindedly before plopping down on the floor and pulling off the backpack that had somehow made it through the chase.

"Bet you're glad I packed snacks now," she muttered to a glowering Freddy. Even Jeff quit his pacing to indulge in the picnic of ready salted crisps, cheese and a handful of grapes that she laid out on top of her backpack. Freddy was examining the odd assortment of items she'd hurriedly grabbed before leaving the apartment.

"I was in a hurry, okay!"

"Is that a whole block of cheese?" a low voice rasped from behind her in amusement.

She spun around so fast she almost kicked sand all over their spoils.

"Dev! Yes. It's a block of cheese. It's Wensleydale though, so it's the good stuff, I'm just glad it didn't melt. Want some?"

He shook his head and laughed, wincing slightly as he tried to ease himself into a sitting position. She offered him a hand and he took it, eyes lingering on her face as he gave her a grateful nod. She shivered as his hand pulled away from hers, surprisingly he was warm and his callouses sent a tingle through her that made her want to punch herself in the face.

"Are you still in pain? Maybe we should get you back in the water."

All three men stopped and stared at her as if she'd lost her mind.

"Into the... water?"

She rolled her eyes, "I know it sounds crazy but when Freddy got us out of there—"

"I didn't get us out of there. I thought it was you."

Well, Dev had definitely been unable to take them anywhere but she had been tapped out – way too tired to take them anywhere.

"I don't think it was me. After bringing us all here, I was all out of juice."

"And how do you feel now?" Dev asked, he had an unnerving sharpness to his eyes, like he was staring at a puzzle he had just begun to figure out.

"Well, fine, I guess. Anyway, when we got here and Dev landed in the water, it started closing up his cuts. You were—" she swallowed thickly past the lump in her throat, "you were bad-off Dev. Whatever's in that pool saved your life."

Freddy was looking skeptical, an eyebrow tilted and a cocky lift to his chin that usually accompanied a sarcastic comment. Jeff spoke before Freddy could even open his mouth and Ivy stuck her tongue out at him, trying not to laugh when he folded his arms in a sulk.

"They... they said you saved my life." Jeff said to Devlin.

Dev looked at him evenly, "I did."

"Well, thank you. I'm not sure how or what from but I trust Ivy and if she trusts you two," Jeff said, including Freddy who watched him intently, "then I do too."

"Just like that," Freddy said disbelievingly.

Jeff nodded and Freddy threw his hands up in the air in agitation, "Ugh! Of course, we couldn't have had the handsome, trusting stranger to save us all. *No,* we get stuck with the sarcastic, distrustful, know-it-all—"

"Aw Freddy, you mean it?" Ivy grinned and batted her lashes while Jeff flushed to the roots of his reddish blonde hair, mouthing the word handsome to himself.

"Ivy, a word?" Dev murmured, ignoring Freddy ranting on. Only Jeff was paying him any attention, nodding and tutting in all the right places, Freddy was preening under the attention when Ivy turned away to face Dev. He had scooted backwards and propped himself up against the narrow wall that acted as a walkway between the pool and edge of the cave. She stood and brushed the sand from her sopping wet cargo pants, hopefully they would dry off soon. Luckily it wasn't too chilly in the cave, though it wasn't exactly balmy either.

Ivy plopped herself down next to Dev and rested her head on his shoulder, soaking in his warmth and presence.

"I really do think you should try getting back in the water. Or maybe you should try drinking it? Maybe it will replenish whatever it is the Guardians took."

Dev smiled slightly, he was facing out towards the pool so she couldn't really read his face, just the curve of his lips. "Sure, maybe I'll try that later. Though nothing but time will allow my power to replenish, magical water or no. That's not what I wanted to talk to you about though."

Ivy shifted uncomfortably, "Listen, Dev, I'm sorry for how I acted when I first opened the door. I was... surprised. I had pretty much given up hope that I'd ever see you again. I know that seems dramatic, but, well, you know me." She let out a weak laugh, "I left you in the Heavens. I know that. But part of me hoped..."

"That I'd come back to you."

She nodded stiffly. Feelings weren't really her jam, she'd much rather offer up a sarcastic comment or better yet – brawl.

"Ivy, I couldn't come back. Not—" he said, as she began to speak over him, "in the way you think. I wanted to, I promise I did. I imagined what I'd say and how you'd look and—" he cut himself off with a blush that intrigued her far more than she felt was appropriate, given he had been mortally injured, they were soaking wet and in a cave with other people. Plus, you know, in hell.

She sternly told herself to get her shit together and tried to focus on what Dev was saying.

"I don't have my wings. It's the quickest way to traverse the planes if you're powerful enough. The angels Michael allowed to keep theirs were not very powerful, it literally took us a month to hop the planes to arrive on Earth. The rest were spent clearing up the mess Michael had made of the Heavens."

"So, what you're saying is... you didn't ditch me and you took the long route home?"

A grin touched his lips now, "Exactly."

"Okay."

The grin vanished, "Okay?"

"Yeah. Okay. I believe you."

"So... we're good?" Dev asked slowly, he tilted his head to look at her. His eyes seemed to glow with the light of the pool and she lost herself for a moment or two staring into them. She gave a slow nod. Somehow the inches separating them had begun to close, she didn't remember leaning in. She wasn't about to pull back. Dev's lips touched hers, a whisper of a kiss that still sent electricity down her spine. Ivy pressed a little closer and then froze when he gave a gasp of pain. God, she had no self-control. Her hand was fisted in his fitted shirt, soggy and flaking blood into her hand.

"Way to ruin the moment, huh?" Dev murmured as she untangled her fist.

She just laughed, slightly embarrassed. Even more so when it came out breathless.

"Anyway," Dev said, lightly clearing his throat, a soft blush still colouring the tops of his cheeks, "that still wasn't what I was going to ask you about. I think you did transport us here. I think for some reason the Underworld is responding to you."

"That doesn't make any sense, why would you even think that?"

For some reason she was disturbed by the thought, like she wasn't freaky enough with her powers, she didn't need any more reason to stand-out.

"Before I passed out, I heard you screaming. You were calling out for help."

Dev looked at her meaningfully and she murmured softly, "Then we were brought here, where there just happened to be a healing pool that you landed in."

"So you agree."

"Well, I agree it's weird. But why would the Underworld help us? Do you think it somehow knows we're trying to find Hades?"

"Maybe," Dev said, his eyes holding hers, "It's just..."

"What?" she said with a sigh.

"Well, it didn't interfere until you asked it to."

"So you think it's me specifically?"

"I think for whatever reason, the Underworld wants you here."

XXIV
IVY

"Do you think we can eat those fish?" Jeff asked from the edge of the pool, peering in cautiously. The silvery light played across Jeff's face, turning his eyes silver and playing in his hair, she didn't miss the way Freddy's eyes lingered.

"Definitely not," Freddy said with a glare of warning in her direction, not quite as oblivious as he seemed, "We don't have a fire or anything to cook them in and I for one, am not a big fan of sushi."

Jeff grimaced as his stomach gurgled loudly and then frowned when the hand he pressed to his stomach came away covered in sand.

"More cheese?" Ivy called with a smirk.

"I can't take this any more," Jeff muttered and Ivy watched in alarm as he took a step towards the pool and then threw himself in.

"Jeff!" Ivy and Freddy called in sync, but Jeff just popped up from the surface of the water with a small shiver, his curls slicked down.

"The sand! God. It's freezing in here but at least I can get rid of the grains wedged in my—" Jeff cut himself off abruptly with a glance at Freddy, "Ah, yeah. Uncomfortable."

"All you're doing is soaking all the sand into your clothes, you should have taken them off first." Freddy called out, his mouth curling into a smile Ivy had ever seen him wear before, almost seductive. *He's flirting!* Well, good for Freddy. It was about time he got over Gabe. Ivy blinked dumbly as Freddy began kicking off his shoes, neatly shaking them out and her gaze jumped to Jeff as Freddy began unbuttoning his fitted fighting trousers. Jeff's attention was rapt as Freddy shook out the rest of his clothes and stepped into the water. It engulfed him nearly to his chest and Jeff's gaze watched the glow of the water play across Freddy's skin before he blushed and looked away.

"What are we watching right now," Ivy murmured to Dev beside her, "I thought Jeff was straight, for one thing, so this is super informative."

Dev gave a low laugh, "Let's give them some privacy. Walk with me?" He pushed to his feet with a wince, swaying only a little and Ivy grabbed a hold of his arm to support him as she rose too.

"I don't know... do you think we should leave them alone?"

Dev grinned, "I think Jeff will be fine."

"It's not Jeff I'm worried about," Ivy muttered as Dev called out that they were going to explore the cave a little more. Freddy waved his hand dismissively, not even glancing back at them as he cut a surprisingly graceful path through the water towards Jeff. Show-off. Walking through water was *hard* damn it and he was showing her up.

There were several dark walkways that lay to the side of one of the pool's edges, they headed down the left one and Ivy shivered as the cool air of the tunnel hit them. She hadn't even noticed it but the air by the pool had seemed to have grown warmer. Well, she was noticing it now. She eyed the goosebumps on her arms and shivered again, pressing closer to Dev. She could barely see him in the near-darkness but she knew his vision was likely better than hers and trusted him to stop her from falling head-first into a shallow pool or something.

Her shoulders relaxed slightly as the air began to warm up gradually, "Do you think we're getting close to another pool? I think it's getting warmer." The pathway curved and lightened, she could almost see what was up ahead, "Brighter too! We must be close to something now."

They had only been walking for a few minutes but Ivy was disappointed when they came to a dead-end. She could see the space nearly perfectly, as if she were walking around with a small candle to light her way. Dev stumbled over a loose rock and Ivy grinned.

"I've never seen you this clumsy, you really *must* have been injured if you can't even walk around in the semi-darkness without tripping – that's usually my role." Dev looked in her general direction in confusion and she saw his eyes widen. "Shame it's a dead-end though. Maybe the other passage is more interesting."

"How can you tell it's a dead-end?"

"Er, by looking at the massive wall of dirt across from us? No don't—" she winced as Dev walked straight into a hanging stalactite, "God, what is the matter with you today?"

"I can't see anything, Ivy."

"You — what?"

"This all looks pitch black to me, but I'm guessing it doesn't to you."

"Are you fucking with me? Because I can see just fine. Maybe a little dimmer than usual but I can see the expression on your face right now."

"All I can see is glowing red eyes."

"Oh okay, I see. I'm sorry, I should have thought taking you into a sort of dark cave after what you just went through with the Guardians wouldn't be the best idea—"

"No," Dev let out a huffing chuckle, "Ivy, I can see *your* eyes. They're glowing. Bright red."

"Bullshit."

"I swear it."

"Why are they glowing? How do I make them stop?" Her heart felt like it was beating too fast, she wiped her sweaty palms on the legs of her trousers and swore. Now she thought about it, the glow of the cave did have a little bit of a rosy tint to it, like looking out through red lenses.

"Dev, what the fuck is wrong with me?"

"Nothing," he said soothingly, fumbling closer to her in the dark, "I think for whatever reason, your powers are responding to the Underworld. We don't really know how or why you have them, maybe they originated here and something in you recognises that."

"Is that really possible?"

Dev tilted his head to the side, "Yes."

"I can see your face right now, you don't look convinced."

Dev winced, "It *is* possible. I just don't know if that's what's happening. It seems more like..."

"More like what Dev? Just spit it out, things can't get any worse."

"Well, it's like I said before. The Underworld seems to respond to you."

"I just haven't seen any evidence of that."

"You haven't shivered for a while."

"Yeah well I—" she paused. She'd thought it was getting warmer because they were getting close to another pool, but this was only a dead-end. "I-I did want it to be warmer," she murmured quietly. "Why is this happening?"

"I don't know," Dev placed his warm hands on her shoulders and stroked a soothing line down her arms, "But we'll work it out, I promise."

This time, when she looked into his face in the dark, she believed him. His eyes were steady, his jaw firm, and Ivy knew in that moment that Dev would do anything to help her. What scared her most was that she would do the same for him. She hadn't let herself truly care about another person since – well, since the night she had found her family murdered in their living room. Hadn't wanted to feel the hurt, the pain. But without it, she wouldn't feel this either, right here with Dev.

"Why are you staring at me?" She said softly.

Dev gave a sharp laugh, "I forgot you could see me. You're glowing Ivy, it's beautiful. Your eyes are as red as rubies right now and I've never seen anything like it, they're badass and unique, just like you."

"I never pegged you for a sweet talker. If I'm glowing it's because I'm sunburnt."

"Good thing it's dark."

She slapped his arm, "God, you must think I'm a freak. Glowing red eyes isn't exactly on every guy's wish list."

"No, but I like it." Devlin said backing her into the cave wall, "It's... sexy."

She hit the wall with a thud, but it was the naked hunger on his face that left her breathless.

"Devlin," she gasped, "wait — I need to say something."

He paused, she could just make out his muscles straining as if sheer willpower held him back alone. She understood, she wanted him just as badly. Here in the dark, it was easier to be vulnerable, as if the words she might say would be swallowed by the cave. She pressed her hand to his chest, "I'm sorry I left you in the Heavens. I told myself I was doing the right, selfless, thing, but I think deep down I knew that wasn't true. I got so used to running and I guess old habits die hard." She took in a shaking breath, "I was a wreck for a while you were gone, I'd lost not only you but Freddy and... Jas. The worst part was that I had nobody to blame but myself. Jeff was a good friend to me throughout all of that."

The words ran out as quickly as they'd come, leaving her hollow but dry-eyed. Devlin took a step closer and she felt more than saw his breathing hitch as her body pressed against him lightly. He could pull away now and she would be okay. She'd leave whatever this was that was between them right here to die in the Underworld and never think about it again. But if he wanted her...

Dev's hands slid from her arms to grasp her around the waist, "Does this make you want to run?" He bent his head blindly towards her, she caught his jaw in one hand and tilted his lips to her mouth. They kissed slowly, re-learning and savouring the shape of each other's lips. Taking their time as they hadn't dared before, drinking in the little whimpers that escaped until she was ignited.

"No," she rasped, "there's nowhere I'd rather be." Her breasts pressed against his chest and she could feel Dev's heartbeat thundering against her skin. His hands slid up from her waist, his callouses scraped lightly at the skin beneath her t-shirt as they travelled further, closing over one peaked nipple and wrenching a gasp from her throat. "Though I'm not sure that this is the best place for this..." she murmured huskily as Dev pressed long kisses to her neck and throat, his tongue flicked against her ear lobe and she groaned, sinking her hands into his nearly-dry hair. She tugged him closer, pressing him into the softest parts of her. Dev whispered her name as his body pressed flush against hers and this time she was certain the breathless quality of his voice came from pleasure, and not pain.

"Why's that?" he murmured between kisses so branding that she knew she would be marked forever.

"Hm?" she was entirely too distracted and pulled back slightly to better focus, "Oh, we're in the Underworld. You were literally almost killed not that long ago, are you sure you should be... exerting yourself?"

She felt his lips against her cheek curve up into a grin, "Oh, trust me. I am more than able to *exert* myself. As for being in the Underworld and the threat of imminent death," he said lightly, trailing kisses down her neck to her clothed chest and sliding the hand still on her breast southward, "there's no time like the present." Dev said, letting his warm hand slide down her waist and deftly flick the button of her cargo pants open as he slid to his knees.

XXV
IVY

THE first thing they noticed when they got back to the main pool was the steam. It coiled in inviting tendrils through the mouth of the passageway as they walked out, curling around their feet. Dev shot her an amused glance and she could feel herself flushing.

"You're cute when you blush." Dev said with a smirk that she could only make out through the haze because he stood so close.

"So are you," she shot back as if it was anything but a compliment. Devlin grinned wider.

"Freddy? Jeff? Are you guys in here?"

"About time you guys got back," Freddy called, appearing seemingly from nowhere amidst the steam. "Aw look at that, you kissed and made-up," he said and then gave her a saucy grin. "*More* than kissed by the looks of things," he added with a wink at her mussed hair and flushed cheeks. There was something a little sharp to his tone, but Freddy looked away before she could press him.

Deciding to ignore it for now, Ivy flicked her middle finger up at him.

Devlin raised an eyebrow, "I don't suppose Jeff is around in this somewhere?"

"Yes, yes, don't worry. I didn't bite. Much."

Ivy rolled her eyes but smiled when Jeff emerged from some steam to her left, shaking out his hair. And in Freddy's shirt.

"Mine had sand in it!" Jeff blurted defensively when he caught her looking.

"So, any idea what's caused it to turn into a sauna in here?" Freddy asked, running a hand lazily through the air, letting the steam dance between his fingers.

"We think that for some reason the Underworld is responding to Ivy." Dev said, she was grateful because she wasn't sure she could pull the words up past the churning of her gut. The blissful minutes she'd had with Dev had finally relaxed her and now she was being reminded of all the ways her life had turned into a freakish mess. Again.

Freddy was nodding like that made perfect sense, "And the steam?"

"Ah," Devlin said, looking positively... well, devilish, and definitely smug, "Let's just say I am particularly talented."

"Gross." Freddy said, rolling his eyes. "Seriously."

"So what's our plan from here then?" Jeff asked, his blue eyes looked worried peering out through the mop of blonde curls that were beginning to frizz from the moisture.

"I guess..." she began and then bit her lip, "I guess if this place is responding to me somehow, then maybe it can bring us to Hades just like it brought us here? Let's try and rest for now and then hopefully we can figure it out in the morning."

Jeff murmured his agreement and followed Freddy through the fading steam to a rounded edge of wall.

"Will it even be morning when we wake up?" she thought suddenly, turning to Dev, "I don't know how time works here."

"It's about the same here as it is in the Heavens, but different worlds do have time differences. I honestly have no idea if it'll be light or dark when we leave here, your guess is as good as mine. Especially because the Underworld has its own set of rules for each domain."

"You mean like the Sun Sands?"

"Yeah," Dev's lashes lowered and his jaw grew tight, he seemed to shake himself and gave her a small smile. "The sands are only ever blistering heat and then night falls and they are desolate and freezing, exposed – they can complete that cycle in a matter of hours. Hades once threatened to send Michael and I there for misbehaving on Earth. We were young and foolish, but the both of us had gained power quickly..." Dev looked equally sad and fond as he remembered, his mouth curled to one side like he'd eaten something bitter.

"I'm sorry about what happened. Jas too. She didn't deserve that." Ivy hadn't really had the chance to say so before she'd taken Michael down to the Underworld. She had pulled the place straight from his mind, had known exactly what he feared most down here and had taken him. Dropped Michael straight into a darkness so complete, so suffocating, she hadn't even heard him scream before she phased back onto the Earthly plane.

It was how she'd first met Jeff actually, he'd found her crouched and pale-faced on the pavement outside her block of flats. She'd been aiming for her bed but simply didn't have enough energy left and had fallen short. He'd asked if she was okay and she'd responded by puking over his shoes. She'd had nightmares about that suffocating darkness more than once since returning home, but she had no regrets about putting Michael in there, not when those nightmares were followed by dreams of Jasmine. Yet Ivy hadn't crumbled, thanks in-part to Jeff, but she also knew it wasn't what Jas would have wanted. She had no plans to tell Devlin exactly what Michael was facing down here, wanting to spare him that much at least. The

Underworld was exactly where Michael deserved to be, but he was still Devlin's brother. Though she suspected Gabe's betrayal hurt worse than Michael's expected brutality ever could.

Devlin pulled her close and pressed a kiss to the top of her head, stooping slightly to do so, pressing her nose into his chest. He smelled like water and sweat and Devlin, sweet and warm.

"I suppose we won't have too much trouble sleeping in here now that it's so balmy," she mused, fanning her t-shirt away from her chest, "do you think if I wished for a burger and a bed right now that it would appear?"

Dev chuckled, green eyes glittering at her in amusement, "I suspect that's not how it works, but feel free to try."

They found themselves their own little corner and she rested her head on Dev's chest as Freddy called out goodnight. Briefly, she wondered what the sleeping situation might look like over where Freddy and Jeff were situated, but the calming motion of Dev smoothing his hand over her hair instantly quieted those thoughts. Devlin murmured something she didn't quite hear and she hummed sleepily in question, he shushed her and she quickly drifted away to the sound of Devlin's heartbeat in her ear.

She awoke to her face still pressed to Dev's chest, a small wet patch marked his shirt where she had dribbled on him in her sleep.

"Morning," Dev murmured gruffly, rolling his shoulders, and she gave him a small smile. Despite the fact that sleeping on a dusty cave floor was ridiculously uncomfortable, she hadn't slept that soundly in a while.

"Sorry, I dribbled on you." Ivy said sheepishly, extricating her leg from between Dev's and attempting to sit up.

"Never," Dev said, sitting up with her and clasping her face gently between his hands, "apologise for dribbling on me." He gave her a sleepy grin that was the most charming thing she'd ever seen and bent and kissed her, tugging her back to lie against him.

"God. I've been awake for two seconds and I've already seen you two sucking face. If this is what the rest of the trip is going to be like I'll just drown myself now."

Ivy really wished she had a pillow in that moment so that she could smother Freddy with it.

"I guess it really doesn't work like that," she said to Dev who looked absolutely lost, "otherwise a big fluffy pillow would have just materialised and smothered Freddy."

Jeff let out a little laugh that came from suspiciously close to Freddy and she sat up and glanced over in time to see Freddy looking mockingly betrayed as he tugged his trousers back on. He clearly did not believe in pyjamas. Or underwear.

"Yeah, well, I've only been awake for two seconds and I've already seen your bare arse so let's call it even, Fred."

Dev let out a deep laugh. Ivy stared at him, she hadn't heard him laugh in what felt like forever, not a full-out one at least. It made something warm curl in her chest and she realised they were just staring at each other like a pair of love-struck teenagers.

"You good?" Dev asked, eyes soft as he reached out a hand and tugged her back to his side on the ground.

"Yeah," she murmured and brushed a kiss across his cheek. "Let's clean up and get out of here. Maybe we need to focus my thoughts a little more when we phase this time, where do you think we'd be most likely to find Hades?"

Dev looked thoughtful, "I mean, he does have a castle."

"A castle?" In hell? *What a bougie-ass bitch.*

"Yeah, well, I guess he does technically rule here. He's basically the King of the Heavens and Hells."

"He's the oldest thing in creation, as far as we know," Freddy chipped in. Ivy sat up and Dev followed suit as Freddy and Jeff approached. "Any chance you could conjure some more of that handy-dandy steam so we can all have a bath?"

Dev smirked at her, the green of his eyes seeming to glow against the golden hue of his skin. Good to know that some rest had definitely replenished his... powers.

"You didn't seem to have a problem stripping off yesterday," Ivy said with an eyebrow raised cockily as she turned back to Freddy, forcing a blush away from her cheeks.

"If you're that desperate to see my pecs again you should just say so, darling."

She stuck her tongue out at Freddy and couldn't help her laugh when he did the same thing back.

"So that's a no on the steam front?" Jeff asked hopefully.

Ivy gave him a pitying look and turned to Dev. "So you think this *castle*," she paused to roll her eyes, "is the best place to start? Isn't that sort of obvious?"

"Well, best to check there first than traipse all over this hellish place and find him tucked up in bed with a cold." Freddy pointed out.

Ivy sighed, "Sure, fine, okay. I need you to picture it in your mind,

I can phase us there if I know where I'm going." Dev nodded and closed his eyes, his dark lashes curled perfectly on his cheeks and she couldn't help herself, leaned in and gave him a quick kiss. His eyes flew open and she could feel her cheeks warm, matching the pink stain spreading across Dev's cheekbones. Good to know they were both equally useless at the emotional stuff. She gave Dev a cheeky wink, slipped into his mind to see the castle and focused on phasing them all there.

She had expected the castle to be some sort of gothic-horror scooby-doo bad-guy monstrosity. Instead, what Dev pictured was a tasteful Nineteenth Century Victorian castle surrounded by green land. It had two, small, turrets. Not a moat or head-on-a-pike to be seen. Taking a deep breath, she focused in on the little details, losing herself in her imagination, pretending she could smell the sweet lilac wisteria. She felt the phase take hold of them, it was as easy as breathing – which wasn't usually the case, further proof of the Underworld's favour it seemed. Normally phasing felt like carving a line between planes or spaces and pressing through jelly to get there. This felt like stepping into a flowing tide of power and willing it to mold to her command, folding space over until they could stroll right through to the otherside. It was an awakening, a feeling of absolute certainty and power. That was until she was flung to the floor feeling like she had rebounded off a wall.

"Ow," she groaned, rolling to her back and spitting grass out of her mouth. Instead of Wisteria she could smell warm cinnamon and the grass beneath her felt silky as she ran her fingers through it. They'd made it out of the caves, but they didn't seem to be at the castle – god, her life was like a game of Super Mario Brothers.

"Everyone okay?" she called out and received a chorus of male groans in response as they brushed themselves off.

"Ivy?" Came a timid voice.

Not. Possible.

Ivy sat bolt upright, her eyes finding the owner of that voice instantly. A river of ice poured through her chest, swirling into panic as she tried to block out the memories that voice accompanied. *Drip, drip, drip.* Blood pooling on the floor. She couldn't *breathe* god damn it. So much for the Underworld's favour. What sort of sick place was this?

"I don't know who the fuck you think you are, but you better back off. Right now."

"Ivy, please—"

"*No.*" The word was torn from her throat in a ragged snarl, half-sob. It felt like the world was pressing in on her, piercing her to the ground like a sword through her skull, driving her down until she could feel nothing but rage. Shit. *Shit.* Was she going crazy? Was Dev seeing this? Could he see *her*? *Breathe my angel, just breathe.* Ivy took a breath and then another, it wasn't helping, they were becoming lost in her chest as she fought to remain in the present.

"It's me," Jess said, she took a slow and small step towards Ivy, as if she were approaching a wild animal. Her jeans cut-off an inch above the ankle in some trendy style Jess had never worn, but she was wearing a red knit jumper — her favourite colour. Red, like the blood that had poured out of her. *Drip, drip, drip.* Staining Ivy's hands, clinging to her skin, her hair — Dev moved abruptly to stand between them, facing Ivy, not Jess. Or the thing wearing her face at least. Ivy hadn't even realised he was next to her, she was too lost in her own head, trapped in her memories.

"Ivy," Dev said, then crouched down and clasped her shaking hands to his chest. His heart beat soothingly against her fingers, steady, "Close your eyes."

Her head whipped up to his eyes and he stroked his thumb down her hand, "Trust me. Take a breath, close your eyes."

Trust him. *Breathe, my angel.* She closed her eyes and inhaled deeply, releasing it slowly, some of the pressure in her head easing with each repetition.

"Good," Dev said, "Now tell me, what do you smell?"

She raised an eyebrow but answered, "Cinnamon. Musk. Warm things."

Ivy felt rather than saw Dev nod, "And what do you feel?"

Now she was calmer, now she could no longer see —

She tugged her thoughts away and gave in to the sensation that had been pulling at her defenses ever since they'd crash-landed, letting her panic and fear drain away. "Peace," Ivy said with a sigh, "I feel peace."

She opened her eyes and saw Dev, Freddy and Jeff peering at her in concern. The grass where she sat had darkened in a large circle, sucking up the negative energy as she released it. Dev reached out a hand to the blighted land but Ivy caught it before he could make contact. Whatever it was she had done to the earth, she didn't want him near it. Wanted no part of him to be tainted by the darkness that had risen up inside her.

"Ivy," Dev said gently, green eyes lighter than she'd ever seen them, "We're in the Elysian Fields."

Ivy's eyes fell again on the young girl standing just behind Dev, cautiously peering around his shoulder.

"Jess?" Ivy's voice cracked and she didn't fight the tear that streaked through the dirt and grime that no doubt covered her face. Didn't fight the rising tide of despair and hurt. Not anymore. She soaked it in, this ragged piece of her soul. Shielded it between two palms in the shelter of her heart as Jess smiled, that great beaming smile that had always taken over her whole face. The gap between her front teeth was still there, but she looked a little taller, her billow of dark hair a little longer.

"Jess," Ivy said again and this time Jess ran to her as Devlin stepped aside. Surprisingly solid and safe, at last, in Ivy's arms.

Her sister.

XXVI

DEV

SOMETHING weird was going on. The way the Underworld was interacting to Ivy was... bizarre. Dev hadn't seen anything like it, except with Hades – which made sense as this *was* his domain. Dev shuddered lightly, remembering the way Hades had once made the earth tremble, thorny vines bursting through the ground and coming within an inch of Dev and Michael's throats. Hades had caught them trying to liberate the soul of Joan of Arc to play 'sword fights' with them in the Heavens when they were just boys. He had made it abundantly clear that the last thing you should ever do was steal from the King of Planes. Then he had laughed, the thorny vines sinking back into the ground as if they had never been there at all, ruffled their hair and sent them on their way, Joan of Arc firmly in hand. Under no circumstances were the souls allowed to leave the Underworld, that was a rule Dev had learned the hard way. He only hoped Ivy wouldn't have to learn it like that too.

He looked to where the sisters were standing together, still clinging to one another. Ivy was clearly trying her hardest not to sob through the reunion, he could see the indentation where she was biting her cheek and he shook his head ruefully as she spat blood when Jess turned to talk to Freddy and Jeff.

There was little resemblance between the two really, Ivy was athletically built but short, her white blonde hair had grown in the

227

six months they'd been apart and now hung well below her collar bones. She was strong, curvy, her face was full and sensual down to the freckle under her pale eyebrow. He'd often found his thoughts occupied for long moments at a time just thinking about the full curve of her lush mouth. Her blue eyes were usually crinkled at the corners from the smirk that perpetually graced her lips. But Jess... she was tall, or at least she would be if she ever grew up. Dev wasn't sure what the mechanics of that were like in the Elysian fields. He had heard stories of course, but he hadn't ever been able to talk to a soul for long enough that he'd found any solid truths. The fact that they had stood talking to Jess uninterrupted for so long was just further, worrying, evidence of Hades' absence. Dev's eyes roved back and forth between the sisters as he compared them. It was clear that the cheeky grin on Jess' face was all Ivy, so was the way her blue eyes danced with mischief. They couldn't have looked more different, seeming more alike in temperament than anything else. Ivy's eyes were icy, a cool, frozen blue. But Jess' eyes churned like the sea during a storm, a deep, dark blue that was closer to denim than Ivy's ice.

The more Dev looked between the two sisters, at Jess' willowy form and Ivy's athletic curves, the more he wondered how they could be related at all.

"Dev," Ivy's voice interrupted the churning of his thoughts, "why are you standing all the way over there?" Ivy tugged at Jess' arm, pulling her forwards as Dev strode to meet them.

"Devlin, this is Jess. My sister." Ivy said, her eyes were lit-up like she couldn't quite believe she was getting to say those words to him.

"It's a pleasure to meet you." Dev said with a smile.

"Ooh dimple!" Jess said with a laugh, flashing her own, "Twinsies.

Nice to meet you too. I wish it could be under better circumstances."

Dev figured she meant the fact that she was dead but her next sentence made his muscles tense in alarm.

"I'm so glad you guys are here to help with the Guard though." Jess paused, eying their blank faces with growing concern. "That *is* why you've come, right? Normally everything is lovely here... Mum, Dad and I have everything we could need."

Dev swallowed thickly, *please don't let her say what I think she's about to...*

"But something's been wrong for a while now. There have been souls wandering where they don't belong ever since Hades disappeared, but when the Guard came back things got worse. Some of the other girls who live here said they never had to fear the Guard before, so they didn't worry when they saw it."

Ivy moved closer to her sister as she spoke and placed a hand on her shoulder in support.

"They said the Guard often plays with the younger kids, and is fiercely protective. It vanished a little after Hades did, but a few days ago it came back and attacked one of the souls."

A few days ago. Around the same time they had arrived in the Underworld. Was this another way that Ivy had affected this place? Dev glanced over and the line between Ivy's furrowed brows told him she was wondering the same thing.

"It's like something crazy has gotten into the Underworld, and nobody has seen Hades for a long, long time."

"What exactly does the Guard... guard?" Ivy asked and Dev had the horrible feeling he knew the answer.

"The castle, of course, and us. Not everyone in the Underworld is happy with their lot, so the entrance to Elysia is protected." Jess gestured behind her. Vaguely in the distance Dev could see what looked like a wall of wisteria on the other side of a forest.

"*This* is the entrance to Elysia?" Dev asked in surprise, it looked like any other dirt path, surrounded by farmland. He could have walked this way a thousand times when he'd been down here and never known how close to paradise he'd stood.

"Well I wasn't too far off when I phased us then," Ivy said, gaze focused on the castle in the distance, "not sure what happened though. It was like I bounced backwards and landed here."

"Well, I'm glad you did," Jess said with a smile, "I'm not surprised you couldn't get in – Hades' castle has very strong wards around it. If you're trying to get there, you'll have to go the long way around."

Ivy frowned and he knew she was thinking the same thing as him, they had hoped to be in and out – naive in hindsight, but they didn't have the supplies for a long trip.

"Back to this Guard," Ivy said with a shake of her head, blonde hair flicking out and shimmering in the spring sunshine, "what exactly does it look like?"

Jess' eyes flickered to the right of Ivy and the blood drained from her face, "That."

Dev spun around fluidly, already sweeping Ivy behind him with Jess. He got his first look at the Guard and swore. *Shit, shit, shit.* He'd never been so sorry to be right.

"Cerberus." Dev groaned, he had encountered the beast as a young angel and had not forgotten the encounter. Though he now realised that Cerberus was likely just protecting the entrance to Elysia, at the time Devlin had just thought him a particularly unfriendly pup.

Cerberus prowled forwards slowly, he was larger than Devlin remembered. He'd heard the stories about Hades' famed guard dog – you did *not* want to be on Hades' bad side, this puppy packed quite the bite. Cerberus' three gigantic heads bent low and sniffed at the grass where Ivy had crash-landed. It let out a low whine and drool slid from its mouth in a long line that puddled on the ground. It was at least double the size of Dev and its mouth was unnervingly large. Sharp teeth glinted white as Cerberus' breath exhaled in a hot pant that blew back their hair. *Those teeth!* The incisor was almost as big as Dev's forearm.

"Beautiful," he heard Ivy murmur and glanced back to see her making swoony heart eyes at the beast.

"Really?" he whisper-shouted, "Cerberus wants to eat us and you think he's *cute*."

"She always did like dogs," Jess murmured thoughtfully, despite her glib words she hadn't taken her eyes from Cerberus since he'd arrived.

"*That's* Cerberus? Oh my..." Ivy grinned toothily and Dev could have sworn that the beast's ears perked up at her voice. This was not what they needed right now. Freddy slid him a sword that he accepted gratefully, Dev didn't want to waste energy on conjuring one. It was slightly warm in his hand and he looked at Freddy with a mixture of suspicion and distaste – where had he been keeping it this whole time?

Ivy grabbed onto Dev's sword arm with a glare, "Don't you dare hurt that sweet puppy."

Jess winced, "That puppy did go a little crazy not that long ago, attack someone, and then vanish."

Ivy made a tutting sound, "Bad puppy."

Dev heard Freddy huff out a laugh but pulled his gaze sharply back to Cerberus when the beast gave a low whine.

"Maybe don't antagonise the huge, slobbering beast?" Dev hissed to Ivy, who just rolled her eyes. Dev froze at the low growl Cerberus emitted and vowed not to take his eyes off it again.

"Well, he only seems to be growling at *you*, Dev." Ivy said smugly and took a step forward towards the beast that made Dev's heartbeat triple, "You're just a big puppy, aren't you? A naughty puppy." Ivy cooed and Cerberus snapped his teeth but gave that same low whine. Dev stared, frozen, reaching out to grab Ivy's arm instinctively as she moved to take another step forward.

Ivy shrugged off his grip gently and moved forwards another step, as though magnetised to the beast. He felt like he couldn't get enough air as he watched Cerberus move one gigantic, black furry paw forwards and sniff the air around Ivy. Its mouths opened threateningly to show his large pointed teeth and Ivy grinned, inexplicably.

"Yes, what a gorgeous smile you have. You're not going to eat us are you?" Ivy moved forward with each word, small hesitant steps and Cerberus just watched her, cautiously sniffing the air as if unsure what to do with this strange girl who just wanted to pet him.

"Ivy don't —" Dev started and prepared to snatch her out of the path of those vicious teeth as Ivy raised her hand and stroked it along one furry ear of the central head. Dev braced himself for the beast to – purr? A soft rumble filled the air as Cerberus' tongue lolled out of his mouth in a disturbingly dog-like grin, his right-head nudging the middle out of the way so Ivy could also pet there. Ivy had a surprisingly tender look on her face as she continued to stroke Cerberus' ear and muzzle, she gave a loud, delighted laugh when he flopped to the ground in a cloud of dirt and rolled for a belly rub.

"I told you," Freddy said with an eye roll, "she can't resist."

Freddy had said as much to Devlin once, back when Freddy was giving him regular updates on the girl he suspected of being the psychic. Dev had heard the smirk in Freddy's voice over the phone when he said, "You've got a good chance I reckon, she can't resist a stray." Dev had sworn soundly at him and hung up.

Dev watched in numb horror as Cerberus wriggled on the ground, demanding more of Ivy's attention and she lavished him with belly rubs and then sat on the ground curled into his side. Dev felt like at any moment Cerberus was going to leap up and smash one of his heavy jaws down on Ivy, quicker than he could move, faster than he could save her.

Ivy laughed from her perch against the furry creature, "You should see your faces right now. He won't hurt us, will you?" she said in that odd baby crooning voice again as she began running her fingers through his fur.

"Okay, this is beyond bizarre," Jess murmured to him, her eyes just as intent on Ivy as his were, "He seems more like his old self, not like he was when he attacked that one time."

Dev wondered... "I think It's Ivy again. Her being here seems to have a weird effect on this plane."

Ivy was now whispering to Cerberus in a voice so low that Dev couldn't hear it, just the sound of Cerberus' hot dog-like pants and chuffs. Abruptly, Ivy stood with a little nod to herself, she leaned against Cerberus' side with absolute ease, her hand buried in his dark fur.

"I think Cerberus knows how to find Hades," Ivy said. "If we follow him I think he can show us the way."

They all stared at her incredulously.

"Are you saying... you can talk to the dog?" Freddy finally asked and gave a jolt when Cerberus' mouth fell open to show his teeth, tongue lolling out.

Ivy shrugged, "I've stopped thinking too hard about all the crazy shit in my life, I just go with it now."

Jeff looked a little dazed, his mouth slightly open as he watched all three of Cerberus' heads lean down and nudge their wet noses at Ivy. She patted them all absentmindedly, the left head whining for more attention.

"Jess... I'm so glad I got to see you. To know that you're okay. Are mum and dad alright?" Ivy asked, brow furrowed. Maybe Dev didn't need to worry about parting the sisters again, Ivy seemed to know that here was where Jess belonged, at peace.

"Yeah, they're both here, they're both fine. Mum watches over you, her little angel, she says," Jess laughed. "Though I can't picture anyone less angelic than you – do you remember that party you went to, the one with that guy who had the motorbike?"

Ivy turned tomato red, "Oh my god, you *know about that?*"

Jess laughed harder, "I watched the whole thing play out. His face when he realised you'd left him with no trousers and no way to get home... priceless."

Ivy gave Jess a wobbly smile and the sisters hugged briefly, but fiercely, before Jess pulled away. "It was lovely meeting you all," Jess said and then set her blue eyes on Dev. "Look after her for me," she said quietly and touched his hand briefly before walking further along the dirt path and vanishing in the mist.

Devlin moved closer to Ivy, who was looking dazed, and tried to keep a healthy distance between himself and the three heads that were trying to sniff him. She took his hand silently and he squeezed it gently.

"Come on then," Ivy called to Freddy and Jeff. Jeff seemed a little uneasy to be moving closer to the triple sets of giant teeth that seemed poised to eat them all and Dev could hear Freddy murmuring encouragements to him as they came closer.

Ivy stroked the muzzles of Cerberus gently, "Show us the way then, there's a good boy."

Cerberus gave what sounded like a cheerful yip that was too bizarre for even Dev's brain to process. The pup began padding towards a small mud trail tucked behind a tree that Devlin hadn't noticed until that moment.

"Glamoured," he said thoughtfully to the others as they began following Cerberus along the narrow dirt path. "Otherwise, we would have seen it before. I bet it's where Cerberus suddenly appeared from and why it looked to the souls like he just disappeared that time he attacked." Dev cautiously peered into the dense trees that suddenly surrounded them on either side, "Keep an eye out. There are probably all sorts of booby traps on this path to keep out intruders if it's glamoured only for Cerberus' and Hades' use. And stick together... something about the trees doesn't seem right."

Jeff, who had been cautiously reaching an arm out to a branch quickly reeled it back in, "I don't think they're trees," he whispered and Dev looked closer at where Jeff was pointing and saw eyes staring out at them from between the bark.

Ivy didn't seem perturbed in the slightest, "We're with Cerberus, he won't let anything happen to us, will you?" she began stroking his side and Dev couldn't help a slight grin when he heard her telling Cerberus what a good boy he was. There was just something so ridiculous about the short, blonde woman cooing at the large, fanged beast.

Ivy began to whistle merrily and Jeff jumped and glared at her, "Seriously? The teddy-bear's picnic? What is wrong with you?"

Freddy let out a cackle and Ivy dropped him a wink before replying to Jeff, "Sometimes you just have to laugh, Jeff. If I don't, I'll cry."

XXVII

IVY

It had been quiet for a while, the trees here didn't rustle, there were no birds or animals that she could see. Some of the leaves looked odd, dense, like they were made out of rubber. Worse was the smell, like cooked meat and death. Cerberus wouldn't lead them astray, but Ivy wanted to get out of these woods as quickly as possible. She felt a little bad for teasing Jeff, he was scared and had been chucked headfirst into this crazy world, but a little distraction was good for the soul. She'd told the guy Jess had mentioned the same thing once before fucking him and stealing his motorbike. And clothes, because he'd ripped hers. It had put Jeff on edge but Ivy... she *needed* that lightness, that brevity. It had always been her way. Whenever life inevitably got tough, she would deflect, use humour to keep things at a distance, stop herself from getting hurt. It had been a healing moment she hadn't realised she'd needed, seeing Jess again. Letting her go was easier now Ivy knew that Jess was whole and at peace.

She jumped as Devlin caught her hand and strode forward to walk beside her and Cerberus. He shot their furry companion a wary look that was all side-eye and bit his lip. Adorable. She smirked inwardly as the head closest to them sniffed at Dev and he winced as if expecting to be chomped.

"It was nice seeing Jess again," she said, trying to distract him. He glanced at her, full lips parting in surprise, clearly not expecting her to instigate that conversation. She couldn't blame him, usually getting her to engage in emotional mush required physical force.

"I'm sorry you couldn't have longer with her." He didn't specify whether he meant in life or in death. Ivy supposed it didn't matter, both were sad truths.

She gave a small shrug and faux nonchalant hair flip, "She'll be there waiting for me, one day. For now, we've got like, several dimensions to save."

Dev's lips tugged up in the beginnings of a smile, "In some ways the two of you are so alike, your stubbornness, your humour, how fiercely you love," Dev raised his eyebrows at her small exclamation of surprise, "Yet, outwardly you are polar opposites."

Ivy gave a small laugh, "Jess looks like our mother, graceful and cool-headed. I take after my father."

Devlin bit down on his lip as he puzzled it out, "*Your* father? You mean —"

"—Jess is only my half-sister. I never met my bio-Dad."

Dev nodded thoughtfully, relinquishing his hold on his lip in a slow slide that brought a blush to her cheeks, "That makes a lot of sense actually, did you ever – can you hear that?" He broke off, frozen in place and looking around distractedly, face pale.

"No," she said, confused, "hear what?"

"I..." Dev sounded breathless, "I can hear Jasmine. I think she's in the forest. I think she needs help!" Dev's voice had grown more frantic the longer they stood frozen. Cerberus began to growl softly, his extra mouths making it sound oddly echoing and harmonious. Ivy patted his side soothingly, and grabbed Dev's arm sharply as he made to leave the trail.

"You said yourself that there could be traps here, we've already seen what's in the trees. Shake it off Dev, Jas isn't out there. She died a hero, she'll be in Elysia, you know that."

"What if she's not?" Dev's whisper was agonised as his eyes roved the trees behind her. "What if Hades being gone messed that up? I have to help her. She's trapped. Ivy, she needs our help, let me *go*."

Ivy had never seen Dev with this sort of harrowed, anxious energy in him before, not even when Jasmine had been killed.

"Cerberus, make sure he doesn't go into the forest." Ivy said, and felt the comforting chuff of air that was Cerberus' agreement as she turned to check on Jeff and Freddy.

They seemed fine, deep in conversation. As she watched, Jeff laughed and colour stained Freddy's cheeks as he watched Jeff. Ivy glanced at Devlin, he was being firmly held in place by Cerberus who refused to let him pass. Dev reached out to grab Cerberus and Ivy gasped but on contact with his fur Devlin's shoulders slumped.

"It's gone," he said, voice trembling. She reached out a hand and placed it on his shoulder, he turned away and she let it fall.

"Hey Jeff, could you come and keep Devlin company while I speak to Freddy quickly?" Ivy called and Jeff nodded with a smile. Devlin clearly needed a little space, sometimes it was better to talk to someone who knew nothing about the situation to get a clear head.

"Hey," Ivy said as she joined Freddy. His smile vanished and she worried her lip, she'd had a nagging suspicion something was up with him and now she was certain of it.

"Hey," Freddy said flatly and she sighed heavily.

"Look, Fred, I'm sorry."

He tilted his face up to her slightly, "You are?"

"I know you said before that the Heavens had nothing left for you, and I left you there. I could have come back for you, and I didn't. I'm sorry."

"Why?" he said, and her heart twisted in her chest when she saw the naked hurt spread across his face.

"Dev needed you more. His people needed him and he would have resented me if he had come back with me. Going back there and seeing him... I just couldn't work up the courage. I ran away again and I'm sorry. I promise I'll do better."

Freddy's brown eyes gleamed, "Don't ever leave me behind again."

"Never," she swore. "I'm sorry about Jas too, I know you guys were friends."

Freddy shrugged and wiped hastily at his eyes, "We weren't close, but I'm still sorry she's gone."

"Did you know my eyes can turn red?" He blinked knowingly at her as she tried to change the subject and hide her discomfort.

"Yes."

"Yes? What do you mean *yes?*"

"I thought I saw them turn red the day you thrust Jas up against the wall."

"Ugh, don't say *thrust,* you made it sound weird. Why didn't you say anything?"

"I figured you already knew you were a devil-woman."

Ivy rolled her eyes, "You're an arse and I didn't miss you at all."

Freddy grinned, "I love you, too."

A scuffle sounded up ahead and she looked up in alarm to see Devlin trying to restrain a struggling Jeff. *Shit.*

He broke free of Devlin's grip just as Freddy reached them,

moving so quickly she hadn't realised he was gone until she saw him ahead, a cool breeze left in his wake. Her legs finally unfroze as she ran over.

Freddy had Jeff by the fabric of his t-shirt as he tried to stop him from entering the forest. With a loud *rip* Jeff's shirt tore and he stumbled into the forest only to be quickly grabbed by a tree. Ivy grabbed Freddy who was trying to run into the woods, yelling Jeff's name loud enough to deafen her as she gripped him about his waist. Devlin had fallen to the ground from the force of restraining Jeff while he struggled, but was now back on his feet. They all froze as Jeff let out a scream that the forest seemed to inhale. The tree that had grabbed Jeff threw its roots through the air. A pair of glassy dead-grey eyes stared out of the trunk at them and the leaves Ivy had previously thought looked rubbery were made of flesh, flapping in the air in a sea of pinks and reds. Freddy let out a shout as the tree drew Jeff into the forest, where a small sapling was rapidly growing. As they watched in horror, it doubled in size, roots reaching out to receive Jeff who was utterly still in its grasp, mouth forming words that they could not hear. Ivy grabbed Freddy's arm again as he made to follow Jeff, she couldn't lose him too. Freddy gave a yell of frustration and flung the sword at his side through the air, slicing through one of the new tree's roots as it lunged for Jeff's prone form.

A shudder wracked the new tree's frame as the root was severed in half, a black substance splattered out and the tree with the eyes gave a groan, as though they all shared in the pain of the youngling.

Faster than her eyes could track, the youngling's remaining root swept out, wriggling through the air and catching Jeff around the neck as the old tree abandoned him. Jeff began to scream as whatever spell the forest had cast receded.

"*Freddy*—"Jeff's scream cut-off as the tree squeezed, the crack of his neck spearing through her. Her lungs seized, her chest burning as her mouth opened, but the scream that erupted came instead from Freddy.

"No, no, no... Jeff!" Freddy rushed to the youngling tree just as Jeff's body began to move, a root hooked around his ankle trying to drag him inside the youngling tree as Freddy fought to free Jeff's body. Freddy was pulled through the black goo and forest floor debris as he was pulled along after Jeff, until with a yell he was shaken off by the root. Blood poured down the bark and a horrifying ripping and shredding sound made her retch as leaves suddenly sprouted from the bare branches, showering Freddy in fresh blood as he stared in horror at the leaves, all in colours of pink and red. Veins highlighted like black shadows in a canopy of flesh. He didn't even seem to notice the blood falling into his eyes, he just kept up that same keening cry as the tree finished its transformation. A tree root snuck across the forest floor towards Freddy and Ivy screamed out a warning, finally broken free from her stupor, her cry brought Cerberus running and the root swiftly recoiled as Cerberus plucked Freddy from the forest floor.

Freddy crumpled beside her, covered in blood and dirt from the forest floor, his curls matted with a grease that smelled foul, like meat gone bad. Cerberus whined from behind Freddy, gave him an anxious lick that probably would have been sweet were it not for the fact that Cerberus had three tongues. Cerberus stood rooted in the place where he had emerged from the forest with Freddy, as if to block the view of the flesh tree.

"Good boy," Ivy said softly to Cerberus, patting the soft nose of his central head as she crouched down next to Freddy. She placed her hand carefully on his shoulder, Dev shared a worried glance with her over Freddy's bowed head. He shrugged off her hand violently.

"Why does this keep happening to me," Freddy asked in a voice so flat that Ivy knew he wasn't expecting an answer. "Why is it that everything I care about becomes rotten. Am I not allowed to ever be happy?"

Ivy flashed back to the mini road trip she had taken with Freddy on the way to the compound, the way he had rolled the word around his mouth as if tasting it, trying it on – *Happy.*

God, this was why she didn't get close, because it was too damn hard to watch the people she loved be hurt.

"Freddy..."

"Guys?" Came a voice from behind Cerberus. "I'm not sure what happened, but I feel weird."

Freddy's head jerked up so quickly Ivy wondered whether he would have whiplash. Jeff stood cautiously behind Cerberus' right front paw, patting him anxiously on the side like he expected to be eaten at any moment. Jeff smiled at Cerberus' fur, "I did it, Freddy, I touched him! And listen," they all waited and heard the deep rumble of Cerberus' purr, "he *likes* it." Jeff looked up smugly but gave a gasp when he saw Freddy, still on the ground and covered in mud and blood, interrupted by patches of skin where he had been cleaned with Cerberus' slobber. His eyebrow hair stood up at a funny angle and his hair had been swept up on one side by Cerberus' giant tongue.

"Freddy what's going on?" Jeff said, peering worriedly at their faces, "You all look as if someone died."

Ivy blinked and Freddy had Jeff in his arms, shooting past her with a speed that astounded even Devlin judging by the slow blink he gave. Freddy pulled back, took Jeff's face firmly in both hands and kissed him soundly on the mouth.

"Dev," Ivy whispered, "I don't understand. We *saw* the forest take Jeff. How is he here?"

Dev's face looked pinched when he replied, "He isn't. Not really. Jeff's dead, but we're in the Underworld."

"You mean, we're seeing his soul?"

Jeff pulled away from Freddy and looked over at them with an expression of horror on his face, "Dead?" he screeched and drew in deep panting breaths, "Oh my god. I can't breathe. I can't be *dead*, Dev and I were just talking and then..."

"And then?" Freddy asked in the most gentle voice Ivy had ever heard him use.

Jeff looked out into the forest and shuddered, "I don't remember," he said but the tone of his voice sounded off. Freddy shot her a warning glance and she closed her mouth. If Jeff wanted to talk about what happened to him he could, when he was ready. For now, she was just glad he was with them.

"What does this mean?" Jeff fretted, a slight sheen of tears in his eyes as he tugged on his springy curls.

"It means you're a ghost. Sort of. You're solid enough here but I think—"

"You're dead," Freddy said, finishing Dev's sentence, "You can't go back to the Earthly plane. I'm sorry."

A muscle in Jeff's jaw ticked when he clenched it, "It's not your fault, Freddy, or anyone's for that matter." He added when he saw Ivy opening her mouth again. "Let's just carry on to Hades' Castle and worry about me later," Jeff added with a weak smile.

"Only in our lives would *carry on to Hades' Castle* be a perfectly reasonable thing to say." Ivy said and Jeff laughed, Freddy's face brightening at the sound.

"Let's stick together a little more this time, okay?" Dev said staring them all down like naughty school kids, Ivy and Freddy instantly stuck their tongues out at his back when he turned to walk away. "I saw that." Dev said mildly and then jumped, muscles in his back tightening in fascinating ways, when Cerberus gave a chuffing laugh and followed him.

XXVIII

IVY

THE smell of decaying flowers hit them first, brown wisteria climbed over the walls surrounding the property. Ivy wasn't a fan of the rotten-sweet smell and Cerberus clearly agreed, he had sneezed at least five times since they had emerged from the dirt track between some shrubbery that faced the walls. She hadn't known fear until she had seen three slobbery dog heads sneeze in tandem repeatedly – luckily, she had avoided a snot shower by lurking near Cerberus' flank. Dev wasn't so lucky and he grimaced as he peeled his jacket off and set it down in the grass with a glare at Cerberus, who gave him only puppy eyes in return. Dev sighed and Ivy couldn't help but grin when he stroked along the jaw of Cerberus' right head ruefully.

It was surprisingly sunny, considering they were in the Underworld. Next to the heat of the Sun Sands, the balmy late-spring air felt soothing and refreshing, it made her only more aware of how sticky and in dire need of a bath she was though. Hades' Castle sat at the top of an incline, the hill hadn't seemed steep when they had been walking here, possibly thanks to the path Cerberus had led them on – she would have loved the pup for that alone, hills were the worst. Standing at the top, however, afforded them a rare and beautiful view over most of the Underworld.

Dev came to stand beside her, wrapping a warm arm around her waist and tucking her into his side.

"It's funny isn't it," she said, eyes on the sprawling view below, "walking through some of the different parts of the Underworld down there, they seemed massive and yet... you see them from up here and they're just like small segments of one big puzzle."

Dev was quiet, just pressed a kiss to the top of her head.

"Like being in the Sun Sands, you wouldn't believe that you could be, what looks like, one very long walk away from the borders of Elysia. I guess the lines between good and evil have always been blurred."

Dev sighed, probably at her incessant philosophical rambling but she tensed at his next words, "I don't see anything, Ivy."

She spun to face him, her eyes roving over his face for a clue that he was joking. Nothing, his green eyes were serious and his arms were tense where his hands rested on her shoulders.

"What do you see, then?" she asked, half afraid of the answer.

"Grass," he said, to her shock. "Just rolling hills. Your eyes are glowing again by the way."

Ivy felt a tug at her waist and looked down to find a surprisingly surreptitious Cerberus pulling on the fabric of her t-shirt very carefully with his teeth, blinking dark, heavy-lashed eyes at her innocently. Glancing behind him she saw Freddy and Jeff standing next to an old-fashioned looking door made of dark wood and iron, set into the stone of the wall. They had obviously been doing the sensible thing: looking for ways into the castle, rather than admiring the view as she had been doing. Or rather, avoiding the fact that she didn't know what they'd find inside. Didn't know what would happen to Jeff, or between her and Dev once this miserable-excuse of a rescue mission was finished.

"Looks like Jeff and Freddy have found a way in," Ivy said, she gently tugged her t-shirt out of Cerberus' mouth, frowning at the now-soggy material.

"Are you ready?" Dev asked, his eyes roved across her face, missing nothing.

"As I'll ever be," she said with a wry grin and sigh, she turned to follow Cerberus but found herself tugged back into Dev's arms as he pressed a sweet kiss to her lips. Well, it would have been sweet had she not pressed closer, deepening the kiss, pushing her fingers through his thick black hair and tugging slightly as he bit her lip —

"Are you guys coming or not?" Freddy shouted from behind her. A deep chuckle rumbled through Dev's chest that made her smile, a real one this time, and he pressed a kiss to her cheek at the sight of it.

"Are my eyes still glowing?" she murmured to Dev quietly and was relieved when he shook his head.

They walked over to Freddy and Jeff hand in hand, and Freddy shot them a smug look for interrupting their kiss. "Pun unintended of course. Hell is certainly not the time or place."

"Funny, that's not what you said to me yesterday," Jeff chimed in and Ivy choked on her laugh as Freddy *blushed,* all the way to the tips of his ears. Dev just smirked and pushed past them to test the circular handle of the door.

"Locked," he said with a sigh, "I guess I could break it down."

Ivy was appalled, "You can't break it down! One, that's solid wood, you'll hurt yourself," she said ticking off her fingers, "and two, sometimes those handles are just a little finnicky, let me try. We used to have one of these doors in the garden at… at my parent's house." She stumbled over the words only a little. Dev looked at her with a proud sort-of smile on his face and she worried her lip ring with her tongue, feeling awkward. It was a small thing, to talk about her past, but it wasn't something she usually ever did. God, being a normal functioning human was hard.

Dev stepped to the side only slightly and she sent him a wry look when she was forced to brush her butt against him just to squeeze by. His eyes were wide with mock innocence when they met hers, but his crooked smile was all mischief. She placed a hand against the door for support and gave a squeal of alarm when it instantly swung open.

"Master locksmith indeed," Freddy said lightly, but his eyes were worried when they flicked away from hers. The creases at their corners deepened in concern when his eyes landed on Jeff, as if making sure he was still there. The two of them sidled past Ivy and into a small courtyard, Cerberus padding softly behind them. Devlin slid his fingers between her own once more as they walked into the home of the Devil.

The pathway from the door to the courtyard was filled with aged beige stones that clanked and crunched as they moved towards the house. An old willow tree stood withered next to the house's approach and a dried-up stone fountain parted the path, they split-up as they moved around it, passing on either side. It was only for a moment but Ivy felt tense until Jeff and Freddy were walking beside them again. The place looked completely devoid of life. The sound of their feet on the stones seemed too loud in the stillness surrounding the manor and Ivy found herself wincing with each step. Her thoughts churned uncomfortably, so much could go wrong. The best they could do was hope that Cerberus was right and that this was where they could find Hades. The grass on either side of the stone path was yellowed despite the sunshine and up-close Ivy could see the wisteria coating the wall was crumbling. Cerberus' paws left deep dents in the grass as he walked and he gave a loud bark when they got close to the castle, running ahead to lay down beside the wide front door.

They caught up to him quickly and Ivy placed her hand on the side of Cerberus' left head, stroking him lightly before stepping away and facing what had to be the entrance. She took a step closer and was tugged gently to a stop by Dev, holding her hand. The tension practically radiated off him, his face was pinched in worry – for her, for Hades, she wasn't sure. Ivy pressed a quick kiss to the back of his hand and said quietly enough for only him to hear, "I love you."

The smile that eased the worry lines on Dev's face was breathtaking, like the sun finally breaking through the clouds. "And I love you."

She stared at him steadily, as she moved another step forward, this time he moved with her. She saw the promise in his eyes, his full faith in her shining out, *I belong wherever you are,* he had said to her. She was starting to believe that, too.

Her hand touched the door and just like the gate, it swung open of its own accord.

"Finally," said a voice. "I've been waiting a long time for you, daughter."

XXIX

DEV

A MAN stood in the foyer of the castle. He seemed no more than thirty mortal years, Dev knew this wasn't the case though. He was tall, with broad shoulders and hair more silver than blonde that brushed the collar of his white shirt. Icy-blue eyes speared him and Dev felt like an idiot. How could he not have seen the resemblance? *Eyes like blue fire,* he thought. Now, if Ivy had been looking at him with that fiery gaze, he would have thought it was hot as hell – but coming from her father? *Fuck, Hades is her father.* They shared the same high cheekbones and full mouth, though Hades' was sans the lip ring. His shirt sleeves were rolled up to show powerful arms decorated with runic bands in a language that Devlin couldn't identify, which in itself was odd, as he could speak most of them.

Ivy had gone pale at Hades' words, she was utterly silent, just staring at her father in shock. If he was reeling then he couldn't even imagine what she must be thinking. Jeff and Freddy moved incrementally closer to Ivy and he felt a surge of relief knowing that who Ivy's father was didn't matter to them. She had picked good friends there. The silence was broken by a loud panting WHOOF. Cerberus stood at the door, one large, wet black nose pushed through the doorway, apparently very happy to see his master.

"Cerberus," Hades sighed. "You know you can't fit through the door when you're that size. Swap back now, that's a good boy."

Cerberus gave a happy bark and with a flash of light stood in the doorway, no bigger than a very large labrador.

This appeared to be too much for Ivy.

"Hold the fuck up," she said, her eyes flashing in anger, Dev wasn't sure but he thought he could see a hint of red in them when she glared at Hades. "You waltz in here —"

"Well actually, you did the waltzing, my love. Not that I'm not grateful, of course."

Ivy looked more enraged at being interrupted, "You waltz into *my life,* shrink my fucking *dog* and what? Expect us all to sit down for tea?" she said, gesturing to a table laid with food and drink that Dev hadn't yet spotted. The teacups rattled as the walls began to shake. Dev quickly glanced back to Ivy, and felt his eyes widen in alarm at the deep ruby pools her eyes had become.

"Well, actually Cerberus is my dog —"

"Finders keepers!" Ivy said with a stubborn lift to her chin.

"Perhaps you should calm down a little and then I can explain a few things —"

Dev winced. He hadn't lived on Earth for very long, but some things transcended the mortal/immortal barrier – *never* tell an angry woman to calm down.

Ivy gave a yell of anger, her eyes blazing as the house's foundations rocked around them. The floor cracked and out shot a barrage of thick thorny vines, much like the ones Hades had once summoned to teach Dev and Michael a lesson. There was no doubting it, she was her father's daughter.

Hades was watching the carnage with an expression of absolute delight, his grin only seemed to enrage Ivy further. The door banged shut and open behind her, groaning, and a furiously cutting wind stormed through the house as black clouds rolled overhead outside. Lightning crashed and set the willow tree in the courtyard ablaze, the light from the fire caught on the brightness of both Ivy and Hades' hair, haloing them. Dev looked on in awe, Ivy looked like an avenging angel. She practically glowed with power, a pale flame against the raging darkness she had conjured. So much power, but she clearly didn't know how to control it. A lightning bolt slammed down a little too close to Cerberus' tail and he gave an anxious wine.

"Enough," said a deep, calm voice. Dev looked away from Ivy to find Hades only a hair's breadth away, eyes glowing a deep red, like blood. Up close, they were deeper than Ivy's, hers were almost feverish now. Tears poured down her cheeks, she was trembling and Dev pulled her hand to his chest, letting her feel the rhythm of his heart.

"I am with you," he said, leaning in close, heedless of the sharp thorns between them. He would bleed a hundred times over for her. "I will not let go."

Ivy shuddered, the red in her eyes fading to a more mortal blue, though they still glowed as if she was lit from within.

"Dev," she whispered, looking up when Hades took a step closer, the wind making his silvery hair dance.

"Enough," Hades repeated softly. Stepping forward, he pressed a kiss to Ivy's forehead and another shudder racked her form. "Relax," Hades said, "don't fight it."

Dev looked between the two of them, confused, and then let out a gasp that was echoed by Jeff and Freddy as the wind and darkness eased and Ivy *changed*. Dev felt a large pulse of energy and a breeze brushed his face. He could only stare.

Ivy's power had been turned inward before flowing out of her in an arc that made his hands tremble. The door righted itself on its hinges and the storm clouds cleared. Her eyes glowed red once more, matching Hades. Dev knew if he looked, the grass and the tree outside would probably be green and healthy again. But he didn't. He couldn't pull his eyes away from the gorgeous, deep indigo wings that now protruded from Ivy's back. They were almost fluffy they were that plush with feathers, tapering to lighter mauve arches on the fine tips of the wings. Ivy sagged forwards, utterly drained, and Hades caught her in his arms.

"Well," Hades sighed. "That could have gone better."

XXX

IVY

SOMETHING felt wrong. The last thing she remembered was the rage and the power, burning inside of her. Absolutely uncontrollable, it had reforged her before sweeping out and away, leaving her burning. It was power she hadn't even known she had access to until she had seen Hades. Her father's power. Fuck. *Hades* was her father. Now all those times her mum had called Ivy her angel made so much more sense. Except he wasn't an angel, he was the Devil, and she was his daughter. Well, as Jess had pointed out, Ivy wasn't exactly angelic in nature. She had just figured it was her mum being sentimental in the past.

Her head felt like someone had taken a hammer to it, even her eyeballs ached. She tried experimentally to open her eyes and retched when it sent a jolt of pain so intense through her brain that she thought she would pass out again.

"Oh good, you're awake. Easy now, wielding that sort of power for the first time is bound to leave you with a hangover."

Ivy heaved open her eyes again, she didn't remember deciding to close them, and winced at the bright light. Hades peered down at her. His eyes, a shade of blue eerily similar to her own, were both concerned and amused. A wry crinkle at the corner of one eye was the only sign of age on his face, he looked barely older than her.

"I'm sorry," he said. "I didn't know what the full extent of your power would be. I would have done things a little differently if I'd known you would be fully awakening when you got here."

"Awakening?" she croaked.

He passed her a glass of water that she took gratefully. She had been angry before, now she felt only drained. "You are of my blood. Well, not blood exactly, I am not a being in the way you are – but my energy. When those energies met for the first time, it unlocked the part of you that being here in my domain had already started to awaken. You are a great deal like me." He said thoughtfully and not without amusement.

"You don't know anything about me."

"Now, that's not true. I've been locked up in this house since the last time I came to Earth, oh twenty-some years ago. I had little else to do except watch you."

She stared at him, "So you've been *spying* on me?"

Hades wrinkled his nose a little as he thought, "Well, I wouldn't say *spying*, is a father not allowed to watch their child grow when they cannot be there themselves?"

Ivy felt her jaw tighten and struggled to contain her irritation for a moment, closing her eyes and breathing deeply. "Start from the beginning. What happened? Why were you trapped here?" Ivy cast her eyes about, she seemed to be in some sort of plush dayroom that had large bay windows letting in the sunlight, "Where are the others? Are they okay?"

Hades seemed to be assessing her face for a moment before he answered, "They're fine. They're cleaning up. As for the rest... It's a long story."

"I have time."

Hades leant back in the armchair he had clearly dragged over to sit next to her, "I met your mother on my first ever trip to Earth. It was not my creation, but a... friend's. I had promised to watch over it for him, and I did. Never interfering. We had designed our worlds to be in conjunction, you see. It was our greatest work, the human soul. To create new energy."

"Where's your friend now?" Ivy asked carefully.

Hades' blue eyes fixed on her as he brushed a stray bit of silvery hair out of his eyes, "Gone. Sleeping. To maintain these worlds, we give our energy. After a time, existence became tiring for him, our kind can sleep for centuries. So that's what he did. He chose to sleep, deep beneath the Earth, creating his angels to supplement the energy that he was struggling to provide as Earth began to flourish. He was not quite so powerful as I... and Earth is a rather more fixed state of reality than my domain. It's why you had so little access to your true power there." Hades looked away from her, not quite able to meet her eyes. Good to know where she got her inability to deal with anything mushy.

"I had avoided Earth. It was hard – to be surrounded by the energies of my friend and yet be without him. But I yearned. I was lonely. Most of my kind were dead or asleep. So, eventually I went to Earth."

"Why didn't you choose to sleep too?"

At this, Hades turned back to her, his eyes burning with an inner flame that made Ivy see exactly why her mother thought he was angelic. The pure power of him washed over her and she didn't have to check to know her eyes were glowing red in response to his power. "I wasn't done," he said simply and she nodded. "I happened across your mother, sweet and beautiful but so young. She knew so little of the world. She probably wasn't much older than you are now when we met. She had been cornered on her way home from work."

"You saved her."

"Of course."

Ivy smiled slightly, imagining this silver-haired menace appearing from the darkness and saving her mother. "I can see why she fell in love."

"We had relatively little time together before I had to come back to my domain. Long enough that I knew I was to be a father. Never had I dreamed of such a thing, I wasn't sure of the limits to the more physical body I had created, but everything seemed to be in working order —"

"I think we can skip over that part." Ivy said hastily. "Why did you need to return home?"

Hades smirked but obliged, "If I leave for too long the land begins to wither, my creation falls apart. The souls of the Sun Sands were either eaten by the Guardians, out of control once my energy had begun to run out, or disappeared altogether as their energy was absorbed by the land in order to replenish it."

"But you've been here this whole time."

Hades gave a light shrug, "I've been in the house, yes. But it is not entirely of this world, and when Michael used his own considerable power to bind me here when I came home to replenish the energies, I could not leave. Luckily, Elysia is well-warded and so was the best protected even when the Underworld was drained dry. Cerberus, however, was not so lucky. Your presence here began feeding the land, returning Cerberus' sanity, and of course, eventually freeing me. What with the energy you generated earlier, the land is almost back to normal." Hades said with an approving smile, just a tilt of the lips really but it hit her heart abnormally hard.

"How did Michael manage to trap you here?"

"Nothing is without weakness," Hades said with a wry smile, "My greatest joy was mine. I told you this house is not truly of this world, it is because it holds the portals to several dimensions. Therefore, it is anchored here but not wholly here."

"I don't understand."

"I was not wholly of my world any more either, I had left some of my energies behind – in *you*, Ivy. My power was reduced when I came back here, I draw power from the land just as it draws power from me, so I didn't notice the difference at first. Not until I tried to break Michael's enchantment and couldn't. He sealed me in here, thinking I would be trapped forever, the door only opens from the outside and would only open to someone recognised by this world as me."

"In other words, you needed a kid?"

Hades grinned, "Exactly. As soon as you arrived, I felt the enchantment begin to weaken and knew I had guessed correctly as to the manner of his curse. Little did Michael know, I had a child. He probably assumed I'd remain trapped here indefinitely. But I felt a flash of your power, several months ago, there for a second and then gone. For the first time, I had hope that we would meet. Fate," he said thoughtfully, "is an interesting and wholly unpredictable frenemy."

Ivy felt an unexpected laugh bubble out of her. He may have looked like a thirty-year-old, but Hades still spouted the same wise old-man crap as any dad.

"I'm sorry I couldn't be there after your mother..."

Ivy blinked back tears, "It's okay. One day that scumbag will get what's coming to him."

"Oh yes," Hades said with a dark smile, "That day is growing nearer by the minute."

She didn't know what to say to that, was it a relief? Maybe. But she felt whole enough now that the burning need for revenge that had filled her before was a low-simmer.

"My powers, they come from you right? I had a vision before that didn't come true."

Hades shrugged, "Some things are set in stone, others are more fluid. Sometimes in trying to prevent a vision from coming true you may inadvertently bring it about, time is not something I would mess around with, if I were you."

Ivy nodded and then froze as an odd rustling noise filled her ears at the movement. This whole time she had been so focused on his story, drinking in the little details of his face when he spoke. Ivy had loved her adopted dad, but she had always wondered who her biological father was, what he might say if they ever met, whether she would recognise him if she saw him on the street. But now that he had finished speaking she became more aware of herself. Glancing to the side she let out a little scream.

"What are *those*?"

XXXI

IVY

"Oн," said Hades, "Yes, yes, I know this one! I had very little else to do except catch-up on pop culture and wait for the day that I might be able to see you. They really are rather lovely, indigo and lavender."

Ivy stared at him like he was speaking another language. Did he think she was quoting *vine*?

"My own are rather nice too, if I do say so myself," he said smugly and whipped out his own wings. They were, admittedly, beautiful. A deep dusky red lightening to orange on the tips and a deep red in the center. *Wings*. She had wings.

"Why—" she choked and had to take a sip of water before she could continue, "Why do I have wings?"

Hades looked at her like she was crazy, eyes comically wide, "Well, you can't keep teleporting the way you have been! It's ridiculously tiring and you won't always be here to access the portals, so it's the easiest way to travel between planes."

Just then, Dev came careening into the room. It was funny really. She knew Dev was older than her, but Hades felt ancient in a way that Dev didn't. In comparison, he now seemed much younger. Ivy liked it. She had realised that he wasn't quite as put-together as he pretended to be and seeing this slightly disheveled, protective side of him was doing funny things to her heart.

Dev blinked at Hades' wings, but immediately shifted his gaze past them to her, still lying on a soft leather couch, "I heard a shout, are you okay?"

Something inside her melted at his concern, "I just discovered I have wings," she said, sitting up so she could admire them a little better. She looked back at Dev and found him staring at them too, had an instant flash of worry that he would be weirded out until he gave her this soft look, full of awe.

"They're beautiful."

"Thank you," she breathed, wishing she could kiss him, wishing her *father* wasn't currently sitting awkwardly in-between them looking both extremely uncomfortable and like he wanted to push Dev through the large bay windows.

Luckily, Jeff and Freddy chose that moment to also walk in the room. Freddy assessed the tension in the room and immediately turned, "Nope. Not today, satan."

"I do really rather prefer Hades," her father remarked in a mildly sarcastic voice, eyes assessing Jeff and Freddy with interest as Jeff pulled Freddy back into the room. Hades stood in one fluid moment, his wings looking like live fire as the sunlight hit them and set them ablaze. "I don't think we've yet had the pleasure of properly meeting," he said striding towards Jeff and Freddy and pressing a kiss to each of their hands. Freddy looked suspicious while Jeff was blushing.

"I think I'm going to puke." Ivy remarked as she drank more of her water.

Hades gave an unrepentant grin, "Did I mention I was trapped in this house for about twenty years? A very *long* twenty years. I have a lot of... energy," he said with a wink at Jeff and Freddy, "to expend."

"Maybe you should use it to sort out the Underworld, seeing as it's a little crazy out there right now." Ivy suggested sweetly.

Hades waved a hand in her direction and continued making eyes at Jeff, "It's already taken care of darling, like I said, your power boost restored the balance."

"What about the portals?" Ivy pointed out.

"You've been here all of five minutes!" Hades said, "We'll get to that. You're not in a rush are you?"

"Everyone I care about is right here." Jeff said and Ivy swallowed past the lump in her throat. No matter what happened next, Jeff had to stay here.

The tension from Jeff's words broke as Cerberus came barreling into the room, barking enthusiastically, still in miniature. He leaped onto her lap and she grinned, despite the spilled water that was now soaking her lap.

"Hello, gorgeous boy. I wondered where you got to. I can't believe you could have shrunk down to this size for cuddles at any point and didn't!" Cerberus only whined in response and Ivy laughed as all three of his heads licked her at once. Slobbery, but cute.

"He's a dog," Hades said with a roll of his eyes, "you have to give him the right command."

Ivy rolled her eyes right back, "Right, the next time I go on a supernatural rescue mission led by a dog, I'll be sure to remember to check how well he's trained first."

"There's only one thing worse than an untrained dog," Freddy remarked but his words held a slightly seductive note that made Ivy want to cut-off her ears.

"What's that?" Dev asked.

"A child." Hades said, deadpan, and then threw her a conspiratorial wink over his shoulder. Did he think they were bonding? This was beyond weird.

The reference went over Freddy's head but Jeff had turned pink trying not to laugh.

"That's not what I was going to say," Freddy said irritably, glancing back and forth between Hades and Jeff.

"Don't worry Frederick," Hades' grin was predatory, "I can assure you, I am indeed well-trained."

Oh god, her ears were never going to recover. Dev threw her an amused look and she sighed, slumping back against the couch with Cerberus lying across her stomach.

"I was wrong before. I can no longer predict the craziness of my life. I give up."

Freddy grinned, momentarily distracted from Hades, "Hate to say I told you so."

Ivy stuck out her tongue and laughed when Cerberus did the same.

Dinner had been an odd affair that evening. Despite everything, it had felt like a family meal, albeit one where your dad hits on your friends. Not that Freddy or Jeff seemed to mind too much. Hades had swept up from the table when he was done eating, having mostly pushed his food around, "I don't need to *eat* darling, terrible waste of time. The energy here is all I really need to sustain me, well that and—" Hades cut himself off, giving Jeff and Freddy a sultry look that made her retch. "Anyway, I'll be in the East wing if you need me." Hades said pointedly and then swept out of the room,

Cerberus looking up briefly as Hades walked by.

"Ugh, beyond gross," Ivy had muttered to Dev. "How am I supposed to eat when there's potentially a menage-a-yuck happening down the hall?"

Dev had just chuckled softly and they had spent the remainder of the evening sitting in front of the fireplace, Cerberus sprawled across their laps. Hades had re-emerged to tell her he had prepared a room for her in the East wing too and that Cerberus could show her the way.

"And you," Hades had said pointedly to Dev, "can have any room in the *West* wing." He had marched out smartly and Ivy rolled her eyes thinking about it now as she made her way down the West wing to Devlin's room.

It was funny to think that Dev had once told her he was the Devil, she didn't think he had a truly rebellious bone in his body. He had gone straight to bed after placing a chaste kiss to her forehead. She snorted to herself in the dimly lit corridor. A plush carpeted runner ran the length of the halls and her toes sank into the fluffy softness with gratitude. She was a creature of comfort and was glad they didn't have to spend another night in a cave, as steamy as that visit had been.

Cerberus pawed at a door to her left and she smiled, bending down to give him a stroke on his silky head.

"Good boy. I'll see you in the morning, okay?" Cerberus looked at her wistfully as she moved towards Dev's bedroom door and then he turned around and trotted back up the corridor.

Ivy gave a soft knock on the hard, dark-wood door.

"It's open," Dev's voice called in from inside.

"Brave of you," she said with a smirk, "Hades is on the horny war-path and you've left your door unlocked?"

"Fortunately, I'm fairly certain he's preoccupied with Freddy and Jeff. Luckily, I'm much more enamoured with his daughter."

Ivy laughed as she stepped into the room, it was dim with only the light from the fireplace lighting the room. It cast a warm glow over the dark wooden furnishings and king-size bed, Devlin looked golden reclining on the bed, arms behind his head and the muscles in his abdomen stretched. He cracked open a lid and regarded her with one brilliantly green eye. The other quickly flew open as he stared at her.

"So, you left your door unlocked for me, then? How presumptuous."

Dev blinked, licked his lips and said in a strangely hoarse voice, "What-what are you wearing?"

Ivy looked down in surprise, she had borrowed one of Dev's clean shirts in the cave yesterday but ended up not having the chance to get changed into it. "Oh, I'm sorry, I didn't think you'd mind. I don't have any clothes here and mine were a little worse for wear."

Dev was still staring at her, his green eyes seeming to darken slightly as he said softly, "Come here."

She walked over slowly, she had barely placed a knee on the white sheets before Devlin moved unbelievably fast, sliding his hands around her waist and pulling her to him. His bare chest was warm against her and she sighed happily as she locked her arms around his neck. He rested his forehead against hers and said in a tense voice, "I'm pretty sure there were clothes in your room, I found these bottoms in the drawer – who knows how or why Hades has them."

"Maybe it's magic," she whispered, her lips almost brushing Dev's and he shivered. It made her feel... powerful, that shiver, knowing that she wasn't alone in this. He wanted her just as much as she wanted him.

"Ivy," he said with a groan, pressing his lips to hers slightly harder, but it was still a whisper of a kiss. "You are torturing me."

Ivy pulled back slightly, surprised and a little hurt. "Torturing you?"

Dev let her go, sinking back on his knees and pushing his hand through his hair, "I'm trying to give you space but it's hard to do that when you come into my room in my shirt, looking like *that.*"

Ivy wasn't sure she could feel any more surprised, "I never asked for space, and what's wrong with your shirt? If you want it back so badly then here," she said and reached her arms above her head and plucked it off. The cool air pebbled her skin and made her breasts tighten, especially when Dev's gaze dropped lower sending a line of heat over the path his eyes had taken.

Dev flopped back onto the bed with a groan, his hand flung over his eyes, muttering something so low she couldn't hear it.

"You may not have asked for space, but maybe you need it," Dev finally said, hand still firmly thrown over his eyes as if he couldn't bear to look at her.

"What on earth are you talking about?"

"That! Exactly that. We're not on Earth, you have wings, you found out Hades is your father and Jeff..." Dev trailed off as if he wasn't sure he could say the words aloud. "So much has changed in a very short space of time. I don't want you to feel overwhelmed."

For a second she could only stare at him, nobody had ever cared that much about her before. Not since her parents and Jess had died.

Gently, she tugged his hand away from his face and couldn't stop the smile that rose to her lips when she saw Dev's eyes, still scrunched tightly closed.

"You said you belonged with me. That you would stay at my side, no matter what."

Dev gave a stiff, firm nod.

"Then I don't need space. I just need you."

His eyes finally opened and he looked at her levelly. "Are you sure?" was all he said.

She moved closer, her knees brushed his side as she laid her palm on his chest, over his heart and nodded. His hand curled around her wrist as he gently pulled her down and over him. The heat rolling off him made her groan as her breasts pressed to his chest and his mouth claimed hers desperately. As if he had been suffering and only her touch had eased his pain.

Dev pulled back reluctantly, his mouth lingering on hers and his green eyes fierce, "I love you."

The words wrung a shudder out of her as they ghosted over her skin, settling into her heart – a new weight, but a welcome one. Their lips met again, more savage than before, tongues tangling as they each tried to get closer still to the other. Ivy's hands moved across the planes of his chest, over the hard ridges of his stomach and paused until Dev's moan of approval drove her on.

Her hand slid slower until she felt him, hard against the softness of the pyjama bottoms he'd borrowed. She let her hand slide gently over him, barely a touch and smirked at the sound Dev made, low in his throat. He gently captured her wrist and pressed a kiss to it as he sat up and impatiently tugged down the bottoms.

"Fairs fair," he said, throwing the pyjamas somewhere in the room and running his eyes over the creamy expanse of skin she currently had on display. Ivy had seen her fair share of male bodies, usually in the near-dark of some club bathroom, but there really was no comparison to Dev. Slowly, as if she might spook, he moved closer on his knees and she rose to meet him. He was still a good head or two taller than her even while kneeling but she stretched upwards, arching her neck invitingly as Devlin pressed a series of delicate kisses to her throat. Ivy loosened her shoulders and let him look his fill, strangely enough, with him she didn't feel naked at all. Dev trailed his lips lower, until his mouth closed over the peak of one breast and Ivy let out a wordless plea for more, pressing herself against him more firmly as his tongue moved over her. His hands slid around her waist, warm and lightly calloused, tightening briefly when she moaned.

Dev's hand slid lower, creating fire as it moved across her skin, getting oh-so-close to where she wanted him to be. Her eyes fluttered open when he only paused there and found his eyes on hers.

"You are... so beautiful." He said softly and moved two fingers over and across her centre, stroking lightly and then harder when she rocked against him. Her eyes had closed again and she forced them open and reached blindly for him, heard Dev groan when her hand closed around him and began to move.

"Ivy," he whispered her name tenderly and pulled his hand away from her, ignoring the sound of protest she made that quickly turned into a squeal as he pressed a searing kiss to her lips and then leaned back onto the bed.

Her breathing felt uneven as she looked at Devlin, kneeling between her legs. He was breathtaking, his golden skin shone slightly with a sheen of sweat and his thigh muscles were coiled tight as he leaned back to admire her. He slid forward to kiss her, his forearms on either side of her as his body moved against her. She couldn't help a shiver when she felt him, hard and hot brushing over her skin.

"Devlin," she murmured, a plea – one that she would never have given to anyone else. He answered with his mouth, knowing what she needed without her ever having to say it, curving his hands around her and pulling her closer to him. Green eyes met hers as she smoothed her hands over his back, stroking lightly over his shoulders as he sank into her slowly. Ivy loosed a gasp as Dev moved deep, bringing them together, clasped her to him like he would never let her go.

"Don't stop," she said holding him as tightly as he held her.

Dev moaned as they moved together, his breaths came faster as he pressed kisses to her neck, her chest, her skin slick with sweat as they drove each other on. Everything inside her tightened and then released in a powerful wave, Devlin shuddered as he came apart and she smoothed a hand over his cheek.

"I love you," Dev said again, the damp hair curling about his ear tickled her cheek as he moved away, collapsing next to her and propping his arm under his head.

She smiled as she rolled onto her side to look at him, "I love you."

Dev gave her a sleepy smile as he pulled her closer. "Your dad's going to be so pissed you came to my room."

"Luckily, I don't give a fuck."

A laugh shook Dev's shoulders as he leaned down towards her, his lush mouth closing over hers in a searing kiss, "Always with that foul mouth."

Ivy grinned against his mouth and rolled so her back was to him, "Spoon me?"

Dev hummed his agreement as the warmth of his chest pressed into her back. Then Ivy noticed the warmth coming from a completely different direction.

"Already?" she said, half in awe, half-concerned but Dev just laughed and it rumbled through her pleasantly.

"Sorry," Dev said and she could practically hear the smirk in his voice, "He'll settle down in a little while. It's just hard—" Ivy laughed and Dev's arms tightened around her at the sound, "when I'm pressed against something as... nice as your butt."

Ivy sat up indignantly, "*Nice?* Picnics are nice, my butt is fantastic."

"That it is," Dev said mournfully and she couldn't help her laugh as she settled against his chest once more. They stayed like that until the sun rose, hands clasped, curled tightly around one another.

XXXII

IVY

HADES, Freddy and Jeff were already at breakfast by the time Ivy and Devlin dragged themselves out of bed – and she really *had* to be dragged. Luckily, Dev was persuasive. *Very* persuasive. Well, that and Cerberus had whined outside their door until they had let him in.

"Morning," Jeff said cheerily when he caught sight of them coming through the doorway, "there's pancakes!" He sounded delighted by this prospect and looked markedly less rumpled than Freddy and Hades.

"Rough night?" Ivy smirked at Freddy and he rubbed his temples with a wince.

"Too much wine." Freddy said shortly but Hades looked like the cat that got the cream.

Before she could comment on *that* further Jeff piped in, "Apparently being dead has some perks," he said matter of factly, "Like no hangovers."

She didn't know what to say to that, and apparently neither did anyone else as it went markedly quiet for a moment before Cerberus gave a loud bark at Hades' feet, demanding the bacon he currently had in hand. Hades gave it to him absent-mindedly and Cerberus looked smug as he chowed down.

"So," Hades said, snapping the odd tension that had taken ahold of the room, "When will you be leaving?" Ivy looked up to see the question was directed at Dev.

"What do you mean?" Ivy asked in a carefully neutral voice.

"Well, you miserable lot came to find me," Hades swept his arms out in a carelessly elegant gesture, "I'm free once more and I imagine you need to be getting back to your angelic lot, make sure they're not off causing trouble."

Ivy glanced at Devlin and found the same look of disquiet on his face that she was sure matched hers.

"You're really going to leave?" Her voice was quiet and her heart thudded unevenly as she waited for his response.

Dev's eyes roved her face and he opened his mouth, to say what she wasn't sure, but no sound came out and he shut it again wordlessly.

Hades huffed in exasperation, his eyes narrowed on Dev, and she was sure she heard him mutter 'idiots' as he stood abruptly from the table and came towards them. "Children, children—"

"I won't go," Dev interrupted, he stared at her father like he would happily throw down if necessary, to ensure that fact. "I already told you," he said, eyes moving back to hers, "I belong wherever you are."

Ivy let out relieved breath and gave him a small smile, opening up to Dev had been hard and last night... well, she didn't think she'd ever had a night like that with anyone else. This felt like the final leap, to know that he would choose her. That he would always choose her. Dev's eyes on hers, soft and loving confirmed it.

"As I was saying," Hades said with an irritated curl of his mouth at Dev, "I said you needed to go back, not that you had to stay. Did you forget you have wings now?"

She blinked. Yeah, she kind of had. Her mind got caught for a moment, thinking about all the interesting positions she could get into with those wings. Mentally, she shook herself and noticed Dev giving her a look like he knew exactly where her mind had gone. Ballsy, to be giving her that sexy, knowing look with her father standing meters from them. It was funny, Ivy thought, how Hades seemed to dislike Devlin and yet they thought scarily alike.

"I feel like I had this exact conversation not that long ago," Ivy said with a wry look at Dev who smiled slightly in response, remembering when Dev had first told her his plan to get into the Heavens.

"Just think of it like one of those day jobs the mortals are so fond of – not like this place, it's a full-time affair. Or at least, it was."

Ivy started to smile at the thought of Dev in some sort of middle-management job in a suit and then froze, "What do you mean, it *was*?"

"Well you know," Hades said, waving a hand lazily through the air, "now you're here and all."

"You expect me to *run* this place? While everyone else gets to go—" she cut herself off, throwing a hand in the air, not unlike her father she realised belatedly. The truth was, Earth didn't feel like home any more. Sure, she missed her flat and knowing that there probably wasn't going to be imminent death lurking around every corner, unlike the Underworld. But... everyone she loved was here.

Hades eyes scanned her face as if he was looking for the unfinished end of her sentence but he continued speaking without asking, "Honestly darling, don't be so dramatic. Your energies are as much tied to this plane as mine is, it will fuel you and you, it. By all means, run back to your mortal job, enjoy. I won't trap you here." He smirked but his eyes were solemn and unblinking on hers, he really had been watching her all these years and it was clear he knew she hated it at the One Stop. "Besides, you'll have company!"

"You don't count. I barely know you." She regretted her callous words almost instantly as a flicker of hurt passed across Hades' face and he bit down on his lower lip as if holding back a reply. Good to know where her poor impulse control came from.

Hades shrugged it off, "I meant Jeff. He's dead, remember? He can't leave. Not," Hades said with a slow smile, "that I'm sorry you have to stay."

Jeff seemed utterly unperturbed by this announcement and Ivy wondered what exactly had gone on last night.

Ivy gave a mock gag before his words sank in, "Jeff really can't leave?"

"Not unless he wants to wander the Earth forever as a ghost. At least here he has a body," Hades smirked and Ivy cut him off, knowing exactly where that comment was going.

"Jeff I —"

"Don't, Ivy." Jeff said firmly but gently, a small smile tugged at his lips, "It's not your fault. I know you don't believe in fate. It was practically the first thing you ever said to me before you puked on my shoes." Freddy went a little green at the mention of puke and quickly took a sip of what looked like coffee. "But if I hadn't met you, I never would have met Freddy. Plus, it's not so bad being dead. So far, it's a lot like being alive, except I don't need to breathe which can come in *super* handy."

"Why would it—" she began and then abruptly stopped with a slight blush, "God, you're both as bad as each other!" Ivy said with a glare at Hades who was looking at Jeff delightedly.

"Oh, I don't know," Hades said, smirk fading slightly as he looked at her steadily, "Fair is fair daughter, or was I imagining you joining us from the *West* wing this morning?"

She said nothing and Hades' smirk returned. "As I thought."

"How will I get back?" Devlin said, his brows were furrowed adorably and Ivy felt a pang of love shoot through her. "Ivy may have wings, but I don't. None of the angels left have the strength to journey here, that's why Ivy brought us in the first place."

"Gabe got his back somehow, can't we do the same for you?" Ivy directed the question to the room at large but her eyes were on Hades.

Dev replied, to her surprise, "He never lost them. It was all a glamour, an especially strong one." Disappointment rolled through her but Dev smiled, "It's okay," he said softly, "I've been without them for so long it would be weird to have them back."

"So what do we do?"

Hades reached for another pancake, "The portals are up and running again now the house is no longer on lockdown."

Devlin looked appeased and Ivy took his hand in hers. "Okay. I'll do it, I'll stay."

A muscle in Hades' jaw ticked, "I don't want you here if you're going to treat it like a prison sentence."

Ivy glared right back, her own hot-headedness reflected back at her in her father and she tamped down on her own temper, deciding to make an effort. "I meant, I'd like to stay. If you'll have me."

Something in Hades softened, anger eased as quickly as it had begun as he closed the small space separating them with a hand cradling her cheek, "I would like nothing more."

Ivy looked away from his intense gaze, "Well, cool." There was an awkward silence and Freddy looked back and forth between her and

Hades with no shortage of amusement before promptly going white and breaking the silence by retching into his porridge bowl.

Hades looked momentarily distracted as he eyed Freddy in both concern and disgust, "I'm not sorry I missed that horror-show of a stomach bug when you were eleven, seeing vomit in person is quite... disturbing."

Ivy couldn't help it, she burst out laughing, tears streaming down her face, "Jeez, how much wine did you give him?"

"A lot," Jeff said gleefully.

Dev gave a short laugh and Hades' shoulders relaxed incrementally.

"Well, no time like the present." Ivy said and focused on the power she could feel bundled tightly inside. Used it to coax the heavy purple wings from her back, loving the look on Dev's face when they sprung free. He stroked down one edge, making her toes curl, "They're perfect."

"Thank you," she said quietly but with a smile. Freddy, looking slightly better after throwing up, clasped her other hand as they prepared to return to the Heavens. Home. Because that would always be where Devlin was.

"Back in time for tea?" she said to Hades and smiled when he did.

"We'll be waiting." Hades said and she squeezed Dev's hand a little tighter as she closed her eyes.

ACKNOWLEDGEMENTS

Thank you first and foremost to Ciara O'Neill, Emily Smith and Callie Keck for all your support, feedback and, in some cases, reading this manuscript a gazillion times. Thank you to my Dad, Justin, for all his help and hard work typesetting and designing the hardcover. Thank you to my lovely partner, Connor, for your endless support and encouraging me to write and push myself... even though it meant less attention for you. Thank you to the amazing Fran (*@coverdungeonrabbit*) for my gorgeous cover, you really knocked it out of the park! Thank you to my Dad, Mark, for your unwavering faith and support. Thank you to the amazing bookstagram community, without whom this process would not have been nearly as fun, your support means the world to me. Thank you to my family and friends for all your support and love. Finally, thank you to you, the reader – I couldn't have done this without you.

Thank you, thank you, thank you.

CPSIA information can be obtained
at www.ICGtesting.com
Printed in the USA
LVHW011745200921
698278LV00008B/1456